THE PAST

PAIGE STONE MYSTERIES
BOOK 2

MARIBETH GARRETT

The Past

Print and eBook editions published by Admission Press

eBook ISBN 978-1-955836-06-7

paperback ISBN 978-1-955836-07-4

1

While darkness consumed the last embers of light, Paige Stone sat staring at the cabin where she died. *He killed me here. If Trin hadn't saved me . . .* She couldn't complete the thought. Paralysis seized her mind. She sat motionless until night completely descended.

Every Wednesday when the sun arched over in the western sky, she drove toward Claremore and the woods that surrounded the log house. She hadn't missed one since that night over six months ago. Each time she promised herself this would be the last trip, but the next week, she found herself here, at the place that changed everything in her life. If this situation didn't suck enough, she thought Hank, her former partner and mentor, knew about her visits.

Finally, she forced herself to open the glove box. Her fingers shook until she grasped the Maglite inside. She stepped out of the vehicle, leaving the door to the compartment open.

The driveway stretched before her. She followed it like she had her first trip to the house. She moved forward through the tall grass that lined her path. The stems, now brown from winter's frost, rustled in the gentle breeze of January. No animals foraged. The silence screamed through her brain, but she made herself continue the short journey.

The vacant house mocked her. Everything looked the same as it did last summer. This time, her mind told her, he's not here. She placed the flashlight to the first window and switched it on. The bedroom remained empty. She checked every corner to make sure. Cold air filled her lungs, and she attempted to steady her hand. The beam of light still quivered.

She forced the light up to the next bedroom window. The bedroll appeared for a split second. Then her vision cleared, and she saw the room as it truly was—bare.

Her leaden feet plodded toward the kitchen's sliding-glass door. She remembered the pink backpack that had triggered her most primal fears. The computer-filled bag had signaled the monster was there. She forced her eyes open. Though the counter tops showed no sign of the laptop or carryall, sweat poured down her back. Her hands felt clammy, and she could no longer breathe. She attempted to walk back to the south end of the cabin, but stumbled and landed on all fours. The sound of the Eagles' "Somebody" filled her brain while she lay motionless in the dead grass. She gasped over and over, her lungs screaming for oxygen.

An eternity passed before she drew her first breath. Tears streamed down her cheeks. Twenty-seven times she'd been overtaken by the panic attack. Twenty-seven times and nothing had changed. *He* still won. He was dead, but still he won.

Her cell phone rang. She wrestled the device from her jacket pocket and glanced at the screen. The number wasn't familiar. She answered anyway. It could be a witness from her latest case. She worked as a homicide detective for the Tulsa Police Department.

"Is this Paige Stone?"

"Who is this?" She still wasn't accustomed to the sound of her own voice. Damaged vocal cords, a constant reminder of what had happened here, were a permanent gift from the monster her soul still battled.

"I'm Josh Stuart. You may have heard of me. I'm a good friend of Ben McCall. We made several movies together." He sounded anxious.

"Who?" *Not* the *Josh Stuart. Shit.* He probably wanted the rights to her story. She'd received so many offers to tell what happened in this cabin. The only person she could talk to was Caroline Montgomery, her televangelist friend, and even *she* didn't know everything.

"Josh Stuart. As in the movies?" She took a breath. "Are you the one who bought the cabin where Grant Windsor was killed? I saw the For Sale sign is gone."

"No. This has nothing to do with Tulsa. Ben's in trouble. We heard how you stopped the man who killed Heather Ballentine. I want to hire you to come help Ben. The deputies put him in the sheriff's station in Malibu."

"You didn't call to buy my story?"

"No."

"Thank God." Her gruff voice didn't convey the depth of relief she felt.

"I need you to come to LA to clear Ben."

"I don't understand how I can help you. I'm a police detective in Tulsa. I wouldn't have any authority in Los Angeles." Her mind raced with options, but none of them included a trip to LA. This was beyond strange. *Josh Stuart. Really?*

"I don't need you to be a police officer. I need you to investigate. A man died at Ben's house. The sheriff didn't look at anyone else. I want you to find out what actually happened."

"Have you spoken to Mr. McCall since his arrest?" Curiosity forced its way in.

"No. The best lawyer in LA and I played phone tag a good portion of the day, and it took some time to find you. Besides, he won't see anyone."

"The only advice I can give you is tell him to keep his mouth shut until he speaks with a good defense attorney. One who specializes in murder. I feel like a lowlife helping you this much. I'm on the other side, ya' know." She rubbed her nose with the back of her hand and longed for a tissue.

"But he asked for you. Tony said he asked for you specifically. It's the least you can do after the way Tulsa treated us when we visited."

"I wasn't a part of what happened to you." She leaned back against the house to give her aching legs some relief.

"I know. If it wasn't for you, we might still be in Tulsa. It's the reason he trusts you. He knows you'll search for the truth. It's warm and sunny here in LA. Why not come and enjoy the weather? At least take a peek."

"I have a job. I can't just take off any time I want."

"It wouldn't be forever. Can't you take a leave of absence or vacation? Something?"

"I don't think you understand." She pinched the bridge of her nose. "I would be out of my jurisdiction. I'm not a licensed PI in California. It would be difficult for me to do anything."

"You could find out who the victim is. Ben won't say anything to me or Tony—or the police. He wants to talk to you. Ben told Tony as much right before he left town for a film shoot. Can't we fly you out for a day or two? The studio has a Gulfstream on standby I can borrow. I could be there to pick you up in only a few hours."

"I don't think so." She sighed. Getting away was actually tempting.

"This is Wednesday. You could come for the weekend. I

could fly you back by Monday morning. Please. My friend needs you."

"I don't know Ben McCall. Why would he trust me?"

"You saved us. You risked your life to find the real killer. The whole episode spooked him. I know he checked you out once we got back. He said if he ever got into trouble again, he'd only trust you with the truth. I didn't think he would ever need you." Josh paused for a moment. "But maybe he did."

"You know his statement could mean he's guilty. If he killed the victim, I won't help set him free."

"You'll come?"

"I'll think about the weekend plan. It's not a done deal. Call me back in a couple of hours. I'll decide by then."

"Okay. I'll give you two hours." She could hear the relief in his voice before he disconnected.

Nothing like this had ever come her way before. The proposal felt bizarre and not in a good way. She'd get Hank's perspective. At least he'd met the three superstars. She hadn't. What interested her was the warm weather in LA and putting distance between her and this cabin.

She wanted her life back. Hank's retirement was proving difficult, and her fifteen minutes of fame never felt right. She wanted to be a good detective with Hank as her partner, but Hank would never work with her again.

The shadows disappeared behind her as she walked back to the car. Josh Stuart's offer gave her something to ponder besides the certainty of her death. The experience six months ago changed her life in so many ways. If Hank knew about her trips, he chose to let her deal with them. She wished she knew the correct path. Victory over the cabin and the panic attacks would go a long way. If only she could figure out how, she could quit these weekly visits.

~

PAIGE STOPPED by Hank Gettering's. The front door to the small bungalow was unlocked. He stopped locking it the day he retired. She didn't know why and hadn't asked. He sat in his recliner and sipped iced tea. Often he laced it with bourbon, but they didn't talk about the liquor either. They both had off-limit areas they never mentioned. She remained hopeful, but they hadn't worked past them yet.

Hank lobbed a volley at her. "I see you're out late again."

"You know how it goes when you're on the job." She hit the ball back.

"You were on the job? Is that why Steve called looking for you?" Point for Hank.

Steve Cook was her new partner. He worried about her, but damn it, he shouldn't call Hank. Her mentor didn't need her problems too.

"What did he want? I saw him a few hours ago."

"He told me the same thing. I think he wants to be a good friend. He mentioned the trips to Rogers County. I don't think he's aware I know about them." Hank's gaze pierced hers.

"I'm doing my job. Did he tell you I wasn't? What the hell business is it of his what I do on my own time?"

"Maybe he's a little uneasy about his backup if the need arises."

"That's low. I've never failed to be ready for backup. If you have something to say, Hank, just say it."

"Fine. I will. You're not the same. Whatever happened out at the cabin changed you. I need to know you're going to pull out of this. I miss the old Paige. The one who flirted with Bill to get her own way. The one who asked a million right questions. The one who met every challenge. I haven't seen her since the night she confronted Windsor. What happened to her?"

Head down, she paced the small living room and lowered her voice. "She died."

They shared the silent room for several moments, staring at each other. Then she sat.

"I got an unusual call today. Do you remember Josh Stuart? He phoned me on my cell. I don't know how he got my number."

"I remember him. We thought he was the one who held you captive because we couldn't locate him. Why would Stuart call you?"

"He claims his friend, Ben McCall, is in trouble. They arrested him for murder."

"I saw the clip on the news. They held him without bail. What does his stay in jail have to do with you?"

"They want me to come out there and investigate what happened. Josh said Ben wouldn't talk to anyone but me. He asked me to fly out for the weekend."

"Huh." Hank scratched at his day-old beard and finished the last of his tea.

"Josh Stuart offered to come get me in a Gulfstream. Can you imagine me flying off in a private jet?"

"So are you going?"

"I told him I'd think about it. Well, I told him no at first. Then I said I'd think about it when he mentioned only coming for the weekend. I could probably go without anyone missing me. Still, it sounds rather crazy. I don't even know these guys."

"You could call the captain and get it okayed easy enough. You're off this weekend aren't you?" Hank asked.

"I don't report back until early Monday."

"It could be a nice opportunity to get away for a few days. At least you couldn't drive to Rogers County from there. It might be good for you."

"I thought about the distance from the cabin too."

She sat on the sofa for a few minutes. They both searched for something to fill the silence. She remembered how she used to sneak down the hall from her bedroom to peek at his case files. The photographs were sometimes gruesome, but she couldn't keep away from them. Most times, she would wake at dawn with a part of the file in her hand, sometimes with the answer to the question that puzzled her before she fell asleep. But always she hurried to bed before Hank caught her.

"This old couch holds lots of memories. We solved some cases when we shared details." She patted the brown plaid seat beside her.

"I know. You hadn't been here a week before I could tell you snooped through my papers. I found different hiding places, but you always located the new one. I knew then I was in trouble. You're a born detective."

"You figured me out so quickly. I wondered why you moved your briefcase around."

"I figured you out real fast. It made you one special girl in my book. Let's find a way to get through this. Go get some sun, and take your mind off whatever's eating at you. A new case, with different evidence, might be the answer."

"I don't think it's that simple, but the sun sounds good. I might never get a chance to ride in a private jet again." Her smile was more genuine this time. "It's so hard to move past some cases. Do you remember the case when I was twelve? I think I was twelve. The one where we lost the guy and he had a young son. The perp beat his live-in girlfriend to death. You know the one I'm talking about?"

"Yeah. We figured his job made him travel. They both vanished."

"I used to worry about the kid. I prayed for him some. I think I asked you about him every day for months."

"The case was a tough one. If there's a child involved, it

always makes it harder to let go." Hank rubbed his forehead, then moved his hand down to brush across his chin whiskers.

"I still think about him. All these years later. I wonder if he's alive or if the old man beat him to death. I guess I'll never know."

"There's a good chance you won't, but we took a lot of bad ones off the street. Sometimes you lose one. It sticks with you, but you can't stop, because there's always a next one. They never quit coming. The bad guys, I mean."

She forced herself to ask the question that wouldn't stop haunting her. "What if I never move past this one?"

The compassion in Hank's eyes squeezed her heart. "Why don't you get on the jet? Go get some sun, and don't come back until you get out of the funk you've been in."

"I don't know. I've never tried to clear a suspect before. It doesn't feel right."

"You could luck out. He could be innocent."

"Yeah, and I could fly without a plane, but I don't think so."

PAIGE RAN FASTER, while Sonya Busby lagged behind. The girl did this when she protested a point. "Come on, pokey."

"I don't want you to go to California. They'll take one picture of you and make you a movie star. I'm not kidding. You don't have to act or anything nowadays to become famous."

"Oh, come on, the town's filled with gorgeous women. I'll fade in the background. You don't need to worry." By this time, their run had slowed to a walk.

"You promise you'll be right back? My mom is . . . You're the only one who understands how hard it is for people my age. You know what it's like."

"Believe it or not, your mother was young once too. I can

tell she loves you. Some mothers don't care what their children do. You need to give her a little credit." She couldn't help but compare Sonya's mom with Caroline's. The evangelist's parent was one cold woman.

"I know, but your advice hits right on. Besides, I don't have any friends who talk with me like you do."

"It's difficult for me to side with you on this subject. I lost my mom at the age of nine. I'm sure your mother does the best she can. It has to be better than no mom."

"I get your point, but you still need to come back quickly. I'll probably turn into a blimp if I don't run with you like usual."

She glanced at Sonya and grinned. The girl had a body like a stick figure.

"We haven't got long, but we'll talk more while I drive you home. I can call you every day. I only plan to be gone for the weekend, but right now, we have to run to keep you fast, so none of the guys who chase you can catch you."

"Oh, you are so full of it. No boys chase me." Sonya's cheeks turned a delicate pink, but she ran even with her the next lap around the track behind Edison High School.

As they completed another lap of the oval, she heard the ringtone that signaled the call came from Captain Underwood. She slowed her pace, grabbed for the phone, and motioned for Sonya to go ahead.

She took two deep breaths and finally answered. "Hello."

"I had an interesting conversation with Josh Stuart. He hinted at a lawsuit if I didn't persuade you to go to LA for a day or two. What the hell's going on, Paige? I didn't think you met those guys."

"I didn't. I received a call earlier this evening. Josh told me some story about Ben McCall and his arrest. He claimed Ben wouldn't talk to anyone else. I told him I couldn't do much. I don't have any authority in LA. I'm not a licensed investigator, et cetera, et cetera. He wouldn't take no for an answer. I finally told him I'd think about it. I ran it by Hank. He seemed to think it's a good idea, but I don't really think so."

"He insisted. He's serious about you helping. Are you going to go?"

"I don't know. I suppose. The warm sunshine sounds good, but if they arrested someone so famous, he's probably guilty. I won't help set a murderer free."

"I wouldn't expect you to, but if it could prevent the department an expensive lawsuit, what would it hurt?"

"What about the case I'm working?"

"Cook will continue to follow it until you get back. Hopefully, you won't be gone long."

Looked like she was getting on that plane after all.

2

———

Paige watched the jet taxi to a complete stop through the large glass window. The aircraft was bigger than she expected. She grabbed the handle of her small blue suitcase and walked out the door, rolling the bag behind her. The trip seemed unreal, but she intended to enjoy herself.

She planned to go through the motions but didn't want to get sucked into the case. A quick check of the facts and her conscience would be clear to bask in the sun and see the sights. Stuart could send her home on a domestic flight. She didn't care at this point, so long as he paid the bill.

The door of the Gulfstream opened, and Josh Stuart filled the space. The steps descended to the tarmac, and the sun lit him like a scene from one of his movies. He looked great even without the makeup. A smile formed on her lips in spite of herself.

He motioned her aboard, and she walked toward the waiting stairs. When she got close to him, his size dwarfed her. She shut her eyes for a second to calm the fear that shot through her veins. He stood nearly as tall as Grant Windsor, her own personal monster. Then they moved toward the creamy leather seats inside.

"You must be Paige. Forgive the hurry, but I want to get back ASAP. I don't think Ben's the type to do well in a jail cell. He'd never admit it, but he worries a lot." Josh stowed her bag under a cushion that hid a small storage compartment. After he twisted back, he seated himself.

She turned her thoughts from his size to the matter at hand.

"Murder *is* serious. What information do you know about the charges against him?"

"Most of what I know I've read online. Which is one of the reasons I need you. You can get in to see him and talk some sense into him. He won't see Tony or me. I don't even have his agreement on what lawyer to hire. He's probably in there staring at the walls, going nuts. They've got him booked in at the Lost Hills Sheriff's Station. It serves for Malibu's law enforcement, but we've got to get him out of there. He'll get moved to the Men's Central Jail in LA, and that place holds every degenerate known to man."

"Do you know what he's told the police?"

"No."

"When did the murder happen? How soon did they detain him?"

"Late Tuesday night. They arrested him that night or the next morning. Someone came forward."

"What kind of someone?"

"The woman who lives next door, I think."

"She said Ben did it?" She knew witnesses could be wrong, but they could sway juries too.

"From what I understand, she did. I've been so busy, I'm not a hundred percent sure of anything. I think the deputy sheriff arrested him so quickly because of her statement."

She sat silent a moment to digest the fact.

"You need to get a lawyer of some kind hired. I need to see the crime scene and the photographs of the victim. It would've been better if I'd been at the scene before the police went through everything, but good photos will help. At some point, I'll need to visit the actual scene. It'll give me insight into the layout and sequence of events that took place. His lawyer has a right to discovery. The information in the murder book and photos would help the most."

"I didn't hire a lawyer. I thought about talking to Jacob Carston. He's well known in LA."

"I know nothing about California lawyers. How many murder cases? What percentage has he won? He should know his way around a court room." She glared at him as he seated himself right beside her. Natural instinct made her want to scoot away, but she forced herself to remain in place.

"My agent is a lawyer. He says Jacob Carston's the best. I've missed the attorney by phone for the last twenty-four hours. We're due to meet sometime tomorrow." He glanced at his watch. "Well, technically today."

She nodded. "Hire him. He can get me discovery. If you don't like him, you can hire someone else later. The first lawyer has to keep privilege. The sooner I get the information I need, the quicker I can come back home."

She surveyed her plush surroundings, glad not to be stuffed into one of the jumbo flights that crisscrossed the nation. She had legroom and more.

"What's the hurry to get home? You got a man waiting?"

"Only Hank. He's more like a father to me than anything."

"So, what's wrong with the guys in Tulsa? You look too good to be running around single."

"I don't know, but let's get something straight. I'm here for the case and the sunshine. I'm not interested in anything else."

"Okay. Fair enough." Josh raised his hands in the air.

They remained silent long enough for her to relax. A few minutes later, she moved to the sofa across the aisle to get some sleep. She'd been up before dawn, and the day ahead of them could be a long one. "I'm exhausted. I think I'll rest a while. We've got plenty to do once we arrive."

A haunting gloom filled the night. Shadows twisted into grotesque beings that chased her through the darkness. She ran as hard as she could. The tormentor's breath burned her neck with each step she took. She stumbled and sensed herself drop into emptiness. The fall seemed to last forever until she landed on concrete.

That's when he snatched her. She felt his hands surround her neck. His fingers squeezed. Her air supply shut off. No oxygen remained in her chest. The tentacles held fast as she clawed at them, still restricting her breath. Her lungs exploded in pain. She longed to scream, but no air made it down her throat. She thrashed for breath and grasped to get a hold on something to stop him. Her hands hunted and searched, but found nothing. The black void came for her, and she separated from her body. She recognized death ever since it claimed her the first time.

"Are you okay? You had a bad dream." Josh's stern voice brought her eyes open.

She released the breath she held. "Yes. I'm fine. I guess I'm not used to flying and sleeping at the same time." She smiled but still shook. She needed to phone Caroline. She always felt the urge to call her after she dreamed like this. "How much longer until we arrive?"

"The plane touched down. We're here."

"Good." Her deep, gravelly voice surprised her again. Her cheeks flared in embarrassment. She moved her feet to the floor and sat up. The nightmare still plagued her, but she determined to shake the effects of it off. She lifted the blanket and laid it aside. She assumed Josh had put it on her.

"I thought we'd go straight to the jail. I want you to get in to talk to Ben ASAP. You can tell me how he's doing. I know I sound worried, and I am." Josh retrieved her piece of luggage and moved toward the exit.

"We can go to the station first, but I need to talk to the detectives in charge. I can't barge in on their case. There's protocol to go through. If some outsider messed with one of my cases, I'd be pissed. They have information I need and we want their cooperation, so I don't want to make them angry." She stared at him to see if he understood.

"Okay. How do we proceed?"

"Let's stick with your idea and see if we can get in to see Ben. It's late. We may have to wait until tomorrow, but we need to talk to the investigating officer in the morning, if we can. They'll probably be around early. You never know how the case will go, until you know how the IO does his work. Finesse is everything with cops. For now, let's go see Ben right away."

"All right."

"Another issue, don't push your weight around. I know you've got pull, but sometimes it's better to wait and see. If you need to flex your influence, we can always use the clout later. I don't want to seem bossy, but the lines of trust between police and outsiders can be a delicate matter. As a woman on the force, I've had my fair share of ass kissing to do. Sometimes it's part of the job. The main idea is to get out of the deal what *we* want."

"I see your point. I'll try to keep my mouth shut."

~

I INHALED the smoke deep into my lungs. The heat from the stub between my fingers burned. I glanced at the short smoldering butt and reached to stab it out in the full ashtray.

The woman strutted her body the way whores do. The cut of her long dark hair reminded me of the memory locked somewhere in my past. While my brain reached for the recollection, it scurried farther away into the recesses of my mind. My instincts pressed upon me the importance of the remembrance. I watched the woman practice her trade. The thought teased me and danced back and forth, but always just out of reach.

I started my truck and drove over to the corner where the hooker worked. The closer I got, the thicker and cheaper her makeup appeared. She turned her head a certain way and walked. The flash of something taunted me again. I decided to hire her until I could decipher what my mind wanted to recall.

"How much?" I asked.

"Depends." Her lewd smile almost changed my mind.

"On what?"

"On what you want, darlin'."

"I want some of your time. Nothing else."

"That's what they all say." She revealed white, even teeth. The perfection of them almost made up for the whorish cosmetics on her face.

I took my time and debated my decision, then nodded. "Get in. I'll make it worth your while." I flashed my own charming smile.

She studied me for a few seconds, opened the passenger door, and climbed in. Girls always found me attractive. Most went with me, no problem.

She settled herself in her seat and slammed the door. I stepped on the gas and we left her corner behind. I drove several miles east on Hollywood Boulevard, away from the area, and searched for a motel. A small row of rooms loomed ahead of me on the right side of the road where a vacancy sign flashed bright red. I pulled in and handed her several twenties.

"Go get us a room. I'll keep the motor running."

The way she moved and the length of her brunette tresses tantalized the memories I longed to unlock. She sauntered toward the office, but something important remained hidden within her undulating movements.

In a few minutes, she strolled back, and we went to room seventeen. The rug was matted with grime. Someone had covered the window and bed in the same dreary pattern of gray and purple splotches. It didn't matter. I needed her to stroll until I brought up the recollection from the depths of my past.

"My name's Hilda. I always like my friends to know my name. You can tell me yours if you want." Her grin became suggestive. She laid her purse down on the dark dresser beneath the mirror.

Her lewdness irritated me. Sex didn't figure in my thoughts right now, but I kept silent.

"Now, what can I do for you?" Her same evocative smile remained as she turned toward me.

"Walk. The way you did on the corner, but not so—just walk normal."

She looked at him strangely and shrugged. The room was small, but she traveled the path between the bed and the tiny bathroom several times. She stopped and looked at me for instructions.

"Walk until I tell you to stop."

She nodded and proceeded to stroll the measured distance back and forth.

I studied the sway of her hips, and the way her hair caught on her shoulders at times, but it wouldn't come to me. While she moved back and forth, I grew more frustrated. I needed a cigarette. I smoked before, and the flashes came to me.

"I'll be right back. I need a cancer stick from the truck. You can rest a moment."

The door to the room closed behind me. I unlocked the pickup and grabbed the pack from the seat. My hand shook as the lighter flamed, and I inhaled until my lungs filled. The nicotine soothed me for a few seconds. As I locked the vehicle, I spotted the Louisville Slugger on the floor. I couldn't afford for someone to steal it, so I opened the truck and picked it up. I went back to the room and leaned the bat against the door facing.

"I don't want anyone to steal my lucky charm. Now, where did we leave off?" I grinned to assure her I wouldn't harm her.

Her eyes darkened with concern, but Hilda didn't reply. She moved along the familiar path.

As I drew on the cigarette, the sight flashed before me. I saw my father draw back and slug a female. The woman had brunette hair and a pain-filled face. She seemed familiar, and for a split second, I thought I'd loved the girl from the vision. The foreign feeling touched a buried emotion that hid dormant inside me. I almost let out a cry of anguish when the illusion left me quicker than it came. My mind struggled desperately to hold onto the image, but it vanished.

Rage filled my head. I gazed at her through a dark cloud of anger. I gripped the bat and lashed out. Hilda threw her arm up to defend herself. The sound of bone breaking gave a loud snap as she whimpered in fear, too stunned to scream. I let it fly again. Her leg went out from under her. Before she could hit the floor, I swung low like a cut at a baseball. The Slugger struck her neck. By the time she landed, her head lay tilted at an obscene angle.

I sat on the bed, finished my smoke, and stared at my handiwork. Finally, I moved to the toilet, and flushed my cigarette. The curtains hung limp until I swept them back and opened the window to the alley that ran behind the squalid motel.

I lifted her dead weight over my shoulder and stuffed it through the window. Her bag still sat on the dresser so I grabbed it and threw the purse outside with her. I closed the opening and put the curtains in place. No one would miss her. The stink would soon bring the police, but by then, I'd be gone.

3

The Porsche sat in front of the Lost Hills Sheriff Station on Agoura Road. The red brick building with white square pillars looked new. Paige felt the salty breeze drift in off the Pacific when she stepped from the vehicle. Its coolness refreshed her tired body. The nap on the flight hadn't done much to stave off the exhaustion that followed her these days. She couldn't figure why Ben McCall wanted her on his case. Something about it didn't make sense. She walked through the glass doors of the building and hunted for someone to help her.

She found a deputy who led her to the cell. A short time later, the muscular man towered before her. The sterile room seemed too small for him. She felt uncomfortable in the tiny space with Ben McCall. Since the incident last summer, she didn't like to share any space with large men. Now she had to deal with two.

She noted his piercing blue eyes as he shook her hand.

"I know you know who I am, even though we've never met, but I can't tell you how good it is to see you." His smile conjured a spark of confidence she hadn't seen a split second before. She wondered if he put on an act for her benefit.

"Only from the movies, but it appears you know me better than I do you. Why did you want Josh to bring me out here?"

"I'm in trouble. I believe you can get me out of it."

"I've heard the same story from Josh. So let's cut to the chase. Tell me what happened?"

"I had a fight with—"

"Before you say a word, I want to advise you to get counsel. If you tell me incriminating details now, I could be called to testify against you." She paused to let the words sink in. If he killed the man, at least she'd warned him.

"I know, we used Miranda in several movies I've done, but I'm not guilty. I promise."

She prodded him when his pause stretched on. "Well?"

"I don't know where to start. I can only tell you certain information. The evening of the murder a visitor came to see me. We did have a huge argument, and I got pissed. He sat and drank my beer by the pool. I had to get away and headed for Tony's, told him to be gone when I got back. He laughed at me and said he wasn't going anywhere." Ben paused and chewed his left index nail.

"So who is the *he*, you're talking about?"

"I can't tell you."

"Really?" She raised her left eyebrow. Surely he joked.

"I've got my reasons."

"You're the one who wanted my help, and now you think you can hold out on me? After I came all the way out here, I need every detail. Especially who the victim is. That's everything. I can't begin to work the case without it." She got up from the bunk, paced, and turned back to him. "Do the police know yet?"

"They've hammered me about it several times, so I don't think so."

"And what's the reason I can't know his identity?"

"If the police knew who he was, what the situation was, I'd never leave this jail cell."

"What makes you believe that?" She wanted to pace again, but there wasn't much room. She rubbed the back of her neck instead.

"I hated him. If I found him drowning, I wouldn't lift a finger to help him. He was pure evil from my past. I waited years for him to make an appearance, but I didn't kill him."

"What do you mean? You expected him to show up?"

"Once I became famous. I always figured someday he'd climb out of his hole, and he did."

"You said you got into a fight with him. What caused the dispute?"

"He needed money. I refused to give it to him. He threatened to expose our relationship from the past. I told him I didn't care. I would never, under any circumstances, help him. He must be crazy if he thought I would." Ben sat down beside her.

She felt crowded, but forced herself back to the issue at hand. "Why did he need the money? Was he specific?"

"He claimed he borrowed twenty-five thousand from a loan shark. I told him the money wasn't my problem, and I didn't care if the bastard killed him. Told him to be gone when I got back. Then I walked down to the beach and hiked to Tony's. At the time, I felt relieved the showdown was over. I thought I'd faced my worst nightmare and conquered it. I came back later and found his body."

"Are you sure the victim was the same person you fought with?"

"Yes, I'm sure. Who else would it be?"

"Did he mention the name of the guy he owed money to?"

Ben got up and paced the few steps the cell allowed, and turned back to her. "Yes, but it wouldn't be prudent to tell you at this time. You would find out who the victim is. I need you to find a way to clear me without his identity."

"Are you serious? I'm not going through this with you again. How can I help you if you won't give me the information I need? You're being ridiculous. I think a good tan might be next on my agenda."

"Well, it's not like I planned it this way. How can I trust you to not tell them who it is? You're still a cop." Ben ran his hand through his hair and left it on the back of his neck for a few seconds.

"You knew the situation before Josh dragged me out here. I don't know why you think you can waste my time. They will get his DNA and test it. Most every department is backlogged, but it won't stay a secret forever. I'm going to the beach. You can stew until you get some sense back in your head. I can use the vacation." She knocked on the cell door to see if the guard lurked close by.

"Wait."

She turned back to look at him, and sat down on his bunk. Her stare dared him to push her.

"I know I'm not being fair, but you don't understand. I can't tell you yet. I can't. But I want you to work the case like you would any homicide investigation, only you know something they don't." His eyes met hers. She saw the hint of fear he hid. His hand quivered. He rubbed it down his pants leg and licked his lips. "I'm innocent."

"People tell me those same words every day. I hope it makes a great defense for you. Let me know how it turns out. I'm through with this foolishness." She got back up and moved toward the entrance to his cell but wondered if he told the truth.

"Please, you've got to help me. I know what I'm asking of you seems unfair, but when I walked back and saw him dead . . ." He shook his head, stopped pacing, and stared down at her. His eyes pleaded. "I knew I was in huge trouble. You're the only one I could think of who could help me."

"I don't know what I can do. You're literally tying my hands. You gave me nothing to work with. How long ago did you know this person?"

"Over twenty years ago. I can't give you any information about what he's done since I last saw him. I truly don't know."

"I need wheels to get around, and someone who knows the area of LA."

"Josh will give you the keys to any car I own, but he'll probably want to escort you."

"Why?"

"He and Tony are my best friends. Of the three of us, Josh has always been the one with the level head. We tease him with the nickname Buzzkill, but he'll worry unless he knows exactly what's going on. I'd trust him with my life. He'll help you any way he can."

"You know someone was brutally murdered. It could put him in danger."

"I assume the same could be said for you."

"I guess so, but I'm not sure he knows how hazardous the case could get."

"Ask him. He'll want the opportunity to make that choice."

"You're so sure of him?"

"Yeah. We never talk about it. Each of us try to keep it real. It's what made us friends over the years. We trust each other. Everything else out here is make believe."

"I guess I'll take your word for it. Can you give me any

other information that could help? I feel like I'm walking blind here. Did anyone see you on the beach?"

"The lateness of the hour . . ." He shook his head. "I don't remember anyone around. I don't think anybody saw me."

"How did the victim arrive at your home?"

"I think he drove."

"What kind of vehicle did he drive?"

"I don't know. I didn't pay any attention. I saw his face, and I guess nothing else mattered."

"Why?"

"It was like I woke up in a nightmare. I only knew I didn't ever want to go back there. I was shocked. I don't think I ever looked out into the yard."

Nightmares. She knew all about those. He could be lying about everything else, but she believed him about this one point. Still, she had to wonder if the police found a vehicle after they arrived. If not, how did it get moved?"

When she left Ben's cell behind, she saw Josh pacing the plain beige tile in the lobby. One thing was certain. He cared a great deal about what happened to Ben McCall.

Josh saw her, stopped, and rubbed his hands against his jean-covered legs. "How did it go?"

"I ought to walk out the door and head straight back to Oklahoma. He wasn't helpful. But I'm already here. I might as well see what's what."

Josh followed her out to the red Carrera GT. "Where are we going now?"

"I'll tell you what I told Ben, I need a place to stay and wheels. I need someone who knows their way around this town. Those are essential." She stared across the top of the car at him. "I don't suppose you could talk some sense into him. He won't give me the man's identity, and he knows. The first step in any murder investigation starts there. You find out everything possible about the victim." She got in and slammed the door.

"Did he say why he won't tell you?" Josh climbed behind the wheel.

"Some rubbish about if people knew he'd never get out of jail."

"Ben's not one to talk about his past. I guess none of us do, but I know him. He wouldn't do something like this. He wouldn't." Josh started the engine and backed out.

"Yeah, well I *don't* know Ben, and I'm not so sure." She leaned her head back on the headrest and closed her eyes. The purr of the engine lulled her to sleep in seconds.

As the motor died, she woke up. She'd dreamed again. The start of the nightmare ran like a familiar theme. The realization made her instantly alert to her surroundings. "Where are we?"

"You fell asleep. I brought you here to my home. I thought you could get a couple of hours rest. In the morning, we can make plans for the next step. The place has four main bedrooms. Take your pick. Mine's at the top of the stairs to the left. The rest are available for your use."

"Are you serious? I expected to stay at a hotel, not your home."

"We have work to do. We need privacy. I promise no funny stuff. Get some sleep, and we'll get back to the job." He got out and grabbed her bag from the back seat.

She couldn't argue with his logic, but as soon as she got some sleep, she needed to figure out a way to change the situation. She felt so tired right now. "Where's the closest room?"

"There's a maid's quarter to the right by the garage entrance to the kitchen, but it's not very nice. No one's ever used it before. I think Greta keeps it clean though."

"I'm sure it's fine." She got out and glanced to the right. He opened the first door, and she saw the accommodation seemed more than adequate. "This will do. Leave my bag for now. I'll see you when I wake up." He set the small suitcase down inside the door. She promptly closed it and left him on the other side.

She surveyed the large tan room and saw a television and a chocolate-brown lounge chair. The full-sized bed in the corner looked like heaven. She threw the covers back, pulled her jeans off, and dived into the softness. One more detail needed her attention before slumber could claim her tired body. She reached down and pulled her cell phone from her pants pocket.

She pressed one on her speed dial, hit the connect button, and waited while the phone rang. "Hello, Caroline."

"Paige, what's wrong?"

"Nothing. I need to ask a favor."

"You know I'll do anything I can to help."

"I know, but this situation is different. I'm in LA. You're supposed to attend a conference scheduled in this area soon, aren't you?"

"Yes, it starts next week. Why?"

"Can you come out a little early? I need you to talk to someone." She hated to ask people for help.

"Sounds rather mysterious. Why are you in LA?"

"It's for a case I'm working as a favor. The problem's twofold. I need a chaperone, and I'd like for you to talk to my client. Well, he's . . . sort of a client. Anyway, could you come out here, if I can get you a ticket?"

"I suppose. I could fly out early to help with the preparations. A lot more goes into a conference than most people realize. How soon do you want me to come?"

"ASAP." Relief flowed through her. Caroline's gentle manner relaxed people so they trusted her. If anyone could get Ben to talk, it would be Caroline.

"Okay. Now, why do you need a chaperone?"

"I'm not sure I do, but in any case, it wouldn't hurt for you to be here. I'm at Josh Stuart's house. They arrested his best friend, Ben McCall, for murder. I'd feel more comfortable with another female in the house. Besides, my weird dreams haunt me most nights. You're the only one who halfway understands."

"When did the nightmares start back again?"

"They never stopped. I handle it better sometimes than others."

"Why didn't you tell me they didn't stop?"

"I didn't want you to worry."

"I don't like for you to face those dreams alone. You promised to phone me after you have one."

"I know, but I'd feel so childish waking you in the middle of the night. You deserve some sleep."

"I'll survive. Besides, I never have trouble sleeping. I meant what I said. Call me if you're down. We'll get through this together."

"I've got to go now. I'll phone you soon with the details on your flight. Talk at you later." She needed to escape Caroline's scrutiny. Her inner voice reminded her she had promised.

"Okay."

"And Caroline?"

"Yes?"

"Thanks."

"I'll see you soon."

She plugged her phone in to charge, and laid it on the nightstand. She pulled the covers up tight around her shoulders and turned over. Weariness pulled her under.

Paige she woke up gasping for air. Perspiration dampened what clothes she wore and terror clung to her. She sat up in the bed and drew air deep into her chest. The room seemed foreign to her, which increased her anxiety until she remembered where she was. Los Angeles. Josh Stuart's home.

As she shook off the last of her nightmare, she threw the covers back, and placed her feet on the floor. She picked up her phone to see the time. Ten till four. *Shit.* After she awoke from the dream that stalked her nightly, sleep was impossible. At least she'd gotten a little rest. It helped. She felt better, if not totally refreshed.

She found the jeans on the floor she'd worn the night before. She pulled them on and opened the door to the right. Josh left through this door so she thought it must lead to the remainder of the house. She found an immaculate kitchen on the other side that appeared perfect. Every Hollywood star probably owned one like it, but she didn't cook so it didn't interest her.

She opened a door she thought might be a closet or pantry. She was wrong. Stairs led to a basement. She searched for a switch and flipped it on. Then she stepped down into the space.

What she found awakened her excitement. She'd wondered how she would stay in shape during her visit here. A fully equipped gym filled her vision. *Sweet.* She retraced her path and grabbed some gray sweats out of her luggage. She'd cut them off several years ago. A white wife-beater covered her sports bra before she returned to the fitness center.

She timed herself on the rowing machine for fifteen minutes and worked up a good sweat. Next, she picked up a fifteen-pound weight and did sets of reps. While she sat on the bench doing curls, she muttered, "Monsters kill you. Monsters kill you. Monsters kill . . ."

She didn't know how long she pushed herself and repeated her mantra. When she glanced up, she saw Josh. He watched her. *Shit.* She felt the burn the instant her cheeks turned red. Blood rushed to her brain.

"Hey, creeper. Do you always sneak up on your guests and try to give them a heart attack?"

"Normally, guests of mine don't work out in the middle of the night. Most girls stay tucked up in bed." He hesitated. "With me."

"Well, I'm not interested. I don't want to sleep with you."

"I didn't say you did."

"Good. We both agree." She put the weight down on the bench and stood. She didn't like for him to loom over her. She stood her ground as they stared at each other.

The silence moved toward uncomfortably long. Finally, he spoke. "What happened to you in the cabin? The expression on your face. The determined way you said those words. I've seen it before."

"I sincerely doubt it. How would you? It's not a scripted story to be acted out before a camera."

"I wasn't always an actor."

"What's that supposed to mean?"

"What I said. I did other things before Hollywood took over my interest."

"What sort of things?"

"I don't want to bore you. Just things. Never mind." He lifted his hand and waved her off.

So Josh Stuart had something in his past he didn't want to share. The potential vulnerability intrigued her. He wore only a pair of low-slung jeans, which left the well-defined muscles of his chest exposed.

"I see you keep yourself in great shape. What's your routine?" she asked.

He seemed relieved she changed the subject.

"It varies. When I'm on location, it's hard to find time. I

usually run if nothing else works, but at home, I change up my workouts. I try to work on each of my muscle groups on a regular basis. The trick, don't let it get boring."

She resumed lifting the weight until her muscles rebelled. Then she carried the dumbbell back to the rack and placed it with the rest of his set. She turned around, and he stood close behind her. Again, she felt oppressed by his height and broad chest. She longed to quell the panic that fought to consume her.

She gazed up at him. "Do you ever spar with anyone?"

"Sometimes."

"How about now?"

She needed to confront the fear head on. She hated that she felt threatened each time he came close to her. In order to function normally again, she must get past the uneasiness. She side-stepped and feigned with her right and quickly followed with a short kick from the left.

He caught her foot in his hand and continued to hold it fast. It kept her slightly off balance. "You don't want to play games with me. You'll lose."

She tore her foot free and wanted to wipe the confidence from his face. She'd known that expression before. Worn it once. Her hands clenched tightly by her thighs. She hesitated for only an instant before she twirled and kicked him in the lower ribs. In a flash, she dropped, rolled away from him, got to her feet, and stood to face him.

"Now look, I don't want to hurt you. You shouldn't ask for trouble." He took a step toward her.

She faked right and caught him in the chin with a short left hook. He returned with a swift jab she never saw coming. His fist landed on her shoulder. She stumbled and took two steps back. Never had she seen anyone move so fast.

Certain he pulled his punch, she needed to see the full

extent of his abilities. She must know she could hold her own with him. It became a compulsion she couldn't stop.

She progressed toward him again. A second later she dived and rolled toward his feet. He jumped over her. Instantly, he faced her again. She barely made it to her feet when he said, "This is not a good idea. I could hurt you and not mean to. Whatever's driving you, let it go."

"I can't."

"Damn it, Paige, don't do this."

She advanced. They both searched each other for weaknesses while they circled for position on the mat. She threw an uppercut at him with her right. He leaned back and easily escaped contact. He had way too much reach on her. Her best option was to use her feet. She bent at her waist and swung her body around as she kicked out with everything inside her. This time she made contact. He staggered back but didn't go down.

As she landed, she stepped into another kick, but he threw his leg up and tripped her. She went down. Terror raced through her veins. *I need to get up. Monsters kill. Get up. Monsters kill.*

She strained to roll away from him, but she was too late. His foot on her chest stopped her before she could respond. He sat on her waist, captured both of her arms, and held them to the floor above her head. He stared intently into her eyes and lowered his head. His lips found hers, but frustration still reigned in her mind. She refused to respond. Josh lingered for a moment and lifted his head.

"Are we through yet? If I let you go, will you stop this madness?"

She kept her eyes closed for a long time and gained control of her anger. It didn't make her feel any better. She understood she'd asked for this. With difficulty she opened them, but still didn't understand why she'd done something so stupid. Finally, she nodded.

He hesitated before he let her go. "What was that about?"

"I don't know."

"Come on. That's no answer."

"It's the best I can do."

"Your dreams turn into nightmares. You start a fight with someone twice your size. What happened last summer?"

"It's none of your business. I came here to do a job. I don't know what I thought. Let's forget it." She flashed him one of her megawatt smiles, but she knew he didn't buy it. "I want you to do me a favor. My friend needs a plane ticket to come out to LA. She can stay here with us. I want her to visit Ben. She might be able to get him to talk. I need to find out the identity of the victim. Preferably before the police do. God, that sounds weird. I've always been the police before."

"Sure. Who we talking about?"

"Caroline Montgomery. Book it from Tulsa to whichever airport you want in this area. We'll pick her up. Let me know so I can call and give her the details."

"I'll see what's available."

"You need to get her here ASAP." She turned from him and ascended the stairs.

4

Paige didn't want to face Josh after her humiliation the night before. She still didn't fully understand what motivated her to do something so dumb. One fact remained: if she couldn't take on an actor who only lifted weights for appearance sake, how could she ever hold her own against a crazed perp who wanted to kill her?

She put on her same workout clothes from the night before. The sun forced its rays through the smog that hung over LA as she walked out of the garage and stretched. She did a few jumping jacks to elevate her heart rate, took off down the drive, and jogged toward the mountainous road they'd followed the night before. At least she thought it was the same one.

As she pushed herself on, her mind sorted through the jobs they needed to accomplish today. She needed to talk to the lead detectives on Ben's case and inspect the crime scene at his house. She knew how to work a case. She'd been taught by the best. She missed working with Hank, now that he'd retired. His gruff manner kept her on her game.

She ran down along the ocean and most of the way back,

then slowed to a walk. She took her cell phone out of her pocket from the cut-off sweats and dialed Sonya Busby's number. She should be on her way to school. It rang five times before Sonya answered.

"Thank God you called. Mom's on the warpath again." Sonya never answered hello. She always started with high drama.

"What did you do now?"

"Practically nothing. She came home from work, and I hadn't done my chores."

"And why didn't you?"

"Well, I . . . James, my friend, was over. Mom went berserk. We didn't do anything. I swear."

"I think we've discussed this before. It's not appropriate for young girls to let guys come over when no one else is home. You're too smart to do something so stupid. Your mother's right. I'm on her side on this."

"We're just friends. We didn't do anything." She could imagine the innocent expression on Sonya's face. The girl pulled the tool out at will.

"It always starts out harmless, but it's where it goes that leads to the problem. After I come home, you've got two extra miles to run each day for a week, and you should be grounded for life."

"Oh, I wish you'd come back. I miss you already. I never get into trouble when you're with me. Are you coming back soon?" The pleading in Sonya's voice made her grin. Somehow, the little manipulator slipped right under her skin.

"I don't know. It shouldn't take too long. Besides, you can't blame this on me. Sometimes I'll need to go out of town. I should be able to trust you to do what's right even if I'm not there. You know we've talked about choices before. I've taught you how to make the right ones. The only one responsible for your decisions is you."

"I know." Sonya's tone made her smile. She could almost see her glum expression.

"We've discussed your dreams. Don't screw up your future. Make the wrong judgement call now, it'll cost you later. You know I'm right."

"Yeah, I do. Hey, I saw the picture of you and Josh this morning on one of the early shows. They talked about your trip to LA to sell the rights to your story. They claimed the house near Claremore already sold and plans exist to shoot the movie. I thought you didn't want to sell the story."

"I don't. They report whatever they want out here." She couldn't believe this place.

"Well, I saw a photo of you and Josh. You were standing beside a hot red car. They did mention you and Josh visited Ben McCall. I guess they assumed Ben, Josh, and Tony Strete made you an offer. You know their new film *Liberty Valance* will come out in a few months?"

"Listen, *they* don't know what they're talking about. I came out here for the reasons I told you. Don't change the subject. I may not be there in the flesh, but I will check on you every day. I don't want to hear any lame excuses. I expect better of you. You won't disappoint me, will you?"

"No."

"You promise?"

"I guess."

"You'd better. I gotta run. Lots to do today. I'll talk to you tomorrow."

"Okay."

She disconnected.

When she glanced up, Josh stood in the drive and watched her while she walked up.

"I thought you'd left." He looked angry.

"Why would I? We didn't get started yet." She forced herself to stare back at him. He couldn't intimidate her anymore.

Finally, he shrugged. "What's on the agenda for us today?"

"First, I want to talk to the lead detectives on his case, and see what I can get from them. I'll need to see the crime scene. While we're there, we should canvass the area for witnesses. We need Q-Tips, plastic bags, and clear tape in case we find fingerprints. Small tools and the like. If we manage to scrounge any evidence the police missed, we'll need to obtain an outside lab, a reputable one. Jacob Carston should know of a company we could use. It'll be a long day." She moved past him toward her room.

"I suppose we should get started."

"Yeah," she answered.

"If you leave those workout clothes in the laundry room, they'll be ready for tomorrow. Greta takes care of those duties for me."

"I could point out I'm not you."

"You could, but she considers it an honor to keep my guests comfortable. I seldom entertain visitors." He shrugged and left it up to her.

She moved past him without a word.

"Listen, we've got to spend a lot of time together. Let's make a peace treaty for the duration. You nailed me pretty good last night. No one's caught me off guard like that in years. If you want, I'll teach you a few moves that might help." His expression seemed sincere.

She knew he meant well, but it still bothered her he'd bested her. His skills were better than her own. He could easily take her in an all-out fight. She nodded. "Where's the laundry room?"

"I'll show you. It's right through here." He guided her back through the kitchen to another door, which led to a small room.

"You can leave anything you need laundered or cleaned. Greta always checks it first each morning. I'm not much of a messy person so she hunts for jobs to keep her occupied. She'll be happy to do them."

"I wash my own clothes. It feels funny not to."

"We'll be much too busy. We need to clear Ben. He means a great deal to me. I don't have a lot of close friends." He closed the door. They moved back into the kitchen.

"I don't either. We actually have something in common?" She laughed at his expression. He must be surprised she possessed a sense of humor.

PAIGE HOPPED out of the car in front of the Hall of Justice on Temple Street in downtown LA. She went inside, where a few stairs led to a beautiful hallway through two white ionic columns. A gold-coffered ceiling with delicate chandeliers ran the length of the lobby. A bank of elevators lined one side. She found the LA County Sheriff's Office on the first floor.

"Who you looking for?" an older gentleman at the desk asked.

"I'm Detective Stone. I'd like to talk to the lead detectives on the homicide that involves Ben McCall. Do you know who caught the case?" If you acted like you belonged, you often did.

"I don't remember you around here before."

"I don't often get this way." She turned on her best smile. It frequently reaped the results she wanted.

"Let's see." He stared down at some paper work. "Curtis Sampson is the lead. His partner is"—he glanced down again and ran his finger over the sheet he held—"Sonny Harmon. I saw them a few minutes ago." He gave her instructions on how to find them and went back to his magazine.

She followed the directions and spotted the two men. One stood a half-foot taller than the other. As he talked, he used hand gestures. His partner, though more handsome, oozed the kind of personality she hated, but she'd humble herself and be charmed, if it would get her the information she wanted.

She observed the two detectives for another minute while they interacted with each other. They appeared haggard. She understood their fatigue. Exhaustion became a close friend, and sleep evaded her most of the time. After she thought she discerned how their relationship worked, she moved to let them know of her presence.

The shorter one walked toward her. "Can I help you?"

"I don't know. Can you?" She grinned.

His eyes moved over her slowly. "I certainly hope so. Sonny Harmon, at your service."

The line sounded old and tired, but she needed to seem impressed. His help might depend on it. "I'm Paige Stone. It's a pleasure to meet you."

"Why are you wandering the halls?" the taller man asked.

"I just got in from Tulsa. A friend asked me to come out here for a visit. I think he's got me on a wild-goose chase, but you know how it is. You must do what the captain tells you." She shrugged. "What's your name?"

"This is Curtis Sampson. He's my partner." Sonny wasn't the type to let Curtis horn in on his flirting.

"I hate to ask, but I promised I'd check into this mess out here. The man who got himself killed out at Ben McCall's place. I could use whatever you have on the case. Might examine a few crime scene photos. Then I would tell them I'd looked into it and be on my way. I mean, if you arrested someone so famous, he has to be guilty. Right?"

"What do you mean, you'd tell them you checked into it?" Sampson asked.

"Some actor threatened to sue the department if I didn't come out here and investigate what happened. You know how actors are. Well, I'm sure you do. You work out here with them." She raised her brows and shrugged.

"So you came out here to butt into our case because some actor wanted you to." Sampson frowned.

"No. My captain told me to. I don't suppose you've ever been between a rock and the crapper before. When he tells me to do something, I don't need to like it. I know, I'd be pissed if someone wanted to nose around one of my cases, but that's not my intent at all. I'd like a quick glance so I can tell my captain I assessed the situation. Report to him that McCall's guilty and be on my way."

"You know that's not the way it works," Sampson said.

"Yes, but I hoped for a little professional courtesy. Then I can get a quick tan before I head back."

"We don't give a damn about your tan." Sampson's face grew red.

"Wait a minute. Her boss asked her to do this. We could be a bit more cordial."

She smiled at Harmon. "Thank you. I figure since you arrested him so quickly, you've got the case gift wrapped with a bow. He has a lot of clout in the media. What's your evidence against him?"

"We've got an eye witness. She lives next door. Saw the whole incident. Called 911, but by the time we got there the guy had died."

"Shut up, Harmon. She's on the other side."

"Not willingly. Where did they find the perp?"

"The patrolman caught him. He stood right over the body. It doesn't get any better," Harmon said.

"And the COD?"

"Blunt force trauma. We think McCall beat him with a pipe or a baseball bat." Harmon talked until Sampson's expression filled with rage.

"Were McCall's clothes tested for blood spatter?" She gazed down and noticed the number printed on a file. One sheet of paper stuck out from the folder with Ben's name handwritten along the side. She quickly put the numbers in her memory bank and gazed back up at Sonny.

"Of course we tested them. Somehow, he got himself cleaned up. Nothing found on the clothes. The murder weapon disappeared, too," Harmon answered.

"No blood spatter. Hmm, interesting." She couldn't help herself. The words escaped before she could call them back, but the numbers still stayed in her mind.

"Okay, big mouth, you've said enough. You open your mouth one more time . . ."

"All right." Harmon put his hands up in surrender.

"You've been very helpful. I'd love to see the crime scene photos. I don't suppose . . ." She grinned hopefully at Harmon again.

Curtis Sampson stepped closer, took her by the arm, and rushed her toward the door. "Our helpful tips ran out. You need to leave now."

"I didn't mean to step on your toes. You must know how it feels to be stuck with a slimy job. It's how I feel about this." She looked back over her shoulder and gave Harmon a pleading expression. "Sorry."

"We don't talk about open cases. Shove off." Sampson closed the door behind her.

When she left the building, she only waited a minute for Josh to pick her up. His eyes questioned hers while she got in his car.

"I circled the block fifty times. Did you get anything useful out of them?"

"Well, my charm only worked on one of them. He did tell me a little, but I didn't get to see the crime scene photos. It's one of the reasons I didn't want you to come with me. They'd take one look at you, and we would've gotten nothing."

"Well?" Josh found a space up the street and pulled over. "What did you find out?"

"If he beat the victim, they didn't find the clothes he wore while he did it. The police can't find the murder weapon. Once I found no blood spatter interesting, the lead detective chased me out the door."

"Why would he? Why so touchy about no blood spatter?"

"I don't know for sure, but it's a weak point in their case. The detail could give them trouble at trial."

"How?"

"I wanted to ask how much time elapsed between the 911 call and the patrolman's arrival, but I didn't get far enough."

"What difference does it make?"

"If the clothes he wore didn't contain blood spatter, and they didn't, he needed time to get rid of them."

"Now we're getting somewhere."

"Maybe." She wasn't sure of anything yet.

Josh pulled the Carrera GT back onto the street.

She needed those crime scene photos. She pulled her phone out and dialed Bill Graywolf. He answered after two rings.

"Hi, slacker."

"Watch the greeting, my friend. I ran at least five miles this morning so I'm not a slacker."

"You get to tool around LA, and I'm stuck here in the frozen arctic. We got one hell of a snow. They've closed most roads in this part of the state."

"You at work or home?"

"Work. I got busy on a case and didn't notice how late it was. By the time I realized, the weather had turned bad. I couldn't leave."

"Have you got enough food and water to get through? I don't remember anything but vending machines in your building."

"I'll survive, if I don't run out of change. I also keep an emergency kit for when I get caught up in a case. I'll be fine."

"Good. I have a problem. I could use your help."

"You always need something. I guess that's good, or I wouldn't hear from you at all."

"That's not true. You're one of my best friends. At least, I consider you my best," she said.

"I know. I only give you a hard time since you always want something out of the ordinary."

"I can do the ordinary myself, but I admit, this time I am asking for a huge favor. I need copies of the crime scene photos from the murder in Malibu. I mouthed off to the detectives, and now they won't share. The sooner I get the pictures, the better. It would be better if you could get the whole murder book, but get what you can."

"You're not the type to mouth off if you need info. What happened?"

"I used the word 'interesting' with the wrong detail. Careless, I know, but . . ." She shrugged. "Will you take pity on me? I need those photographs."

"I'll give it a try. What's the case file number in case I get lucky?"

"Lucky my foot. It's a piece of cake for someone like you." She gave him the information and ended the call.

~

THEY ENTERED Ben's estate through a wrought iron gate held up between two huge pillars made of stones. The half-circle drive exited through an identical set of columns and gate. The massive front door appeared to be carved from solid wood and stood at least eight feet tall on the mid-century modern dwelling. Inside, black leather furniture prevailed. Windows along the high ceilings flooded the space with light. Everything tastefully done, of course.

She figured someone else had decorated for him, but it still gave away a few details about who he might be. She sensed he cared more about what others thought of him than he thought of himself. Last night at the jail for the first time she'd posed the question he might be innocent. Still, at the back of her mind she understood he was a skilled actor.

She'd see what the day revealed. It made police work interesting and each day different. You didn't know where a new lead might go until you followed it to the end.

Ben's house hugged the bluff near the ocean, but still included a large swimming pool. It seemed like overkill to her. The patio revealed the markings where they'd found the victim outlined in blood spatter. At least, it helped her perspective.

She studied the crime scene for several minutes. Was the murder weapon here, or did the killer bring it with him? Did he take it with him? If not, where did the murder weapon go? More important, why did he take it with him? Or did Ben manage to get rid of it before the police entered his residence?

Dried blood spatter covered every surface in a twenty-foot area surrounding the position of the body. In some droplets, she could tell they'd sampled for testing. Lots and lots of cast-off pattern. When she received copies of the crime scene photos, she would come back, but for now, she took pictures of every detail that might be pertinent. The weapon might not be a bat, but she discerned from the blood spatter that the killer had used it like one.

From the excessive quantity and type of spatter, she knew the murder was rage induced. This amount of fury always meant a personal motive. Whatever caused the wrath, it built inside the killer for a long time. She questioned what trigger set the violence free. Most likely, the victim never saw it coming.

She looked over at Josh. "Did you bring screwdrivers? We need to check every drain in this house for samples. Whoever did this would be covered in blood, hair, and tissue. If Ben killed him, he needed to clean up somewhere. If we find nothing in the drains, that fact could help clear him. I'm sure the crime scene unit checked everything thoroughly, but you never know what they might have missed."

"Will these samples be legal in court? Aren't we wasting our time?"

"I don't know California laws specifically, but I'm certified to take samples at home. The thing is, I know the techs in Tulsa. I don't know the ones out here. Even in Tulsa some are better than others. We have techs that seem to find what others don't. If I can show reasonable doubt, that may be all we need. But the truth is, I want to know what happened here. Did Ben do it or not?" She continued to stare directly at him.

"I left the tools we brought out in the car. I'll go get them."

"I'd like to study this area until you get back." She wanted to make sure she took enough pictures of the house. The weather would contaminate the crime scene the next time it rained. With the salty air, the damage could already be done so they really needed whatever evidence remained available.

After Josh returned, they worked together and opened the drains in every conceivable place. They swabbed and pulled hair samples. They ran cotton swabs around every pipe and threading possible. They carefully labeled the contents and location of every plastic bag as they put the evidence inside. Several hours elapsed before they finished.

"I didn't know this kind of work could be so tedious." Josh broke the silence that grew between them.

"Boring's why I'm not a tech. I like to interpret the evidence the techs find. They give us the results, and we try to figure exactly what happened and sometimes why."

"But you still know how to collect samples the way they would."

"Any decent detective knows how to take a sample, but one summer I followed the crime scene techs around Tulsa. I did a research paper on it later. It also helped keep me occupied while Hank worked a tough case. Of course, I didn't tell him I worked the case, too, in my own way. That's part of how I qualified."

"So did you always know you wanted to be a cop?"

"Oh yeah. I moved in with Hank when I was ten. I became interested in what he did for a living. I studied the murder books and anything I could get my hands on. I thought Hank didn't know, but the night you called we discussed it. He figured me out the first week. I should have known. He's always been too good at his job."

Josh nodded and moved up beside her. "We need a box to move these samples to the car."

"Did you always know you wanted to be an actor?" The question was simple, but instantly Josh's demeanor changed.

"No." He didn't add a word to his answer.

She found the omission insightful. These buddies held onto a lot of secrets. Ben wouldn't reveal who the murdered victim was. Apparently, Josh didn't like to talk about his past. She decided to let it slide. If they got better acquainted with each other, she might corner him about it then.

"Okay. Where would Ben keep an empty box?" She wanted to lighten the mood.

She searched for one and didn't find it, so they placed samples in the back of the Porsche for twenty minutes. Once they finished, they raided the fridge for cold drinks. Josh handed her a beer.

"No, thanks. I hate the taste. I like Pepsi if he has it."

Josh moved objects around and pulled one from the back of the refrigerator. "I never heard of a cop who didn't like beer."

"I get plenty of crap about it back home. I don't like coffee either. Hank never lets me hear the end of it. Keep me stocked with plenty of soda and bottled water, and I'll be fine."

She took a long swallow from her plastic bottle, and wiped at her brow with the back of her wrist. "Do you know any of his neighbors? We need to canvass this area."

"What about the samples?" Josh asked.

"Let's park the car in the garage. We'll lock it up tight. It should be fine until we get back."

"Sounds like a plan."

Her phone interrupted their discussion. "Hey, Caroline. What's up?"

They spoke for several minutes and disconnected.

"The good news. Caroline managed to snag an earlier flight. The bad news. She is already en route and will be here in a half hour. We'll need to put our canvass on hold. Can we get there in thirty minutes?"

"Maybe. Depends on traffic. The freeway's usually a bitch in this town."

"Let's go. I don't want her to wait any longer than necessary."

As they left Ben's house behind, Josh asked, "Do you think she'll make any progress with Ben?"

"If I didn't, why would I ask her to fly out here? Besides,

after she prays for me, good stuff happens. If anyone has an in with the man upstairs, I figure it's Caroline."

Josh's tight expression lifted. He'd make his own judgments about her best friend soon enough. For now, she watched the road and kept track of landmarks. The sooner she got her bearings in this town, the better.

5

———————

Footsteps made Ben McCall glance up. A sexy redhead entered the hallway outside his dismal new quarters. She strolled beside Jerry Martin, his jailer. He noticed her black tailored slacks fit loosely over shapely hips. When Paige Stone mentioned some evangelist would come to see him, he didn't dream she'd look this hot.

Then he remembered his whereabouts and the futility hit home again. She was the type a man wanted to impress, but she'd never be interested now. Who was he kidding? No girl would be interested in him again, ever.

Jerry opened the door to his cell, and she walked inside. She offered her hand and introduced herself. "I'm Caroline Montgomery." He took it in his, grinned, and ejected his recent thoughts.

He motioned for her to sit on the bench and took his seat on the single bed. "Welcome to my humble abode, as the saying goes."

"I see your taste runs toward minimal." Her smile lit up an already perfect face.

He didn't expected her sense of humor or the way her beauty affected him. He paused and searched for something to say.

"You must know why I'm here. Paige did tell you I'd come to visit you," she said.

"She sent you to unlock my darkest secrets."

She rolled her eyes. "No. I think she's only interested in one." After a short pause in their conversation, Caroline placed the Bible down beside her.

For an instant, he recalled his mother's Holy Book and longed to hold it to him. He missed the lost innocence from his youth and the only woman he'd known who had brought him peace.

Caroline sat and studied him while his silence grew longer. "I've gotten to know Paige well over the last six months. She wants to investigate this case. You asked for her help. She's here, but you don't seem to trust her. You surely don't think you can have it both ways." Her words sounded reasonable.

"I can see your point, but you don't understand. The man who was murdered at my house was a monster. I have powerful reasons to hate him, but I didn't kill him. I'm not sure what will happen when the truth comes out." He hung his head and focused on the beige paint splotches that made random patterns on the floor.

"Surely you've been told life holds no guarantees. In a situation like this, you must trust someone. You're in trouble. The kind that doesn't go away easily. If I picked sides, I'd choose Paige first." Her brown eyes, flecked with topaz, showed no guile as she gazed into his.

He wanted to trust her, but he couldn't let anyone see the disgrace of his past. People didn't know him, not even Josh or Tony. He couldn't explain the shame he felt. He'd sooner die than expose his family secrets to another person, especially this gorgeous girl in front of him.

"She gave her life for me. Paige never talks about it, but once the serial killer pointed the gun at me, she distracted him. She made him go after her again. She let him strangle her, and he'd already choked her several times before. She died right before my eyes. Special Agent Trinity resuscitated her and brought her back. You can trust her with your life, Mr. McCall."

They remained quiet for a time. He stared directly at her for a few moments, then dropped his gaze. Finally, he broke through the silence. "I'd offer you something to drink, but the hospitality here isn't what it should be."

"Cut the BS. You're wasting my time. Whatever you think is so terrible you can't reveal it, isn't anything new. Everyone has something in their past that isn't appealing. Paige has seen everything on her job. Bottom line. You want her help, you need to trust her with your secrets."

He searched his mind for words, any words. He opened his mouth, but nothing came out. She stood and glanced at the door.

"You remind me of her." He didn't want Caroline to leave. Her manner reminded him of old memories. Fond periods of the time when his mother nurtured him.

"Who?"

"My mother. She read her Bible sometimes."

"So she was a Christian?"

"Oh, yeah." He nodded.

"She was a good influence on your life?"

"The only one. I remember she loved me."

"Do you have any siblings?"

"No. Only me."

"Were you a lonely child?"

"My mom was always there for me. Well, until she wasn't."

"What's your father like?"

"I'd prefer not to discuss him. How about you read to me like my mom used to do." He would do anything to get her off the subject of his father. He hated to think about him. He kept the old man safely locked in a compartment he never visited. Besides, he needed her to stay. He didn't want to be alone with his fear. Not now.

"What type scriptures did she read to you? What would you like to hear?"

He didn't speak for a few moments. "Proverbs 31 in honor of my mother, the virtuous woman."

Caroline turned several pages back and forth until she found the correct one. She cleared her throat and read.

He sat on the edge of his bunk, gripped the sides, and listened.

"'Who can find a virtuous woman? For her price is far above rubies.'"

My father found one and beat her most of the damn time, the son of a bitch.

"'She will do him good and not evil all the days of her life.'"

She did her husband good, but he gave her nothing but evil. He chewed the inside of his lip.

"'Her children arise up early, and call her blessed; her husband also, and he praises her.'"

The asshole never said a kind word to her. Ever. He felt the hatred for his father steal over him like a cloak.

"'But a woman that feareth the Lord, she shall be praised.'"

His mother. The only person he knew for sure lived in heaven. She'd been at peace for many years, and he missed her with an ache that gripped his chest tight.

PAIGE SAW Caroline at the door of the building. Her friend walked out, and the sunlight turned her hair to flame. Caroline spotted them across the street. She wove her way toward them, opened the door, and climbed in the back of the black Escalade.

"Did he tell you the victim's name?" She turned and stared at her.

Caroline shook her head no. "He isn't ready yet."

"Shoot," she mumbled. When the evangelist was around, she attempted to never let a curse word slip out.

"I know, but he still needs your help. You can't give up on him." Caroline's right brow lifted.

"I haven't, but I need to know who the victim is. Homicide 101. Motive equals who wants to kill them and for what reason. It's impossible to find out if you don't know the person's identity."

"I agree with her." Josh turned and nodded toward Caroline. "We can't give up on him. I know he didn't do it. He's not the type of person to kill someone."

"I didn't say he did." She turned back to face forward and motioned for Josh to pull out into traffic. "We need to get those samples to the lab. So let's take Caroline back and get her settled in. While she unpacks, we'll take care of the evidence."

"Sounds like a plan." Josh started the engine.

After they got back to his home, they unloaded Caroline's luggage and carried it into the house. Josh took the two larger bags into a gorgeous bedroom that overlooked the Pacific Ocean. The heavy drapes stood open and let in light. He set the suitcases down next to a gold velvet bench at the foot of the bed.

An antique dresser with four large drawers rested against a rich brown wall. Luxurious carpets in matching colors hid sections of inlaid burl wood floors. Dark rust and burgundy silk covered the mahogany four-poster bed. Paige thought the space was too perfect to live in, like rooms she'd seen in designer magazines.

Caroline chuckled. "This reminds me of the home I left behind years ago. It's lovely. Thank you for your kindness. It's a treat to stay here."

"I'm lucky you agreed to come. I think Paige might have fled back to Oklahoma if you hadn't." Josh nodded.

"Oh, good grief. I wouldn't go home." She set the two smaller cases on the floor near the others.

"You know, I'm capable. I can carry my own bags." Caroline moved toward the seating area on the right and touched various objects along the way.

"Wouldn't hear of it. You're my guest. Besides, it's no big deal. Let me be a gentleman."

"When do you think you should go back to see Ben? We need to apply steady pressure on him. The sooner I know the victim, the better." She changed the subject and walked back toward the door they'd entered. She crossed her arms.

"I guess the next time I can get back in. He needs company. He won't say it, but this frightens him."

"He's more sensitive than he lets people know. I'm glad to see you understand." Josh walked over to join her at the door.

"We can take the samples to the lab. You can relax a little. Put whatever you want away. We'll come back and pick you up. Our errand might take a while. You know LA traffic." She glanced at her wrist as if to check the time even though she hadn't worn a watch in over a year. She always used her cell phone now. She hadn't broken the habit yet.

Josh moved toward the antique dresser. He opened the top drawer and took out a tablet. He pushed an icon, and a beautiful painting on the wall slid to the side, revealing a TV. "You can watch something if you care to. Refreshments are in the kitchen. Help yourself. I would offer to fix them for us, but

Paige is hell bent on getting us out the door." He bowed like a servant.

She signaled him with scornful eyes and nodded toward Caroline. "Try to watch your language."

"Sorry, I'm not used to proper company." His mischievous smile wasn't contrite. Josh showed Caroline how to use the programmed device.

"Okay, Josh, we're burning daylight, as the saying goes. Let's get the samples to the lab." She tapped her foot.

They left Caroline and moved toward the garage where the Porsche contained their morning's work. The black Escalade sat right beside it. After they got in the Carrera, Josh turned to Paige.

"Caroline seems like a nice person. I think she believes Ben is innocent."

"You never know how a case will turn out. You follow where the evidence leads you. I hope it leads to anyone but your friend. In cases like these, most of the time, the police arrest the right guy."

"Are you saying you think he's guilty?"

"Right now, I don't know. He sounded straight with me when I saw him, but I know he's an actor. Which makes it more difficult for me to judge his reactions. No matter what I think, I intend to treat this like I would any other case. Watch, examine, and follow leads. Those steps will get me to the truth. I won't cover for him if he's guilty, but if he's not, I won't let them convict him."

"I guess that's all anyone could ask."

Josh didn't appear too happy with her statement, but he couldn't find fault with it either.

A big traffic jam slowed them down, and they arrived to find the lab they'd chosen closed.

~

THE DARK-HAIRED ONES always caught my attention. This prostitute was beautiful. She barely covered her body with her tight black shorts and midriff tank top. The heels stood at least four inches high. She looked exactly like what she was, but I didn't care. The way her hips weaved back and forth as she walked reminded me of the image from the night before, the identity of the mystery lady, and the memory I glimpsed for a second.

I needed more insight into my recollection. Somewhere in my brain lurked the answer. Why was the brunette in my vision so important? I took my last drag on the stub and felt the heat between my fingers. I watched her ply her trade and promised myself I wouldn't hurt this whore. The smoke calmed me a little. I put my cigarette out, started the engine of my truck, and drove to her corner.

She flashed me a seductive smile when she walked up to my window.

"Need a lift?" My eyes contained a knowing expression of their own as I flirted with her.

"If the price is right."

"It might be."

She gave me a figure and hoisted herself up into the cab of the pickup. I nodded agreement to the amount.

I glanced at her again. The smoldering intensity her eyes revealed and the redness of her lips teased the image hidden in my memory, but it dangled just out of my mind's reach. This hooker resembled the woman in my mental flashes more than the one last night. I needed to get her to move again. I felt the answer would come, if she would pace for me in her sultry way.

I pulled into a park away from the streetlights. She could

stroll farther with the extra space. The room had been too small for Hilda to move properly. This would work. I felt it.

"Okay, Honey Bun, I need you to walk for me like you did on the corner. It's what a man needs to get his juices going." I lied to her. I wasn't interested in what she sold. Only the images and the secrets that remained hidden.

"How did you know my name?" She stared up at me with the first hint of fear in her eyes.

"I didn't know your name. You smell sweet like a honey bun." I grinned and got out of the car to open her door.

6

———

Paige stretched both calves several times, bent at the waist, and touched the ground flat handed. Both leg muscles pulled tight. When her head came up, Josh stood right beside her. He threw a small towel at her and put another around his neck.

"I figured I'd find you here. The morning's perfect for a run."

She didn't answer him and took off toward the Pacific, which waited for them at the bottom of the mountainside. She could see the gulls fly above the surf, searching for breakfast. They ran closer to the beach, and the bird's cries screeched louder.

"Have you figured out our plans for the day?"

She continued to ignore him, trying to hold on to the unspoiled atmosphere of the scene surrounding her.

"Are we no longer on speaking terms?" he asked, intruding into her solitude for the third time.

"I'm working to maintain a peaceful start to my day. I never invited you along. If you don't enjoy the quiet, please take another route." She increased her speed and pulled slightly ahead of him.

"I see you're in a good mood." Josh brought himself up even with her.

"Actually, this is my good mood. Sorry you don't find it charming enough." She tried to focus on the mystery. Who died on Ben's patio? Why would someone want the victim dead? Most important, why was Ben so reluctant to identify the man?

When she ran, she liked to let her mind ponder the events on her current case. She worked best that way. She'd solved several cases after she mulled over the facts and listened to the rhythm of her own jogging. The evidence seemed to fall into place after she perspired and her feet slapped the ground ahead.

"I'm sorry. You're right. You never invited me along. Do you want alone time?"

"I've already lost my train of thought. You might as well stay. Sometimes I get my best inspiration during a run, but Sonya talks incessantly. She's my running partner. What's on your mind?" She turned her head in his direction.

"I'm not sure. You're different from what I expected, and Caroline's like no other religious person I know. Not that I know that many evangelists. Who's Sonya?"

"Sonya's a kid I mentor back home. I caught her smoking pot, so I make her run with me. Caroline's different than I expected, too, but I like her. I trust her. Those two don't always come in the same package."

"I know what you mean."

Their conversation lagged for several moments.

"So what's bothering you? If you don't beat around the bush, we'll get there much sooner." She glanced in his direction. They turned right and moved north along the highway.

"Do you have any idea why Ben's so hesitant to tell us the guy's name?" Josh asked.

"I'm working on it. Obviously, he knows him. I figure it's somebody he probably would want dead. The motive must be strong. How much do you know about his past?"

"Not much. Tony, Ben, and I cemented our friendship over the years. We worked on several movies together years ago. Our bond has strengthened since we first met. We don't talk about our pasts much. I figured if they wanted me to know, they would tell me. Ben never mentions his at all. Tony rarely does. We only found out he had an old-maid aunt during filming on *Liberty Valance*."

"So what do you all talk about?"

"Mostly drink beer, joke about our lives, girls, and things that don't matter."

"I see." She hesitated for a time and considered how he referred to women, but decided the information she needed led in another direction. "Why do you suppose that's true? Ben is a good friend. You told me he is. Why don't you know more about him than his favorite drink and how many women he's scored with?" She watched his expression turn thoughtful because she'd forced him to see something he'd never examined before.

"I'm not sure how to explain it. Our friendship exists because we know we can trust each other not to ask the wrong questions. I think we each have areas we never discuss. We know we don't need to. We accept each other without every detail. I don't need to know Ben's secrets to know he didn't kill the man. I know he didn't." Josh's certainty would persuade most people, but she didn't convince that easily.

"Unfortunately, your opinion won't hold up in court, but I'll keep it in mind. However, I'll also bear in mind you wouldn't be surprised if he had something shady in his background."

"Now, you're putting words in my mouth. I didn't say shady."

"No, you didn't, but you know there's a gray area there somewhere."

Josh ran in a half circle and reversed their direction. "What do you want for breakfast when we get home?"

She allowed him to change the subject and followed him while they increased their pace toward his residence. "I don't know. I hadn't thought about it. We need to go check with the lawyer. See what angles he wants more information about. I want to check my laptop. Bill might have my crime scene photos ready, and we need to let Caroline work her magic on Ben. He'll talk to her sooner or later."

"You know what I don't understand?"

She shook her head and ran toward the road up the mountain.

"How can a TV evangelist look so damned good?"

"Beats me, but she's my friend. Keep your testosterone to yourself."

He laughed aloud for several seconds. "You needn't worry. I'll consider her off limits."

She turned on him and stopped. "I'm serious. She's my friend. Put a lock on your zipper. I won't let you hurt her over this. She's doing you a favor."

"You think I'd leave her with a broken heart."

"I'm not taking any chances. Caroline's an evangelist. It doesn't mean she's a pushover. Besides, you flirt with every female in sight."

"So you did notice I flirted with you."

"You're about as subtle as the Hollywood sign. I'll race you home." She knew the challenge was a mistake the minute they turned the corner onto the mountain road. He left her behind. She would smile if it didn't hurt so bad to run up the elevated grade of the mountain.

After she reached the gate to his property, he held a sports drink out for her. She took the cold bottle and walked past him without saying a word.

"You're not a poor loser are you?"

"Not at all, but I hear a shower calling my name."

When she got to her room, she reached into her pocket to empty the contents. The phone vibrated in her hand before it started playing Bill's ringtone.

"I've got your crime scene photos."

"Hello to you too, Bill. Are they on my laptop, yet?"

"I sent them a minute ago. Is it sunny in LA? The snow's deeper here than I've ever seen it."

"I just got back from running several miles. The fresh air felt great." She put the phone between her ear and her shoulder.

"We've set record lows over the northeast part of the state. I think I hate you right now."

"Are you still snowed in?"

"Yes, and the snack food machines don't tempt me anymore. What I wouldn't give for a hot cooked meal, not to mention a shower."

"I'm sorry, but I'm heading for one right now. Believe me, I need it. Have you talked to Hank? Is he okay in this weather? " She sat down on the bed and took her left shoe off.

"He called my cell this morning. Claimed he was fine."

"Thanks for the pictures. I know I asked a lot." She wiped the sweat on her brow with the shirt she'd taken off.

"I had nothing else to do. The night crept by. They'll probably get a few roads open today. I might get out later."

"I hope so. I'll talk at you in a bit."

She went straight to her laptop, turned it on, and waited to enter her password. Then she hustled to the bathroom to rinse off while the computer uploaded.

The shower didn't take long. She could hardly wait to see the gift Bill sent her. Crime scene photos were her favorite. She studied them growing up. If their techs knew how to do their job, she should unscramble a few of the theories that remained tangled in her brain. She dried with Josh's plush towel and heard her phone ring again.

She glanced at the caller ID and snatched up the phone. "Why aren't you in school?"

"There's snow up to my elbows. No school," Sonya said.

"Sorry. I forgot. My mind was on other business. So what's up?"

"You're not back, and I'm bored. The snow is so deep outside, it's like we're prisoners. Haven't you solved the case, yet?"

"No. You called to pester me. I can't get any work done. Are you and your mother okay with the storm and all?"

"Yeah. She got food in before the weather hit. We're lucky. We still have electricity. Part of Tulsa lost power. So, what's Josh Stuart really like?"

"I guess he's okay. I'm still a little pissed. He went over my head to get me out here, but he's treated me all right since I arrived."

"Did he get you in trouble? He might be worth it. He's hot."

"Not trouble. How did we digress to this subject? I've got to go. I'll never come home if I stay on the phone with you all day."

"I know, but I miss you."

"I miss you, too, even if you're a mess most of the time. I'll see you when I get back."

She laid the phone down on the bed and walked over to the

computer that sat on the dresser. Several strokes later on the keyboard, the photographs she needed appeared on the screen.

"Gotcha." She grinned.

A knock on the door made her frown. She grabbed the towel from the floor and wrapped it around her. *Shit. Would people never leave her alone this morning?* She opened the door a crack and saw Josh on the other side.

"Are you ready to go?" he asked.

"I've been interrupted so many times, I'm not. Do you own a good color printer? I want to print photos from my laptop."

"Yeah. I have one in my study we can use."

"Give me five minutes. I gotta put clothes on. I'll meet you in the kitchen." She closed the door, dropped the towel, and hunted for something quick to put on. Jeans and a red V-necked T-shirt would do.

A few minutes later, she arrived to see Caroline sipping coffee and Josh munching on a granola bar. They sat around the breakfast table and looked comfortable. The glow from the morning sun came through the bay window and washed over them. The scene resembled a Norman Rockwell done in a California style. She broke the golden spell that rested on them.

"I need the printer." She held up the flash drive that now contained the crime scene pictures.

Josh got up and motioned for her to follow. They moved through the main part of the house and up the stairs. His massive bedroom had a private study attached. The office contained a desktop computer set up with a three-in-one.

He plugged the thumb drive into the USB port and turned the computer on. She waited for a few seconds while he typed in his password. The computer hummed, and he turned back around.

"Did you get a chance to go through them?"

"Barely a glance. I can tell more once I get them to Ben's

and compare them to the scene itself. The body's a mess. No way to tell who the victim is, unless the fingerprints come back with a match."

"Won't the police have run them by now?"

"I'm sure they did. That's why we need to get Ben to talk. We need to stay ahead of the police, not behind them. They may already know. States require prints when you get a driver's license. It's only a matter of time." She gathered the considerable stack of eight-by-tens, and they walked back to the kitchen.

"What do you want to eat this morning?"

"Let me grab a granola bar and a Pepsi, but I'm okay if you don't have either."

"We've got to work on your eating habits. They're horrible." He tossed her a can of Pepsi and she grabbed a nutty oatmeal bar and moved toward the garage.

"Thanks for inviting me." Caroline got up from her chair, emptied her cup in the sink, and placed it in the dishwasher.

When she saw Caroline following behind them, she changed her direction to the black Escalade. They climbed inside, and she turned to Caroline in the back seat. "Do you want to go by and see if Ben will talk to you? We need the victim's identity ASAP."

"I'll give it another shot, but I can't promise anything."

"What Josh and I are going to do won't be a picnic. After this long, it'll stink. You're better off with him." She turned back around and settled into the quiet that filled the SUV.

After they left Caroline at the jail, they drove back to Ben's home in Malibu. Josh used his key to let them in. The house smelled stale and felt stuffy like so many crime scenes left empty too long. She strolled through the house and examined it thoroughly. Something felt off. She was certain she'd been careful not to move anything when she took samples the day before.

When they got to the place where Ben discovered the body, she sorted through the photos until she found the one she wanted. The victim was a mess. He wasn't just dead. Someone bludgeoned him repeatedly after his last breath.

Josh interrupted her contemplation. "What is it? What did you find?"

"I'm studying the pictures. You need to search them. Concentrate on what fits and what doesn't. You can tell a lot from the victim for example. The murder was rage induced. So much anger means this was personal. The killer knew him well."

"You think that's why Ben won't tell who the person is, don't you?"

"It could explain the reason, but jumping to conclusions doesn't always pan out. I need to know for sure. So do the police."

She pulled several more photographs from the stack and moved around the room. First one and then another, she compared them to the scene before her. Fifteen minutes passed before either spoke again.

"I didn't want to say anything, but I'm sure someone has been in here since we were here last. Several objects aren't in the same place. You were careful the day we took samples, weren't you?"

"I only touched what you told me to. Why?"

"I noticed the drawer in the other room wasn't pushed in all the way. I'm sure the front was closed tight after we came here before. This photo confirms what I remembered. Go see for yourself. Someone moved the patio chair. See how the rust print around the bottom is off a little? In the picture, it's perfectly in place. I'm sure it was in place when we visited yesterday. Someone was careful, but not careful enough. It's been searched."

"Why would anyone want to go through the place? What would be the point?"

"Exactly my thought. I'm not sure. I don't have a theory, yet."

BEN PACED HIS NEW CELL. They'd moved him overnight. He wanted to know what the detective and Josh discovered. Had they made any progress? He pushed his hand through his hair for the twentieth time, stopped, and threw himself on his bunk. His feet hung over the edge. The damned bed was too small. The cell was too small. His life was too small. How the hell would he ever get out of here?

Jerry Taylor walked up and tapped on his bars. Since he was a celebrity, the same guard moved with him to this horrible hole. That surprised him, but the deputy acted like a standup guy.

"You got a visitor. It's the redhead, again."

The news distracted him from his morbid reflections. He got up off the bunk and put on his winning façade. A few minutes later, he faced her, separated by a thick layer of glass.

He expected his smile would surely disarm her like it did countless other women, but her expression gave no sign she was captivated.

"Have you decided to participate in your own defense?" she asked.

He stopped all pretense and stared at her.

"I won't beg you. If you decide to help yourself, it'll be your choice."

He ran his hand through his hair, but he stayed mute. She watched him for several moments that seemed to linger forever.

She got up. "You know I have better places to spend my time."

"No. Don't leave." He wanted to hide, but he had no place to go.

"Tell me, why do you want me to stay? Will you still dance around the answers we need to defend you? Who is he? Was he your father?"

He searched her eyes and recognized, she knew the answer. "Why do you say that?"

"I feel it's true. Your reaction confirms it."

"Does Josh know?"

She shook her head. "Did you hate him so much? Is that why you don't want to tell anyone his name?"

"A person like you could never understand the filth that I came from. Tom McCall was the lowest scum ever born, and he fathered me. I've waited my whole life for him to show up to destroy me, but I swear, I didn't kill him." He sat back down and stared at the floor. He didn't want her to see him like this. The shame ran too deep.

He paused a long time before he continued. "My earliest memory is of my mother. In it, she read to me from her Bible. The house is tranquil. I sense my mother's love for me. I know everything is secure."

His expression turned to a frown, and he hesitated again. "My second earliest memory, I hear the front door slam and harsh footsteps cross the room. Every drop of peace flees from his presence, and I feel my mother's arm shiver beside me. I can't explain it any other way." He examined Caroline's eyes, and found no judgement in them.

"You must have been young. I assume the person who stole your peace is your father."

"He claimed to be, but I don't possess any real knowledge of what a father should be. I only remember the way he punched my mother. I saw her covered in bruises, sometimes she could barely stand upright, and our hugs were always careful ones. Later, I learned his fists felt like pistons of steel."

They both remained silent for a time.

"Sometimes I try to remember her face. To me as a young boy, she was so beautiful, but it's been a long time since I've seen her."

"Why?"

"She died."

"How did she die?"

"You know the answer, don't you?"

"You mean your father killed her."

He nodded.

~

The Past

"WHAT'S YOUR FAVORITE PSALM?" Ben asked.

"I love so many." His mother looked thoughtful for several seconds. "I'd choose Psalm 91. It promises to protect you from harm."

He didn't understand how that worked. His father seemed stronger than God, but he never said that to his mother. It confused him at five years old, but he knew she continued to believe.

The sound those powerful footsteps made echoed from the porch outside. His mother's face filled with fear.

"Hurry, Ben, go to your room."

He scooted down from the couch and ran as fast as his legs could go, but the front door exploded open. He rounded the corner to his bedroom and closed the door without a sound. His closet provided darkness where he crawled in and hid. He heard his father's voice yelling at his mother. Then the lamps crashed against the wall and furniture scraped the floor when his mother landed on it. The slap of flesh pounding flesh. Sounds of terror and fear choked him to silence, though he wanted to scream for his daddy to stop.

Under his breath he whispered, "*Psalm 91, Psalm 91, Psalm 91.*" Over and over again, he chanted the name from the *Holy Bible.* Still, loud noises came from the other side of the wall. He didn't know how long he stayed there, but eventually, he became aware of the warm pee running down his leg.

A few seconds later a different fear crept over him. He must clean himself up. *No, no, no. My father will kill me. I must hurry. My father will kill me.*

7
———

Buck Tillman gazed down at the broken mass that had once been a female. The carpet of grass soaked up her blood. More than likely she'd been a prostitute. Black shorts revealed her bare flesh and the snug red top implied a working girl. Still, she deserved better than this. He'd like to castrate the SOB who'd done this to another human being. Didn't the asshole know that kids played in this park? What if one of them found her? The scumbag didn't deserve to breathe.

Vern Dowdy, his thirty-year partner, walked up beside him. He didn't need to say a word. They could finish each other's thoughts. It came from working together so long.

Neither he nor Vern touched the victim. The ME wasn't through with the body yet, but he got as close as he dared. He didn't see any ligature marks on the wrists or ankles. With an attack like this, he wasn't surprised. She'd come with the perp willingly. Probably assumed he was a regular john.

"Do you see any signs of sexual activity?" he asked his partner.

"No. I don't think he touched her that way." Vern shook his head.

"Me either." Which didn't make sense. Why bother to get a hooker and not at least get your rocks off before you kill her. He had a bad feeling about this one. In his tired bones, he knew another victim would turn up soon. The bastard's a psycho. The kind who didn't stop until you stopped him. He glanced up at Vern and figured he agreed. *Son of a bitch.*

"Damn it, Vern, I should've retired last year. I don't need this aggravation."

"I knew you'd say that. This guy's only begun."

"My thoughts exactly."

"Let's start a file on her and gather what little information we can. When we find out for sure, I guess we'd better warn the pros." He walked back to their vehicle and grabbed more yellow crime scene tape.

As Pete Goad climbed into the worn out pickup, he saw a black Escalade slow down and pull into the property he'd vacated. *Shit, that was close.* He wondered who the hell they were. The police didn't drive Cadillacs, and the owner was in jail. He slammed his door and decided to see what they were up to.

He moved his truck to a convenience store a block away and grabbed a tool belt with his Glock tucked inside. The sun warmed his back as he walked down the street toward the beach house. Several times along the way, he stopped and stared up at the power lines. His uniform suggested he worked for the electric company. No one paid attention. He wove his way closer to his target.

The wind tunneled from the Pacific between the two walls

that lined the estates. He jumped over the fence to the left and eased around the corner to view the patio. A woman stood sorting pictures. She held them up one at a time and compared the photos to the crime scene. The scene he'd left fifteen minutes earlier. He figured she was a detective, but she seemed young for that. The woman didn't look familiar, but the male did. He couldn't place him. At least not yet.

He still wondered about the two and continued to spy on them. The more important issue, how did they fit into the puzzle with the father and the son?

If the bastard had left Selena alone, he'd be on Paukea, his island in Fiji, minding his own business. Instead, he stood here in the States tracking down the piece of shit who killed his daughter.

The phone in his pocket vibrated. He stepped back to a safe distance and peeped to see who called. The display gave his business contact number. He did well enough that he didn't need the money. Hell, he'd stored enough away, he'd never need to accept another contract.

The pisser was, he'd squirreled away the money to leave for his only child. He knew she'd never be proud he fathered her. He'd stayed away from her life and let her mother nurture her. The careful plan he'd killed men for meant nothing. Selena was dead. The fortune he'd made no longer had purpose.

He replaced the cell phone in his pocket while his eyes scanned one more time around the corner. Then he retraced his steps to the street. A quick glance for the license plate number on the Escalade, and he returned to his vehicle. He waited.

He plugged the digits into his phone app. A minute later, the name Joshua Stuart popped up. With the address not far away, it seemed reasonable the man was Josh Stuart, Ben McCall's actor friend. Everyone knew the actors hung out together. One or the other managed to show up on the front page of the gossip rags weekly. That's why the guy was familiar.

But the woman acted like the one trained to investigate. Why would an actor drive a police detective around? Ben might have hired a private eye, but she acted and moved like a cop. Whoever she was, she looked damned good. He smirked. The dude was in jail. Still the hot chicks swarmed around him.

The sun beating down turned his vehicle into an oven. He rolled the windows down, but it only helped so much. An hour passed, and his throat felt parched. He walked into the store and grabbed a cold Gatorade. Through the glass door, he watched for the Escalade, threw a five down on the counter, and returned to his wheels.

What took so long? Surveillance was a bitch, but it always paid off. He liked to know what the hell went on so nothing caught him unaware. Patience rewarded him in his line of work. He'd been trained by the best, the U.S. government. Damned shame they didn't need him anymore, but shit happened. That's what his old man always said. More than thirty years passed, and he'd finally agreed his father was right.

He saw the black Caddy nudge through the gate from Ben McCall's estate. His hands touched the wires together. The truck started. He eased the pickup into traffic with a car between them. It surprised him the PCH wasn't busy at this time, so he didn't trail too close. He followed them several miles and figured they were headed back into LA. The traffic increased so he shadowed their SUV closer again.

They parked outside the Men's Central Jail, and a redhead got in their Escalade. They went around several blocks and drove back toward Malibu. A few miles farther, they turned into an In-N-Out Burger joint but didn't stay more than twenty minutes.

He tracked them to a place in Malibu up the side of a

mountain. It matched the address given for Josh Stuart's license plate.

This could waste a lot of time. The problem was, he needed to pursue this situation. He didn't have any other leads. If it weren't personal, he'd go back to his island near Lakeba, Fiji.

~

PAIGE COULD TELL when Caroline first spotted them. Josh pulled the Escalade next to the curb. She quickly climbed into the automobile, and they drove away.

Her friend barely got the door closed before she delivered the news. "The victim is his father. Name's Tom McCall. Says he hated his father and wanted him dead, but swears he didn't kill him. Before we go any further, to add my opinion, I believe Ben."

"Thank God. You don't know how much it helps. We can finally start to investigate the victimology," she said.

Josh slowed the SUV and turned his head. "Thanks."

Caroline nodded.

"Let's get something to eat. We need to play catch up. The day ahead will be a long one." She grabbed her phone from her pocket and dialed. "Hey, Bill, the photos turned out great. I compared them to the crime scene. It gave me better perspective. Could you run a name for me? Tom McCall or Thomas. Send it to me as soon as you find something."

"I'm on my afternoon break. I'll see what I can do. Is the weather still good out there?"

"Clear. Sixty-five degrees, headed to seventy."

"Now I know I hate you. We're still buried in snow. I've never seen this much in Oklahoma at one time. Weatherman said some places got two feet," Bill said.

"Wow. That is deep for Tulsa. I gotta run. There's an In-N-

Out Burger. I want to try one while I'm here." She motioned for Josh to pull into the establishment.

"You're all heart, like usual."

"I'd bring you one if I could, but it would be soggy and cold if I did. I'll see you when I get back, and I do appreciate your help."

"I know." Bill broke the connection.

"I see you've chosen lunch for us," Caroline said.

"Everybody always tells me to eat here if I come to California. You don't mind, do you?"

"No. How about you, Josh?" Caroline asked.

"It's fine. They're quite good. Especially these funky fries they make."

She had to admit, the hamburgers tasted good, but the Animal Fries with their cooked onions, cheese, and the rest were awesome.

Josh drove back to his house in Malibu. She checked her laptop first thing. Bill had already sent an e-mail.

I found what I could under the name you gave me. He has long periods of time unaccounted for. Had a wife, Martina, and a son. The boy's name is Benjamin Thomas McCall. Is it the same case you're working on? Thomas worked for a trucking company at that time. If he continued to do so, he used a false identity somewhere. I attached a picture and what I could dig up on him under his name.

Bill

She clicked the attachment to open it and stared at the photo for a long time. The face seemed familiar. She told herself Ben favored his father, but something about the picture nagged at her memories. She let the idea go for now. If she didn't worry an issue, the recollection came to her. It always did.

She examined the file that Bill gathered. A new mystery

presented itself for her to work. Bill was right. Huge holes in his timeline riddled the life of Thomas McCall.

~

BUCK TILLMAN PULLED up to the old motel and parked. The manager had called in a body behind the building in the alley. He got out of his car and moved toward the group gathered ahead. As he got close, he motioned everyone to get back.

"You'll contaminate evidence. Back up," he said. Frustrated the black and whites hadn't kept their distance and marked off the crime scene with tape, he barked orders for them to do so.

The first detail he noted was the amount of decomposition. The victim laid there for more than twenty-four hours. The eyes appeared cloudy. Larva crawled over the nose and mouth. The stench was detectible for at least fifty feet. Death never produced anything pleasant.

When Vern walked up, he shook his head. Buck knew what his partner was thinking. They'd caught another one. The black matted hair, the excessive makeup, and the stiletto heels. All trademarks shown by the previous prostitute. He suspected this victim was their first. The amount of decay put her death before the woman found in the park. *Damn it.*

"You thinking what I'm thinking?" Vern asked.

"Yeah. This one's an earlier victim," he said.

Vern nodded and leaned over the stiff to examine the corpse. He lifted the skirt. The lingerie remained intact. "No sign he messed with her. We'll have to wait for the autopsy to confirm."

"Son of a bitch. We've got another sociopath on the loose."

The medical examiner rolled in a few minutes later followed by SID. The group scrambled around to examine the victim and photograph everything in sight. After the Scientific

Investigation Division finished, the ME moved the body to his vehicle and left. He estimated the deceased laid there thirty-six to forty hours.

While Vern stayed in the back, he walked up to the office to interview the manager, and the techs went to the motel room to collect more evidence.

The name tag on his narrow chest read Larry. At a little under six foot, he looked lanky and frayed.

"Did you work night before last?" he asked.

"I'm damned near always here. I sleep in the back every chance I get."

"So you checked the guests into room seventeen the other night."

"Yeah, a brunette paid cash for the room. Most do pay with the green stuff." Larry rubbed at his nose and sniffled.

"Did you see the gentleman with her?"

"Nope. He parked to the side of the building. Left his lights on. I couldn't tell you if it was a guy. I assumed so." Larry grabbed a tissue from the box and blew his nose. "Trying to get over this sinus infection. I felt terrible the last few days."

"Could you tell anything about the vehicle he drove?"

"No. Like I said I felt bad. I took the money and gave her a key."

"Did you rent the room out last night to anyone? We need to know about contamination."

"I rented a pair the room for about an hour. I was up front and filled out the paperwork for another couple when they took off. Sorry, but I didn't know the dead woman was back there at the time."

He left a card and asked the man to call if he remembered anything useful. As he got to the door to leave, Larry spoke. "I think he drove a pickup. I remember the lights set up high, but I don't know what color or make."

"At least that's something," he said.

He walked back down to the room.

"Did the manager contribute anything helpful?" Vern saw him and came out to meet him.

"Not much. The vic came in to pay for the room. He thought the guy drove a truck. No color or model," he said. "The room was rented last night for about an hour. I'm sure SID won't like that."

"Can't catch a break. I hate to chase these sick bastards. I sent patrol to canvass, but I wouldn't hold my breath. We through here?" Vern asked.

They both walked to their shop, got in the vehicle, and headed back to the station. The captain would need a full report. He hated that they'd found so little information to put on it.

Paige and Josh parked the Porsche near the Bradbury Building at Broadway and Third. The structure appeared mundane from the outside. After she entered, a delightful surprise awaited. Charlie Chaplin sat on a long park bench with his cane tucked over his arm. She smiled at the statue.

"They filmed *Blade Runner* and *Lethal Weapon 4* here. It's the oldest commercial building left in Central LA. We researched the place once for a film I worked on, but we decided we didn't need it," Josh said.

"Are you sure this guy knows his way around a murder case? This is too theatrical for a law office." She walked with Josh away from the silent movie star.

"He's supposed to be the best. My lawyer checked him out."

"If you say so." She shrugged and glanced around while

they moved toward the elegant antique elevators. The most intricate scrollwork made from wrought iron trailed along the stairs and balconies that looked down on a central courtyard. The glass dome above let in light and brought life to the potted palms and greenery that peeked from behind the delicate black metal.

She and Josh walked into Jacob Carston's office. The décor blended naturally with the structure's interior. It reminded her of an elegant southern home in New Orleans. In her mind, it didn't fit with the LA scene. Nor did Mr. Carston.

"We need to cover a lot of details. Josh, you got to scram. You can't remain party to our discussions. She'll be the investigator of record. If you stay, you'd get called to testify. We don't want that." The man stood five feet six. He chewed vigorously on a short cigar that remained unlit. Anywhere from mid-forties to mid-fifties, she could tell he didn't waste time on foolishness.

"Detective Paige Stone." She reached out to shake his hand. "I'm sorry. Here it's just Paige."

"Yes. You can't consort with the police on this case." Jacob examined her eyes. "You're on our side. Right?"

She nodded, but her eyes didn't want to meet his yet. She still felt like a traitor.

"Okay, Josh, out the door." Carston pointed to the opening.

"I'll call you once I'm done," she said.

Josh left the room, and the lawyer turned to her. "I know you talked to Ben. What did he tell you?"

"He only told me he's innocent. You didn't go talk to him?"

"No. Not yet. I don't waste my time butting heads with a mule. If they don't want to talk yet, they only burn my daylight. I'm too expensive to squander my time. Headline it for me. What did you find out? What are we dealing with?" He commenced to chewing the cigar again.

"He wouldn't talk to me much except to say he went down the beach to Tony Strete's house after he had a confrontation with the victim. Claims he left the guy there alive, and when he came back the man was dead."

She followed him across the room where he sat behind his desk and left her to sit across from him. "A good friend got him to reveal the victim is his father, Tom McCall. The computer search shows he used to drive a truck, at least part of his life, but holes in his timeline appear throughout his history. We still don't know the whole story on the father because we only found out the name a few hours ago."

"What else did you accomplish since you've been here?"

"Josh and I took the house apart. We resampled everything. Can you recommend a reputable lab where we could take them? Who do you want me to use?"

Jacob took the cigar from his mouth and stared at it. He gave her a name and address.

"I want to get out to Ben's and canvass the neighbors. See if we can produce a witness to verify his story. I need to talk to the eyewitness the cops found. Did they give you discovery yet?" she asked.

"Not a thing, and they won't until they absolutely must."

"Now I know who the victim is, I want to talk to Ben again. See if I can pry any more information from him. The guy's been famous for some time. There must be a reason the old man showed up now. Do you plan to go see him again soon?"

"Tomorrow. He'll be more malleable by then. If they think they're big shots, it's best to show them the law doesn't care once murder is involved." He put the cigar back in his mouth and chewed while he leaned back in his burgundy leather chair.

"All right. Anything else on your list? I'll keep Bill on

McCall's background. We need to see what the old man's been up to."

Jacob's eyes moved up and examined her. "You're way too pretty for this line of work. We don't have to worry about you going Hollywood on us, do we?"

"God, no. A police detective raised me. It's in my blood. Call me if you need something more." She left her card with her personal number and walked to the door.

"Keep in touch. I need to know where the investigation leads at all times."

She nodded and left.

When she exited the Bradbury Building, Anthony Quinn stared down at her from a Victor Clothing Co mural across the street. She got in Josh's Porsche, and he quickly pulled away.

"How did it go?" Josh asked.

"Everything is about show business in this town, isn't it?"

"A lot. Why?"

"There's a huge mural with Anthony Quinn on it back there. I've noticed several others around town of various stars. It seems different to me. Are there any of you or Ben somewhere?"

"Not yet."

She nodded and pulled out her notes for the name and address. "We have to get these samples tested."

After they left the lab, they drove to see Ben. She'd given him a few hours to adjust to the idea that they knew who the victim was. He'd surely figured out the world didn't come to an end yet.

The county guards ushered her to a visitor's waiting room and went to retrieve Ben. He appeared more pale and dogged than the last time she'd seen him. She hadn't grasped how much jail changed a person. It gave her a new perspective she wasn't sure she wanted.

Once he sat on the other side of the clear thick divider, she smiled at him to reassure him she still worked for his side. "Look on the bright side, many people hate their father. We know about him, and the sun is still in its orbit. You okay?"

Ben nodded.

"I want to know more about the relationship between you. What was he like as a father? Did he beat you? Why did you hate him? The fine details of your life and his. It'll get personal, but I have to know. The police will uncover everything about you. They will violate everything in your existence and learn every little secret, but your lawyer and I need to know this information ahead of time. We can't be blindsided in court. Your life could depend on it."

He stared at her. His countenance lay bare with shame. Her eyes moved down. She didn't want to see the despair he exposed.

She cleared her throat and began again. "What was your father like?"

"He drank most of the time. When he did, he beat my mother. I hated him from the time I can first remember."

"What about your mother?"

Ben sat there and stared down at his hands for a long time. She figured he wouldn't answer. He opened his mouth twice, but closed it each time. Finally, "She's gone."

"What do you mean gone? She's deceased?"

"She's dead. I helped bury her." His voice sounded lifeless.

"How did she die?"

"After I turned twelve, my father beat her to death. I tried to stop him, but I took too long. I remember her eyes rolled back in her head, and I knew she was hurt bad. I got behind him to trip him, but then he beat me. It never brought her back. Nothing could."

"I'm sorry. Why didn't you get help?"

"We took off in his truck. He drove a tractor trailer. He kept a close watch over me for several years. Eventually, I got away and wound up in LA."

"At what age did you get away from him?"

"Fourteen."

"How did you survive?"

"I learned women found me attractive. If I pleased them, they gave me fancy trinkets and money. A few took me in for a time. I did all right."

"You made money as a male prostitute?" She hadn't expected his answer.

"I couldn't work legally. I had to do something."

"What about school?"

"Before I got into acting, I completed my GED. I kept it secret, but I needed to learn how to handle my money. I didn't trust anyone. I studied finance on my own. If *Liberty* takes off, I'll have more than I can ever spend."

"That's the movie you made when you came to Oklahoma?"

"Yeah."

"How did you meet Josh?"

"He was a stuntman in an early movie I made. We hit it off."

"We need to get back to your father. What jobs did he do once your mother died?"

"Mostly drove a rig. One time, he worked on the docks for a few weeks."

"You've been in the movies for years. Why now? For what reason did he seek you out?"

"He needed twenty-five grand for a loan shark. Said he lost at cards. I laughed at him and left. I told him I'd be dead a long time, and he still wouldn't get a dime from me."

"What happened next?" She knew, but she wanted to test if he'd told the truth earlier.

"I went down the beach to Tony's. I knew he wasn't home, but I have a key. I didn't want to be around anyone. Not after I saw that son of a bitch."

"Did your father mention the loan shark's name? I need to talk to the person who gave him the cash."

"I don't know. Mike? No, Mark. Last name started with a B, I think. He acted like I should know what a badass the guy was. As if I should know him or something." He shrugged and shook his head. "Wait. I remember. Bader. His name's Mark Bader."

8

———————

Twenty years earlier

Ben flipped the light switch and entered his room. A rat scurried for cover. He walked to the single mattress and flung himself down. With his head pushed against the wall, his feet hung over the end. He looked older than his fourteen years, but could he make it on his own?

He'd saved every penny he could scrape together from odd jobs and the little his father gave him for groceries. In the back of his closet, he hid the stash under a floorboard to keep it safe from the sneaky thief. When he drank, Tom McCall went through all the cash he could find. If Ben had to start his nest egg over, he didn't think he would make it out alive. He needed to escape soon.

Certain the son of a bitch would kill again, he figured he'd wind up in the system if the asshole got caught. He didn't know what living in foster care was like, but every friend of his who'd been placed in DHS claimed nothing could be worse.

He slid off the bed and went to his hiding place. The old

board creaked as he lifted it. He didn't see the faded red coffee can. He reached farther into the hole and moved it around. Desperately, he stirred his arm another time. *Oh my God. It's gone.*

A sunken feeling overwhelmed him, his mouth went dry, and his fingers searched in vain again. A few seconds later he heard pounding footsteps on the porch. The bastard he hated came in the front door.

"Ben, where the hell are you?" Tom McCall's voice carried down the hall.

He quickly pushed the oak board back into place and scrambled toward his bed. By the time the dirtbag arrived in his bedroom, he rested safely on the twin mattress.

"What did you do after I left?"

"Just hung out."

"You know I hate that answer. Why the hell do you always say it?" He pulled his belt from his waist.

"You'd better not touch me. I already told you what I'd do if you did."

Tom grabbed him by the neck and raised him up from the bed. "You're nothing but unwanted sperm that got caught in a trap. I can always put you down next to your mother."

Certain he meant it, he saw the hatred in his old man's eyes. He had to escape from him before his dad did what he threatened. The piece of garbage threw him against the wall and let him slide onto the bed. The scumbag grinned, turned, and left down the hallway.

He laid there for two long hours and waited to hear him snore. Silence reigned when he got up and put his few clothes into his backpack. He would crawl under the house to find the money. It had to be there. He needed it to be there.

Twenty minutes later, with his stash planted at the bottom of his pack, he carried it out to hide under the white crepe myrtle that grew beside the house. For his plan to work, he must complete one last thing before he left. He needed to stop the sleazy snake from following him, and he needed more money.

The darkened room loomed before him as he snuck inside. His dad always left everything in his jeans when he went to bed. So he dragged them from the room, down the hall. The belt loop snagged on a piece of loose trim board barely attached to the wall. The noise sounded a vibration in the walls before it came loose. He paused several seconds, heard nothing, and then took two more steps.

"What the hell you doing with my pants?"

He jumped and twisted his head toward Tom McCall in the same motion. He knew he was a goner the split second the jackass came fully awake. *Son of a bitch.*

He ran toward his room but realized he had nowhere to go in that direction. The slimeball would trap him. He changed course, threw the jeans at his dad, and struggled to slip by him. He pushed with all his might and hoped to catch the drunkard off guard.

His father's head made a loud crack as it hit the edge of the door trim behind him. The old fart went down hard and didn't move, but Ben saw his chest move. He was still breathing.

He grabbed the jeans and took the billfold from the back pocket. Inside he found over five hundred dollars. The amount would more than double his stash. The bastard won at poker tonight. Thank God.

After what he'd done, he could never come back here. He stuck the money in his front pocket and hurried out the door into the night.

For the first several blocks, he moved through the alleys and roused dogs while he went. Their barking signaled his movements, but it kept him out of the streetlights. He walked on past the bus stop closest to his house. He couldn't afford to get caught by taking the nearest one. When the murdering thief came awake, he would surely check there first.

He'd dreamed about this night for so long, but it still scared him. His bed didn't wait for him anymore. Food and water were his responsibility. He kept up his pace until he rounded a corner and saw a police cruiser. He ducked behind a bush and waited for the vehicle to disappear. Someone might have seen him go through the alley and called the cops.

He turned, increased his pace, and took off in a different direction. Sweat moistened his temples, but every step took him farther from the nightmare behind him.

Sunshine fell across his eyes and woke him from the niche he'd found under the overpass the night before. His stomach growled with hunger. He must look a mess. Without permanent shelter, keeping clean would be difficult, but in southern California, his cash wouldn't last long. Besides, he had to keep moving. His father would look for him—he'd want his money.

He dusted himself off and started down the road again. He walked a block over, turned, and moved parallel to the main highway. He'd like to catch a ride, but lowlife traveled every street around here. The chance he'd get caught on the busiest road was too high.

By noon, his stomach ached so bad he couldn't resist. He found a McDonalds and went inside. He could eat something and clean up in their restroom before he left. The line at the counter ran long, but he didn't have anything to do but wait. The smell of hamburgers cooking tormented his empty belly.

A woman in the line next to him had the biggest diamond ring on her finger he'd ever seen. He hoped she wouldn't notice the dust he hadn't been able to get off this morning. He smiled, feeling very shy, but she was hot.

Her return smile exuded confidence. She moved closer and bumped into him. He could feel her breast on his arm. He didn't know anything about women her age, but he felt certain she'd done it on purpose. He leaned into her and upped the wattage on his smile.

"Now aren't you somethin' to behold." Her slow drawl intrigued him, but he wasn't sure how to follow up on her comment.

"Cat got your tongue?"

"No, ma'am." Her old saying startled him. No one her age ever used it around here. He couldn't help but wonder where she called home. Certainly not southern California.

"So you can talk."

"Yes, ma'am."

"My name is Cathy Crowder. What's yours?"

"It's Ben."

"Well, Ben, you seem kinda' lonely here. Where you headed?"

"LA. I'm going to interview for a job," he lied. He figured she understood exactly what he was. But what the hell, she was pretty and somewhere under forty he thought. She might show him what life was about. Every guy had to start somewhere.

"You're in luck. I'm headed there myself. Want a lift?" She pointed at a golden Mercedes convertible he couldn't take his eyes off of.

He nodded.

By this time, they'd neared the front of the line. He ordered a hamburger, chocolate shake, and a bottle of water. She paid for both their orders, and they left.

Several miles flew by. She parked in front of a small motel and sent him to pay for the room. "You'll need to clean up for your interview. Come on back, and I'll make you look real good."

He wasn't in panic mode yet, but he'd never been involved with this type of arrangement. Should he tell her he hadn't ever? No. He felt certain she'd already read the situation. She appeared experienced with what she intended.

He came back out and handed her the keys.

She dangled them from her index finger. A lazy grin swept over her face. Though he didn't know what he was doing, she certainly did. He climbed back in her convertible and rode to their room.

His mind went blank. He wanted to impress her. He wasn't a total idiot, but no words came. He didn't want to make a spectacle of himself. He was hard as a piston ready to fire.

She unlocked the door and spread herself across the bed in a pose that said, *come and get it.*

"Why don't you climb in the shower to take the dust off? I'll stay right here."

He moved toward the tiny bathroom, turned on the shower, and dropped his clothes on the floor. It didn't take long to scrub clean. He turned the water off and grabbed a towel to wrap around his waist. He opened the door—and didn't see her on the bed anymore.

He quickly scanned the room to see where she was but couldn't find her. He moved to the door and swung it open. Her car had vanished. *What the hell?*

He turned back to search the room again. The zipper on his backpack hung open. He grabbed the bag and pulled the contents out. Thank God his mother's Bible remained inside, but the old coffee canister didn't.

Son of a bitch. She robbed me. What will I do now? A few seconds later he remembered the money in his pants pocket. In the bathroom, he checked his jeans to see if she'd gotten it all.

He pulled his hand out, and the five hundred bucks came with it. He sat on the toilet and put his head in his hands. At least she didn't get everything.

He decided to stay in the room until check-out the next day. He worried at first about how little money he had left, but for tonight, he had the roof over his head and water to drink.

By morning he'd made a decision. If Cathy Crowder could prosper by ripping people off, so could he. In order to con women, he must keep his body in great shape, his clothes clean, and his personal hygiene up. Women liked men who smelled good, had white teeth, and stuff like that.

He got up from the bed and did twenty-five pushups. The room key was deep in his pocket when he let himself out with his backpack firmly in place on his shoulders. He ran about a mile, turned, and made the return trip at a dead run. After he got back, he set the lock and chain and brought everything he owned into the bathroom with him. His shower was long and cleansing.

Once he got out, he groomed himself the best he could with what he owned and started on his new profession. At least his father couldn't kill him now. The police would never know he'd gone missing. The old man couldn't afford to report him.

Paige dialed Caroline's cell number. It rang four times before she answered. "What are you up to?"

"I walked into town to see what stores are here. I needed the exercise and found this darling little shop. They have a lovely bag in yellow. I think Marjorie will adore it."

Marjorie owned the garage apartment where her friend lived. She'd fallen out with her parents, and the Jones' took in the teenage girl. As time passed, the evangelist loved the woman like a mother.

"I might have known you'd find a way to shop, but I'm glad you did. I want you to enjoy yourself while you're here." She couldn't figure out why her friend liked to pick over stuff so much. It seemed a huge waste of time to her, but Caroline often bought gifts for others. She'd received several frilly tops and scarves she'd never wear. Her new friend possessed a generous nature.

"I plan to."

"Good. What's on your agenda for this afternoon? Josh and I need to canvass the area around Ben's place."

"I intend to study for the conference next week. So I'll be fine. Will you come back in time for dinner?" Caroline asked.

"More than likely. If something comes up, I'll call and touch base again."

"Okay. See you this evening."

She hung up and called Bill. "I have a name for you. Mark Bader. He's supposed to be a loan shark out here. Will you see what you can find on him? I need to talk to him so an address would help. Are you still snowed in?"

"No. I got out this morning, but I only had time to go home, turn around, and get back. The roads sucked big time, but the shower felt good."

"Is Hank all right? I haven't talked to him in a day or so."

"He sounded fine the last time I phoned him. I plan to stop by this evening on my way home. I'll go buy him a few items to get by. It looks like the snow will hang on for a while."

"Good luck with that. He hates when I treat him like an invalid, but I do appreciate the effort. I'd prefer he didn't get out in the icy weather."

"I have my ways with him. I may mention I want to spend

the night and need a few toiletries. He won't want me to travel back to the farm again."

"Great idea on both counts. You don't need to get stranded out in the boonies, anyway."

He laughed. "See, I knew you cared."

"Of course, since the accident, we've only got each other and Hank. You're the best friend I've got. I don't want anything to happen to you." She felt odd talking to Bill this honestly. She rarely told anyone her inner thoughts. It still felt like she betrayed Crissy, her best friend, who died a year ago on Christmas Eve.

"I know. I feel the same way about you. Promise you'll be careful out there in la la land. Whoever you're tracking is a killer. They may feel like they have nothing left to lose."

"I promise, I'll stay vigilant. Now, I need everything you can find on Mark Bader and every little detail on Tom McCall, too."

"I figured you'd butter me up for my talents."

"You know I meant the other stuff too. Now get to work so I can." She disconnected, glanced up, and noticed Josh in the driver's seat. Her cheeks warmed. She'd forgotten he was beside her. She rarely ever forgot the presence of another person. Was she getting too comfortable with Josh?

As she glanced outside the window, Ben's place came into view. The phone call had lasted longer than she realized. Josh parked in the drive and turned the motor off.

Before he could speak she asked, "North or south to Tony's house? Ben said he went toward Tony's. Let's start the canvass in the direction he lives."

"His home lies about a half a mile to the north on the beach."

"Yeah, he said he walked along the beach." She got out of the vehicle while Josh did the same.

"Let's try the house next to his first."

She knocked loudly on the ornately carved front door. After they waited several moments, a stately, older woman with silver hair and black framed glasses opened the door.

She gave the woman her best smile. "I'm a friend of Ben McCall, your neighbor. We wondered if you witnessed the events that occurred Tuesday night and early Wednesday morning."

"The police stayed here for hours. The inconvenience was extremely annoying." The woman scowled.

"I'm sure it's true. Are you acquainted with Mr. McCall?"

"Yes. He's lived there for seven or eight years. Has women in his home at all hours of the day and night. Sometimes it gets loud over there. I've seen the gentleman with you at his place on more than one occasion." Her frown indicated her intense displeasure.

Josh only nodded and produced a polite smile.

"Did you see what happened before the police arrived? Was the noise loud enough to get your attention?"

"I already told the police what happened. You know the man who lives next door did it. I saw him. He shouted at the older man. They both yelled. I couldn't hear the distinct words, but they made a big racket. Mr. McCall appeared to leave for a few minutes. He came back and grabbed the bat from against the wall over there. It startled me. He beat the older man with it. I stood there and watched. I couldn't believe what I'd seen. The whole event seemed like a dream or something. When I finally called the police, it took them too long to get there."

"You actually saw Ben hit the other man with the weapon?"

"Sure did. Worst thing I've ever seen."

She remembered the discrepancy with the blood on Ben's clothing. "What clothes did Ben have on?"

"A white T-shirt and dark jeans. Wore a dark baseball cap, too."

She sifted the woman's words through what she'd already been told. Josh opened his mouth, but she interrupted. "What's your name? I'll need it for my records."

"Hannah Evans."

"Does anyone else live with you at this residence?"

"No. My husband passed away a year and a half ago."

"Did you see anyone else around? Did anyone walk on the beach who could have witnessed the attack?"

"No. I watched the gentleman get murdered. I didn't look around."

"You've been very helpful. If you think of anything else, anything at all, please call me." She handed Hannah her card with her cell number on it. She needed to get Josh away from here before he said something she couldn't control. She took him by the arm and dragged him along behind her.

Devastation etched lines on his face. She understood Josh believed in his friend, but in the face of evidence pitted so strongly against Ben, it could overwhelm like the smell of bacon first thing in the morning. She moved him toward Ben's drive and the car that waited there. After she put him in the passenger seat, she walked around to the driver's side and got in. He handed her the key fob.

"Draw a breath. Calm down if you can. It's times like this, we need to keep rational more than any other." She watched him closely. His reaction during this test could give her information about the relationship between the two men she might not learn any other way.

"It doesn't add up. She didn't tell the truth. I know she hated when Ben partied, but to say she saw him murder someone . . ." His voice trailed off. He sat quietly for a time. "I wanted to shake her to stop her from lying. I guess I'm an awful person."

"I don't think she lied. She saw something, but eyewitnesses are not always reliable. It's a proven fact."

"You think she told the truth?" Josh stared over at her.

"I said I don't think she lied. Not on purpose. She witnessed the murder, but what she saw might not have been what she assumed she saw. We've got a long way to go before we know what actually happened. Hang in there. I won't quit on you yet."

"You're not? Thank God."

She mulled the details over in her mind and reminded herself she couldn't rely on anything said by a trained actor. But evidence never lied. For the time being, the case still intrigued her. She knew she wouldn't stop until she got the facts to line up. Until she finished and every detail fit.

James Silsby drove west through the Arizona desert along Interstate 8. The night settled in and brought many stars with it, but the beauty in the sky didn't interest him. He yearned for a swallow of tequila. His brain constantly teased him with the idea that one drink would be enough. The same lie enticed him for too long now. Tension locked his shoulders, and the grip on the steering wheel strained his knuckles. Finally, he reached for the radio and searched for a country station until he heard Garth Brooks singing "Wild Horses."

He'd managed to stay sober since the morning he woke up after it happened, but he'd gone from one pack a day to three. His hands still shook two long years later. He'd started with Jose Cuervo, but quickly declined to whatever he could get his hands on. Anything to stop the craving that drove him.

He forced his mind to concentrate on the man who'd killed his baby sister. He only had the name his sister called her latest boyfriend, but he suspected Sam was a fake one. His buddy passed on information about a tractor trailer driver who worked around the docks in San Diego. The description matched the guy he'd seen only one time. Supposedly, the driver ran short hauls between there and LA. It would take a miracle to find him, but San Diego seemed a better place to start, considering the smaller population.

He cracked a window and pulled a cigarette package from the roll in his sleeve. Smoking was a filthy habit, but he'd loved James Dean as a child. His father watched reruns of *Giant* every time it came on TV. Back then his father had eyed Liz Taylor, but he'd taken the young male star for a hero.

He felt a kinship. They shared a first name, and the actor wore cool like no one else could. From that time on, he never missed one of Dean's movies. Too bad he only got to make three.

Once his father turned fifty-five, he'd married a woman who looked a lot like Liz. Gina was much younger and got pregnant with Marcia. The young girl delighted everyone in the family. After his father died ten years later, he'd moved back in to help support his stepmother and sister. He felt the need to protect her from every wrong the world sent her way.

Marcia grew into a dark-haired beauty like her mother. Men swarmed around her. He'd run off more than a few, but he didn't count on the animal who'd beaten her, raped her, and left her dead. The bastard needed a lesson in correction. He wanted to teach the scumbag the price of raping and killing women.

When he'd heard about the trucker in San Diego, he took two weeks of his vacation and drove west. He inhaled the last puff on his cigarette. The heat scorched deep in his chest, and the relief the nicotine brought soothed him for the moment. He crushed the stub in his ashtray and continued another twenty miles before he pulled into a truck stop for an hour's sleep. San Diego would wait a little longer.

He parked and leaned his seat back, but his brain wouldn't shut down. Though he'd been drowsy a few moments ago, the call of tequila was too strong. His mouth felt dry and his tongue thick. *Son of a rotten bitch, I need a drink.*

He got out. Diesel fumes attacked his nostrils. By the time he walked into the café, he wanted to tear the head off every asshole in the place, but that's how the last fiasco started. A waitress with more lines on her face than a worn-out map strolled up to take his order. Hell, he couldn't catch a break on the scenery. This one had the shape of a broomstick and was about as appealing.

"What's your pleasure?" she asked.

"Not you," he mumbled and grabbed a menu. The scent of old grease and stale coffee enveloped him.

She brought him a chipped white mug and poured coffee before he could stop her. He didn't needed caffeine or any other stimulant. Sleep already eluded him, but he decided to let her continue. If he drove straight through, he'd get there sooner.

"Where you headed?" She finally lifted the pot.

"San Diego."

"You've still got around two hundred fifty miles to go. Do you know what you want to order?"

"I'll take three eggs over easy, whites done, and a nice piece of ham . . . and biscuits if you got some handy."

"We ought to. You been on the road long?"

"Too damned long." He didn't want to waste energy talking, but the waitress wasn't at fault. The call from the bottle wouldn't leave him alone.

She wrote on a small pad and walked toward the back.

His focus changed from the notched cup in his hand for a second, but his thumb still rubbed the rough edge. He felt someone watch him and casually surveyed the area. At first glance, he didn't notice anyone. The place wasn't that busy. He figured he was paranoid since he wanted a drink so bad. He stared down at the mug between his hands. Finally, he picked it up and sipped from the burnt liquid. Sure enough, it tasted scorched. Probably been on the warmer all day.

He set the coffee down and took time to better search the room. The feeling someone watched him lingered. He spotted a man near the restroom hallway. The man was six feet plus an inch or two, mid-thirties, and balding. He didn't recognize the guy, but he met a lot of people. He put his head back down but looked up through his brows so he could study the stranger without the man knowing.

The guy definitely had a bead on him. Something didn't feel right, but he'd already ordered. With the few customers in the diner, his food should arrive soon. He added a little sugar to his coffee and stirred profusely. He hoped to get a better view of his stalker.

The waitress came by and slid his plate covered with scrambled eggs before him. He glared up at the woman. "I ordered over easy, whites done."

"I'm sorry, Henry only knows how to scramble eggs. He's sorta learnin' how right now."

Too frustrated to argue, he picked up his fork and ate what sat before him. At least the whites didn't run, and the biscuits were warm. He reached for the condiments, grabbed two packs oof orange marmalade, and finished his food. He drank the crap they called coffee, and motioned for his receipt.

He didn't want to stay any longer than necessary. The stalker didn't move from his position near the restrooms. By this time, the guy should've memorized every postcard on the rack. He needed to relieve his bladder, but he wouldn't go near the man. Not in this mood.

When he got up to pay the cashier, he watched the guy until he finished the transaction. He walked out the door to his car. He squatted beside his vehicle and peered over the hood of the Impala to see if the stranger followed him. Several minutes later, he felt certain he'd imagined the whole episode. He went to the end of his car by the back fender and opened his fly. After he finished the job and zipped up, he turned around. The stranger stood right beside his front bumper.

"Aren't you the man who murdered my brother a little over two years ago?"

He couldn't breathe for a second or two. "I think you got the wrong man. I don't believe I know you."

"You wouldn't know me. I wasn't there at the time you killed him." The man's grin turn into a sneer.

BUCK RELEASED HIS SEATBELT. He climbed out to start a street canvass with Vern. They hoped to find the corner one of the two dead prostitutes walked. This area of LA was one known for solicitation, and the perp dumped their bodies in close proximity. Once they located where they had worked, they could start to profile their victims. It would help if one of the other working girls saw one of the women get in a vehicle. Any help from the pros would be a long shot. Hookers didn't like cops. They hated talking to them even more.

The day progressed into night without any leads. Several ladies sauntered along the streets as they worked their way into the evening. He and Vern walked closer. A woman with a yellow boa and Crayola-red hair headed south. He took off toward her, and Vern followed the other pros who worked the corner.

She increased her speed. He quickly caught up to her, took her by the arm, and stopped her. "Are you in a hurry or something?"

She turned on him. "I didn't do anything wrong. Let me go."

"I only want to ask you some questions. We need to find out information about a . . . a working girl we found. Well, two actually." He took the two photos from his shirt pocket.

The woman stared straight ahead, not at the pictures.

"What's your name?"

She hesitated for so long, he didn't think she'd answer.

"My name is Sylvia. Sylvia Striker, and I don't like to see dead hookers."

"How do you know they're dead?"

"You wouldn't be here if they weren't. Cops like you don't care about people like me unless we wind up without a pulse."

"Did you know her? This time at least take a peek." He put the prints right in front of her face.

"So what if I did."

"Which one?"

She pointed to the face of the first victim they'd found.

"We discovered her body in the park. Someone beat her to death. Did you see her night before last?"

"I don't know. They ain't my problem."

"They who?"

"Other women."

"Why aren't they your problem?"

"Cause, you know. We're both after the same men."

"Yeah, but you'd notice if one went missing. You'd remember. You'd know it could have been you." He hated to rub it in, but she must be glad she wasn't the victim.

"Hell yeah, they called her Honey Bun, but I don't know anything about her. I took a meeting with a friend. I came back, and she'd gone."

"But you at least know her?"

"We didn't hang out, but I know her street name."

"Who'd she run with?"

"I don't know. I'm not her pimp. She hung around. I saw her sometimes."

"Where did she work the last time you saw her? What corner or on what part of the block was she standing?"

"I don't know which corner she worked, but when I saw her last, she was across the street on that corner." She pointed in the diagonal direction from where they stood.

"If you think of anything at all, or if you hear something, please call me."

He handed her his business card. She took it, rolled her eyes, and stuck it in her bra.

"Yeah, I'm sure gonna do that." She shook her head like he was the dumbest cop in the world, walked off, and left him to stare at her back.

He joined his partner.

"The redhead said she saw Honey Bun Thursday night, but didn't see her picked up by our perp. Did you learn any new information?"

Vern glanced up from writing in his small note pad.

"Not much. One of them said the victim we found at the motel might work two blocks farther down. She didn't know for sure."

"We'd better check it out. We don't have any other leads to follow up on. Damn it, this case sucks," he said.

As they moved down the street, they questioned several other women, but none admitted they knew either vic.

They walked into the Naughty Lady Bar, standard fare. Several pool tables in the back kept half a dozen guys busy. The name tag on the man behind the barrier read Steve. He got the man's attention.

When the guy brought his head up, he saw a faded scar that ran from his sideburns to near his hairline. "Hey, Steve, you seen either of these women around here before?" He placed both pictures down on the flat surface before him. The barkeep studied them for a minute and nodded.

"This one they called Hilda. She worked around the corner at the end of the street. The other one didn't come in often, but I've seen her around."

"What was she into?"

"I'm not sure, but she never got got much to drink. She mostly came in out of the rain." Steve looked up and smirked. "Like we get showers here anymore."

"Ain't that the truth. Can you tell us anything that would help us? We need to find someone who'd know more information about her or Hilda."

"You didn't hear it from me, but I think they both worked for Terrell. It's the only name I know him by."

"Do you know where he calls home?"

"Not a clue, my man. Not a clue."

He slipped him a card. "Thanks. Give me a call if you think of something else."

After they left the Naughty Lady, he turned to Vern but saw he'd already called vice for a location and info on Terrell. Several minutes later Vern disconnected.

"They got a file on him?"

"They're supposed to call us back."

"Let's take a break. It could take a while. I don't want to drive halfway across town and back." He walked to the corner. Vern followed him.

Out on the street, everything appeared normal. Cars whizzed by, lights glittered on many buildings, and a killer hunted his next victim. Why the hell did this, their last case, turn out to be such a bitch? Tired frustration hugged him like a tight dinner jacket.

"Our favorite deli's over a block. We could grab a pastrami on rye. If we're lucky, a beer could enter our future."

Vern gazed at him. "Sounds perfect, but we're still on the clock. You know you won't take a drink until we're off for the night."

"I know, but I can dream can't I? It won't be long until we can grab a cold one any damned time we want."

"I live for the day." Vern's phone sounded. He stuck a finger in his other ear so he could hear above the traffic. "You got anything for me?"

He spoke for a minute and turned back to him.

"They got nothing on this Terrell guy. If he runs a string of women, he's not on their radar. So no help there."

"Son of a bitch. Did I mention I hate this damned case? Who ever heard of vice not having info on a pimp?"

He pushed the door open to Henry's Deli. Notorious for their pastramis, he felt he could eat a dozen right now. He'd been busy this long day. They found more bodies, and no one would talk. His feet already ached, and he needed a break. Vern walked up to the counter and ordered three on rye, while he hunted for a booth they could share.

Seven minutes later Vern joined him. His partner took his note pad out and reviewed his notes. The scratchings were illegible, but his old friend could make them out okay.

"We got an idea where he took Honey Bun from. We need to pull film footage, see if we caught him on tape when he took her. So I guess we go back and look for security cameras in the area." He put his notes away and took a sandwich from Vern.

"Sounds like a plan, but my feet feel like nubs."

"Mine, too." He paused. "We're already here. We'd have to come back tomorrow. I say, let's get it over with."

"I know you're right, but damn it anyway." Vern took the third sandwich, cut it in half, and handed one to him. They didn't say much during their meal. Ten minutes later they exited back to the street.

They retraced their steps the way they'd come. He pulled a flashlight from the glove compartment. With so much neon in the area, they hardly needed it, but it helped them to see in dim places that the light didn't reach.

They walked around each corner where the dead hookers most likely worked their trade. After forty-five minutes, they got enough information to get warrants for the videos. Within fifteen minutes they'd arrived back at headquarters.

THIS TIME PAIGE left Josh at home with Caroline while she canvassed Ben's neighbors. The rest of the day passed swiftly. She talked with dozens of people from the beach houses lined along the Pacific Coast Highway. No one saw Ben the night the murder took place.

She asked about security tapes that might have faced Ben's house and learned the police had taken them. She didn't see any that faced the front of Ben's property. Most were too far away and pointed back at the owner's homes. If Ben had a security system, you could bet the authorities had taken the hard drives from those, too.

She noticed the Escalade was gone when she pulled the Porsche into the garage later in the evening. Tired and aggravated, she opened the door to the kitchen and found the house dark and quiet. They'd probably given up on her and gone out to eat. She left the access open. They would be back soon. She entered her room. It didn't take long to change into her cutoff sweats and top. She went into the kitchen, intent on a workout in the gym.

She saw a silhouette move. A blur really. It brought her

heart rate up. She froze midstep, as a figure in black emerged from the living room doorway. *What the hell?*

Nothing in his hands. Not a burglar.

"Josh?"

He stopped. The gun came up next.

She didn't have time to think.

She took a step back, slammed the door, and set the lock. The egress seemed flimsy at best. The protection it provided wouldn't hold long. She went for her gun holster, pulled the Glock out, and hurried to the door that led to the garage. The overhead remained open, but the intruder came through the kitchen door at a right angle to her. He seemed determined to move past her and escape through the outside opening.

"Freeze. Hands in the air." She took her stance and pointed her weapon at him.

He ignored her and continued forward.

Ferguson, Missouri and the riots there flashed through her mind, plus a dozen since. She left her doorway and cut him off. As she tackled him, they both rolled to the ground. He kicked hard and shoved her away from him. Pain erupted through her ribs, and the pistol flew out of her hand. By the time she managed to get up, he stood on his feet, ready to land another blow, but this time with his right fist. She countered with a block from her left hoping to protect her ribs.

He must have known his boot did its damage because his blue eyes dared her to try again. She dropped her left shoulder and kicked out with her right foot. It hit him and glanced off when he twisted away and ran. She fell to the concrete floor.

She picked herself up, grabbed the firearm, and started after him. The darkening sky and the vegetation hid the perp. She searched the perimeter around the house and grounds. No trace of him.

She went back into the house and pulled her top up. A

faint discoloration covered her ribs. The angry red would turn purple before morning. She checked her backside, painful from her last landing. Soreness might last for a day or two, but she'd be fine.

She strolled through Josh's home and searched for any signs of disturbance. One drawer in Caroline's room gaped open, but the contents didn't look moved. Only her friend would know if she missed anything. She pushed the dresser closed and walked away from the area.

Did he take anything? She didn't think he had time since she'd interrupted him. Besides, his hands were empty when he fought her. Who could the man be? She could only attest to blue eyes because he wore a ski mask. Unless Ben was innocent and this guy the killer, she couldn't figure out why anyone would want to take Josh's home apart. What motive would the perp have? Nothing here would affect the case.

But he might not know that. Did he lose something at the crime scene and thought they found it? What other reason could he have? The ideas that ran through her head were only conjecture.

He could be a burglar, but in her experience he didn't feel like one. He wore gloves and didn't feel threatened when she pulled her weapon. He handled himself like he'd been trained. Someone searched Ben's residence. Now this. Her instincts told her he acted like a pro who wanted something specific, but what?

Before she stirred everyone up or called the police, she needed to figure out what exactly went down here. Too much didn't add up. Besides, she'd learned from her work, on a small crime like this, her brothers on the job couldn't do much.

She went to the gym. The rowing machine held her attention for about twenty minutes. It didn't seem to bother her ribs too much. She figured it would, but she still needed to go slow and easy. She worked to strengthen her arms with weights. Though she refused to say it aloud, in her head she still repeated, *Monsters kill you. Monsters kill you . . .*

Sweat poured down her back. Her breathing felt labored. Still, she continued to lift and repeat in her head the words she was determined to remember. She moved to the bag and punched without rhythm or gloves. Only frustration and fear drove her until she collapsed on the floor. She sat and leaned against the heavy bag while her hair dripped and tears slid down both cheeks.

She strained to gather enough strength to go up for a shower and didn't notice the shadow approach. A second later, she felt a presence, jumped to her feet, and took her position to defend.

"Whoa. I came to find you." Josh stepped toward her.

"You startled me. I need to go up for a shower anyway." She attempted to walk around him, but he reached out for her.

"Are you all right? You look exhausted." His eyes searched hers.

"I might have worked out too hard. I wanted to smash something. My afternoon was wasted. I didn't find anyone to corroborate Ben's story." She felt totally defeated. A part of her wanted to believe Ben. Caroline did, but she strived to keep her objectivity. She'd learned if a person got tunnel vision by believing one line of thinking without proof, it could blind them to the facts. Evidence led to the truth, not believing in people. Anybody was capable of doing horrible damage to another person when cornered. She'd seen it too many times not to know that truth for a certainty.

"We picked up food. You're probably hungry. Come on."

He sounded so hopeful she didn't have the heart to bring him down. The intruder was probably just that. Since she'd interrupted him, she doubted he'd be back. The guy knew she had a gun.

"You're right. What did you bring me?"

"Steaks. Caroline has the grill heating. She cleaned out the salad aisle too, but I'm okay with green veggies. Sound good?"

"Let me shower and change. It sounds great." Her legs trembled, but she moved ahead of him up the stairs. He left her in the kitchen. She walked into her bedroom and didn't stop until she reached the bath. Hot water soothed her exhausted muscles and steamed up the mirror. Finally, she adjusted the temperature to cold. The blast got her moving again.

She emerged from her room twenty minutes later feeling much better. The smell of grilled meat assaulted her empty stomach. "How long before we eat? I'm famished. Do I have time to dry my hair?"

"Not if you want your T-bone hot. Come on. You're fine. We planned to eat outside by the pool anyway." Caroline walked past her carrying a huge bowl of salad.

She followed. The glass table held casual dinnerware. A small fridge contained wine, water, and most importantly, Pepsi. She went to retrieve one, then decided she needed to hydrate with water first after her workout.

Josh came through the back door in a white T and cutoff jeans. The clothes looked immaculate on him. She noted his fantastic chest muscles move beneath his shirt. She wondered if she would find him more attractive if she still didn't dream about Bobby several times a week. Her smile of appreciation faded. Over a year passed since the accident that claimed Crissy and Bobby Youngblood. It changed her life so much.

They sat down together. Caroline suggested they hold hands during her short prayer to bless the food.

She cut into her steak with determination. She quickly finished her meal and took seconds on the salad.

Caroline and Josh continued the small talk. The trio relaxed as the last of the light faded from the mountainside. She mentioned she felt tired and moved toward her bedroom. Caroline claimed she still needed to finish the notes for her sermon. So they both went inside, while Josh reclined beside the L-shaped pool.

She closed the door and felt antsy. She paced for several minutes. She grabbed the remote and turned on the TV. She flipped through channels for a bit. Her sports bra and jeans came off next, and she pulled an old gray T-shirt over her head. When she glanced up, she saw two detectives on the news. They worked a case concerning prostitutes. She turned the sound up and listened.

A woman from the local news station interviewed a homicide detective named Buck Tillman. He discussed the bludgeoning deaths of two prostitutes.

"Isn't this the second prostitute you've found this week? Does it mean a serial killer is loose in LA?"

"It could, but we can't panic. He's only killed a specific type. Prostitutes with shoulder-length, brunette hair. So if you're a working girl who fits the description, you should be careful."

"Is there a certain area we should be aware of?"

"We only give out the pertinent information. The investigation's ongoing. We don't discuss details. If anyone out there has information regarding this case please call us." The detective gave the contact information.

Once the taped portion flipped back to the news anchor, she smiled and thanked the reporter. "In other news, the case against the Oscar winner, Ben McCall, may take a turn for the worse. A secret source told our entertainment liaison his fingerprints matched those found at the scene of a double homicide more than twenty years ago. We asked the lead detective,

Curtis Sampson, about this report. He declined comment. The tongues in Hollywood should wag for a long time."

She rewound the remote and watched the news anchor's report again. *Shit. The lying ass.* He never mentioned he'd been involved with another homicide. How could he be so clueless? Did he not consider that the police would run his prints?

After she turned off the TV, she seethed in silence. She hated working for the other side. Suspects always lied. If not outright, then by omission. Ten minutes later she turned out the light. Tomorrow would come soon enough. She would confront him. When she got through with him, he'd know better than to do anything like this again.

10

Special Agent Jordan Trinity sat in his sterile apartment and thought about the one person who'd taken up residence in his mind over the last six months. Paige Stone left her mark on him and didn't know it. A mixture of wholesome beauty and innocence made a man imagine fantasies he shouldn't. The fifteen-year age difference bothered him, and his jaded experience would eventually corrupt the ideals he loved about her. The transition into maturity would come to her like it did everyone who lived a long life. He didn't want his disillusionment to change her sooner rather than later.

He cleared his mind of thoughts of Paige and pulled the file up on his computer. His boss had sent a text with the case number to him a few minutes ago. While the laptop hummed, he stared out the window at the overcast sky. The weather in DC called for more snow. LA offered a nice change.

He paused to consider how he could justify a stopover in Tulsa. They'd spoken on the phone a few times, but their relationship didn't feel the same through the cell towers. Hell, he couldn't tell if she liked him or not. She wasn't the easiest person to decipher. Of course, he'd spent more time with Hank than Paige when he worked the case there. A day or two off on the way back sounded good.

He forced himself to concentrate on the new murders again and gazed at the screen in front of him that displayed photos of the victims before the psycho got to them. It helped him remember they were people, not statistics.

Every streetwalker hailed from somewhere. Hanny French, the one called Hilda, grew up in Des Moines, Iowa. Her father pastored a small church, and her mother taught the third grade.

The second victim, called Honey Bun, came from a small town in New Jersey. Her real name was Henrietta Barton. No father in the picture. Her mother a drug addict. Cliché all the way on her. She'd run away into something worse. He shook his head at the hopeless situation.

He studied the photos that revealed how the unknown subject pulverized his victims. If no one told him, he would still know Hilda was murdered first. The snapshots revealed it all: the blows delivered with more force on Honey Bun, the increased number of bashes to her body postmortem, and the escalated fury.

He read a little more and turned off his computer, closed the top, and planned everything he needed to accomplish before he left. If the unsub's interim remained the same, he would bludgeon the third body over the weekend. He needed to add his last minute items to his go bag, make sure he cleaned perishables from his fridge, and left the trash in the dumpster on his way out. After so many trips to forgotten places, his life felt like a routine.

He stared at the framed art that still sat on the floor. He'd planned to hang it for over a year but constantly went out the door on trips that often lasted months. When he didn't work cases, he testified at others already solved. He hated to give up on a regular life like most nine to fivers enjoyed, but he might not have time for a relationship. In his heart he hoped he did. He'd like to give it a go with Paige. She was smart, fearless, and a beauty in one terrific package. Like his, her apartment walls were bare. They had a lot in common.

He walked to the window. The evening sky spit a few flakes. The wind whipped them in diagonal dances as they eventually landed on the ground. He watched his reflection in the window pane and spotted the disarray in his black hair. He finger combed it back in place and made up his mind. *I'll stopover in Tulsa.*

Sweat beaded on his back while James Silsby focused on the switchblade tucked inside his boot. He bought it to kill the asshole who murdered Marcia, but he might have to use it on this son of a bitch.

The man who stood before him didn't look like an assassin —more like a tall nerd. The important issue, was he here to do serious damage or swap fists? He could handle a beating and probably deserved one. After all, he'd taken a man's life. He didn't mean to, but he did.

The man's challenge hung in the fumy night air. He no longer wanted a drink. He *needed* one, to the exclusion of everything else. Thank God, he didn't have that option.

The stranger took the decision from his control. He saw the gun come up in the man's right hand. He heard the words. "David Renfrow was my brother." The muzzle flashed in his peripheral vision as he hit the ground and rolled away from the shot. He grabbed the knife and flicked the switch. The blast penetrated his ears. When he came up in a sitting position, he hurled the blade into the stranger with enough force to stop his heart. *Son of a bitch.* The man collapsed, and he rolled away from the body. Gunpowder from the fired shot overwhelmed his sense of smell, and his ears still rang.

He pushed himself up, stood over the corpse, pulled the steel out, and wiped the bloody edge on the man's shirt. In an instant, his life had turned violent again. He didn't take time to feel for a pulse. His own blood raced through his veins, but he made himself drive quietly from the parking lot. A minute or so later, he wrapped the dagger in a paper napkin from his front seat.

For the next ten miles his eyes searched the rearview mirror for any lights that didn't belong, especially flashing ones. He saw a rest area ahead and took the exit. Once he stopped, he reached over and took a cleaning kit from his glove compartment. This particular one he'd made special for his switchblade. He got out, locked the door, and walked to the restroom.

The florescent lights hurt his eyes while he moved into a stall. He sat down and ran a hand through his hair. He relived the scene from two years earlier. The man was tough, but he had a mouth, which he ran more than any asshole he'd ever met. That mouth had started the fight that ended in the creep's death—a death that still weighed heavily on his conscience. Cuervo had numbed the guilt for a time. The cleaning kit rattled as his hand began to shake. He swallowed hard.

He got up, flushed the toilet he hadn't used, and pushed every door open to make sure no one lurked inside a stall. He checked for cameras as he walked to the sink. He laid the plastic box down, opened it, and took out the small screwdriver. He took the knife completely apart and scrubbed each piece. A small bottle contained bleach, which he poured over them. Three minutes later, he scrubbed the chemical off the parts. He blew each component with the hand dryer, carefully reassembled the weapon, and inserted it back in its sheath still strapped to his ankle.

Proper procedures seemed tedious, but lazy men got convicted. If the law found him now, at least his weapon didn't contain viable DNA. He used the urinal and left. San Diego was still over two hundred miles away. The darkness outside matched his mood. He walked toward his car.

He got in the Impala, placed the cleaning kit back in the glove box, and locked it. Still, something gnawed at him. He pulled onto the interstate. A partial detail of what he'd done still resided in the Chevy. He needed to be thorough.

At the third exit off the interstate, he drove into the desert a ways and stopped. From here, he could see every star in the blackened sky. He got out of the car, dry sand blowing across his face. The breeze would erase his tire and foot prints quickly.

He moved to the trunk of his Impala and removed a shovel. Fifty feet from the road, he dug a hole several feet deep and left his light for a marker. He went back for the special kit he'd made and removed it from the compartment. Once he put it in the ground, he covered and smoothed the dirt. The wind should do the rest. He grabbed the flashlight, got back into his car, and drove toward his destination.

Dawn swept over the mountains as he passed the El Cajon city limit sign. His head ached from no sleep. The thirst for tequila never abated throughout the night, and his eyes felt gritty. The trucking company would wait for a few hours. He needed a cheap motel that accepted cash and rest before he continued his search.

PAIGE STRUGGLED with familiar dreams throughout the night and felt relieved the phone awakened her. Bill's voice on the other end brought her to attention. "Mark Bader's a known loan shark. His business covers a good portion of southern California. Your information's correct on him. He has an office at The Faded Pea restaurant. From what I could find out, I think he owns the place he frequents."

"Hello to you, too." She placed her hand over her mouth to cover a yawn.

"You sound half asleep."

"I was, but I'm glad you called. I have a lot to accomplish today. Did you find any more information about Tom McCall?"

"Not much so far. It appears he moved from town to town a lot. The gaps are consistent. I assume he used various identities. I may need to use creative thinking to trace his movements. His truth can't hide from me forever, but not every state required fingerprints back then. Might take time."

"All right. You work on him, and I can check out our moneyman. The way traffic backs up out here, it may take me a while. Give me a call later to let me know how your search progresses. A change in events occurred here. I may need the murder book more than ever. Any chance you can get it?"

"I'll see, but I have other work to do."

"I really appreciate the help. Do what you can. I'll squeeze more info from their prime suspect. I promise a steak dinner when I get back. How's Hank?"

"Ornery. He misses the job."

"I know. I've made efforts to involve him on a few cases. You know, ask his advice, but he won't take the bait. I'm not sure what to try next."

"The problem is he knows you're good enough you don't need his help."

"Well I've got to try something. He puts bourbon in everything he drinks. We already know liquor didn't worked out for Bobby's dad. Besides, he's not supposed to drink with his heart condition. Did he let you spend the night?"

"Yeah. I didn't give him much choice, but we talked. You're right. We need to find him something to do, or at least, get him away from the house more."

"After I get back, we'll conspire against him. Surely we can figure a plan of some kind."

"While I eat the steak dinner you owe me."

"It's a deal."

She grinned, disconnected, and flipped the covers back. The smile lingered. She stretched for a few seconds and climbed out. She checked the time. If she skipped breakfast, she could go for a short run. Her workout clothes from the night before smelled, so she decided to wear old jeans and her sleep T-shirt. They'd do. She hoped Greta would launder them before she arrived back later in the day.

She used the door to the garage and pushed the button to activate the overhead. She took off down the drive to the gorgeous view the Pacific offered. Once she completed two quick miles, she headed for the shower.

When she came out, Josh sat on her bed. Her body jerked and the towel slipped lower on her breasts.

"What the hell? You nearly gave me a heart attack."

"I was afraid you'd leave without me." Josh watched the top edge along the terrycloth.

"I planned to, but I had another idea. We need to get a different car. The two you own stand out too much. I think a brown one, several years old. A Chevy, Ford, maybe a Toyota. What do you think?"

"I think in LA you stick out if you don't drive a Porsche." His eyes never left her cleavage.

"Ha-ha. I'm serious. We can use an old junker if it doesn't

smoke. I may need to do stakeout work or tail someone. Something nondescript." She grabbed clean clothes from her bag and secured the towel with her left hand. Her underwear slid to the floor.

"I haven't seen any of those in . . . in maybe never. Do you actually wear those?" Josh laughed aloud.

Her face flamed. She picked them up and walked with purpose into the bathroom. Once she closed the door firmly behind her, she clicked the lock.

Several minutes later she came out and sat in the chair across from her bed. She put on her socks and shoes and refused to let him intimidate her. "So I don't wear sexy panties. What business is it of yours? You won't see them anymore. Hank always bought me those when I was young. I never saw a reason to change." She shrugged.

"He bought you old lady panties. Surely, men have commented on them before."

"I don't care if you're not a fan of plain cotton briefs. Not your concern." She gave him a pointed look. Her cheeks burned.

He shook his head, but the grin still spread across his face. "I suppose you're right." He opened his mouth to say more, but she cut him off.

"The investigation needs our attention." She walked out of the room and to the garage, where she climbed into the Porsche's driver's seat. Josh's expression implied she should give him the keys.

"This time I know the way. Besides, I might never get another chance to drive a Porsche again. So I'll take advantage while I can." She patted the steering wheel and smiled at him like she'd already won the battle.

He hesitated a few seconds and got in the passenger's side. "Where're we going?"

"I need to verify a few details with Ben."

"What type of details?"

She glanced his way. "Questions I have that you need to let me get answered. Remember, what you don't know, you can't testify to. You've got to trust me a little, if this . . . whatever you call it, will get us anywhere. I need to talk to Ben without you."

She backed up and stomped the gas pedal when she took off through the gate to the drive. Josh grabbed the door handle. His knuckles turned white. She chuckled.

They'd turned her life upside down. The time had come to get a little back.

The vehicle performed like she imagined an Indy car would. She sprinted a short stint with a heavy gas pedal and eased their speed to five miles past the limit. She slowed for heavier traffic. Before long she parked in front of the jail and got out. Josh came around, climbed in, and drove away to find parking until she finished with Ben.

She saw McCall's expression change once he recognized her. He couldn't hide the disappointment as they brought him into the room behind the clear thick partition. She hoped it didn't mean he had ideas about Caroline. He wasn't the right guy for her. Caroline was the real deal when it came to her beliefs. She figured she didn't get through to Ben before.

If Caroline got hurt over this trip, she'd be pissed at herself. She brought her friend out here to help him. Guilt leaned heavy on her heart. If Ben imagined he could play with Caroline and throw her aside like he did other women, she'd set him straight.

He sat down. She did likewise. He lifted the phone and waited for her to speak. She wanted to scream at him her suspicions, but they needed to come last, after she got what she wanted from him.

She sat quietly for another moment before she finally

spoke. "I need answers to a few more questions. Did Jacob Carston visit you yet?"

He nodded.

"Did you agree to hire him?"

"Yes."

"Good. I need the best answers you can remember. What clothes did you wear the night the police arrived?"

"I hadn't been home long. I still wore my brown slacks and a gold Polo shirt. Why? Is it important?" He chewed the side of his lip.

The clothes didn't match the description for the ones Hannah Evans said the killer wore.

"It could be. Did you mean you hadn't been home long from Tony's, or did you mean you went out for the evening or something?"

"Both, actually, but earlier. I went to The Grove for a few items. I ate dinner and drove home. I hadn't changed yet before the doorbell rang."

"So you didn't change at any time from the period when you went to The Grove and the time the police arrived?"

"No. What's this about?" He lifted his right brow and tilted his head a little.

"I need to get your timeline in perspective. While you walked around at The Grove, did anyone want a picture with you? Did someone recognize you? Anyone who could prove your alibi?"

"I don't remember, but people approach me every time I go out. I don't think about it anymore."

"Where did you eat?"

"The Cheesecake Factory."

"What time?"

"I'm not sure. Seven or eight. I'm just not sure." He shrugged.

"Think about it later. If you remember anything, let me know." She switched the receiver to her other hand. She wanted to verify he didn't lie to her. "Now, after I get discovery, the clothes you wore will show brown slacks and a gold Polo shirt, right?"

He nodded.

"What brand were the pants?"

"Armani. What does it matter?" He shrugged again.

"Because whoever killed your father would be covered in brains and blood. So their clothes would be too. You can't inflict so much damage to someone and not coat yourself with the evidence."

"My clothes were clean. A little sand and sea water on the cuffs, but nothing more."

"This could help you in court. We'll see what happens. How about the murder weapon? Did you see one when you got back, before the police got there?"

"No."

She could tell from his expression he held something back. "No more bullshit. What aren't you telling me?"

"Nothing."

"Don't give me your innocent look. You already gave yourself away a minute ago. What did you do with the murder weapon?" She watched him for a tell.

"Nothing. I swear."

"Answer my other question. What are you *not* telling me? I know there's something. What is it?"

He hesitated for a moment. "My Slugger's missing."

"What do you mean your bat's missing."

"I used it out by the pool earlier in the day. I practiced for my next role. After I got back from my walk to Tony's, I didn't see it anywhere around the pool or patio area. The police got there so quick. I think it's gone, but I couldn't ask them. I figured I was in trouble. I didn't want them to know I owned what might be the murder weapon."

She rubbed her thumb along the scratched edge of the table top and sat in quiet thought. "How long ago did you buy the bat?"

"About a week before my old man showed up."

"So the police can prove you bought a brand new bat."

"Yes." He nodded and stared down at his hand.

"Why?"

"I owned an old metal one. My film director wanted me to practice with a new bat. One closer to the real weight I would use in the film. So I went out and bought a Louisville Slugger like the one used in the screenplay."

"Did you use a credit card?"

"Doesn't everyone?" He rolled his eyes at her.

"No, everyone doesn't. The credit card will link it back to you. The police run a credit check first thing. So by now they already know you bought one. Which was right before your father died, almost like you knew he would show up. Believe me, it's what I'd think if I investigated this case. It shows premeditation. Which means they file murder one on you."

"I didn't kill him. I swear I didn't." He gazed at her, and fear crept into his expression.

"Yeah." She raised her eyebrows. "So can you explain to me why the police found your prints at a double homicide, and you didn't tell me about it? What do you think I am, stupid? I found out on the news last night. The whole damn town knows, but you didn't think to tell me."

He ran his right hand through his hair and gripped the back of his neck. But he wouldn't answer.

"You got nothing for me. You screwed me over, and still you got nothing for me."

He barely moved his head and indicated no.

"I know it's in every program you've ever watched, but it's true. Keep your mouth shut. Refuse any interview without your lawyer present. You need to tell him everything you haven't told me. He can't repeat anything you say. It's privileged conversation so don't hold anything back. The dumbest stunt you can pull is lie to me or your lawyer. It's how people get convicted."

His expression bereft, he nodded and swallowed.

"One more thing. Keep your mouth shut, and I mean it. Your guard or other inmates are often used for snitches. So when I say don't talk to anyone, I mean not a soul that breathes, not even Caroline. The details of this case go only to me and your lawyer. Don't think about looking tough in front of others to impress them. They'll sell you out for a single cigarette. Remember, they're in it for themselves only. Not you."

He met her gaze and nodded.

"Now, we have something else I want to clear up. Caroline's too good for you. You need to leave her alone."

"Okay."

"You say okay, but I saw your face after you recognized I wasn't her. I've helped you against my better judgment, so don't mess with me on this. I don't know how to make it any clearer. This time take it seriously."

"I'm the first to agree, she's too good for me. I know that only too well."

She nodded, but watched him. "The clothes give me more information to work with, but the fingerprints hurt us the most. You pull this crap again by not telling me everything the detectives could use against you, and I'm gone. I've never meant anything more. You still got nothing to say on the prints?"

He shook his head.

She crammed her receiver into its hook and left him to replace his, while she fumed as she stormed out the door.

11

———————

A hammer pounded in Cherry Pie's head. Terrell got her drunk again last night. She closed her eyes and rolled over. He'd wake up soon and her life in hell would continue like it did every day until he passed out for the night. She lived like his prisoner. He'd trained her like people did their dogs, but men cared about their pets. He wasn't capable of feeling anything for anyone but himself.

The bed shifted. He'd woken up. She felt herself fly as he kicked her to the floor. She landed hard and pain shot up her back. He gripped his gun and brought it up. In her peripheral vision she saw it pointed at her. She ran for the kitchen as he pulled the trigger. Thank God it fired on an empty chamber.

"Get me something to eat, and hurry your ass up."

When she came back, his legs hung over the side of the bed. With his elbows on his knees, he held his head with both hands.

"The asshole cut into my cash flow. He's taken two of my women and brought the cops around way too much. I'm gonna kill the bastard."

She moved hesitantly toward him and handed over a peanut butter and jelly sandwich. In her other hand she grasped a glass of orange juice.

He took them both and glared up at her like she was stupid. And she was stupid, since she ever believed he'd loved her.

"Who ever heard of OJ with a peanut butter and jelly sandwich? You bitch, get me some milk."

"We ain't got none. Beside I heard orange juice is good for hangovers."

"Stuff it. You don't know anything but how to move your ass."

He sneered made but took the juice and emptied the glass. He threw the glass at her. She managed to catch it, watched him quietly, and wondered what he'd do next. There was no telling. He let her continue to breathe if she performed whatever he commanded her to do.

He sniffed once and finished the sandwich in only a couple of bites.

"The douchebag made me look bad." He pulled the drawer out beside the bed and reached for something inside. He inserted a clip into his Glock, injected a cartridge, and winced at the sound.

She figured his head felt like hell this morning. He drank more than a quart of Wellers the night before.

When he threw the sheets back, she saw the scars. A knife wound ran up his thigh, and he carried a red pucker from a bullet hole someone put in his shoulder. Pistol in his hand, he walked naked to the bathroom, placed the gun on the toilet, and climbed into the shower.

She longed to find the nerve to go pick up the weapon and shoot him through the glass, but she stood there and chewed her thumbnail in an indecisive trance. She hungered to do it so badly, but fear of him paralyzed her. Tears ran down her cheek. One day she hoped to get the courage to finish him off.

As steam filled in behind the partition, she wanted and stared, and wanted and stared, and didn't do. Soon he turned the water off, stepped out, and pulled a towel from the stack on the shelf. She watched him rub himself dry and didn't know how to conquer the demons that filled her life. She'd live under his control until he or a john killed her. She sighed. It might bring relief.

"I'm gonna kill the bastard. I've been thinkin' on the situation. He's got a type, and it'll be his downfall." He gazed into her eyes, and his grin grated on her nerves. "And you're gonna help me."

She figured he saw the terror fill her face. He strode over and slapped her so hard her neck made a cracking sound and her ears buzzed, but she understood instantly. She was already dead.

At ten in the morning Buck and his partner brought twenty-three videos into LT's office for the techs to go through. Catching the SOB on tape while he picked up one of the two hookers could give them a huge break. He wanted to put this case behind him. He could hear retirement calling his name. After too many years on his feet as he chased around town, he found it harder each day to stay enthused about the job. He didn't want to end up like those who finally quit and kicked the bucket two weeks later.

Most cops weren't ready for the easy life, but he was. He'd never needed the glory like a lot of his brothers on the job. All he wanted when he started thirty years ago was to do a decent job and serve the people without getting himself or anyone else killed. Up to this point, he'd managed to do both, but with psychopaths, no one could tell what the hell would happen. They were a rare breed with no conscience. He'd never wanted any part of them. Leave them to the cowboys who loved the big thrills.

LT Bennett glanced up. He laid the stack of videos down on his supervisor's desk. "Perfect timing. Someone reported another one at the Delilah Inn. You need to get out there. The ME already left for the crime scene."

"We'll get right on it, boss," he said.

Vern, his partner, turned for the door. He followed right behind.

The Delilah Inn gave "rundown" a whole new meaning. Another squalid place to die. Their victim had been dumped behind the seedy motel. A cloudy film covered the eyes while maggots squirmed under the top of her lids. Brain tissue oozed from the elongated gash on her head. Even for a veteran, the stench and the scene before him made him gag. He couldn't help but think the blow fly that crawled in her gray matter was one brave creature.

Vern peeked up under the short skirt. "Her underwear is still in place, like the other two."

"Figured." He asked louder. "Has the ME finished? Can we move the body for an ID?"

The medical examiner, Gene Shaw, nodded.

"With the amount of decomp, I assume she's our Friday night vic," he said.

"Probably. I'll know more once I get her to autopsy."

Vern moved her leg to pick up the hand bag. He pulled the wallet out and read aloud. "Christine Petty, Pocatello, Idaho. She's twenty-two. Damn, this one's young."

He'd never felt the urge to throw up his hands and walk away more than at this minute. *The son of a bitch.* He had a daughter her age. After his many years on the force, he still couldn't fathom how people committed such atrocities against each other, but many times over he'd seen enough to know they did.

He started to walk the crime scene and to develop insight into his opponent. With psychos like serial killers, he didn't want to get a feel for them. It made you sick inside. He closed his eyes for a second to rest them from the horror in front of him. Then he plodded on and saw details no human should imprint on their brain.

His phone rang. He gazed at the screen and saw LT's name.

"Buck, they found another one. So wrap up there and go to the next one. Apparently, he won't stop until we catch him," his boss said.

"We'll get there ASAP." He waited for the address that LT gave him and disconnected the phone.

PAIGE HOPPED into the Porsche and sung the door closed with a loud bang. "Do you know where The Faded Pea restaurant is located? If you don't, Bill sent the address to my phone."

"I've heard the name, but I've never been there." Josh's questioning glance reminded her he didn't know the reason for her anger.

"We're headed there so let's get started." She entered the address on the GPS in the dash. Josh backed the car around and drove away. "I'm sorry I snapped, but your friend pisses me off. He held out on me again."

"Held out? We know who got killed at his house." He eyed her like she'd lost it.

"That isn't the problem. Every time I start to think there's hope for him and he's innocent, I find out the police found more evidence against him, which he didn't tell me. If he pulls this stunt in court, he'll get convicted for sure, whether you think he didn't do it or not."

"What happened?"

"On the news last night, one of the commentators mentioned his prints were found at the scene of a double homicide more than twenty years ago. I don't suppose you'd have a clue what that was about? I asked Ben. He gave me nothing. No excuse. No explanation. Zilch. How am I supposed to investigate zero?"

"Calm down. He might have a reason."

"I'll bet he does, but he has to understand at some point he can't continue to do this to his defense team. It's like he wants to commit suicide. I work hard on my cases. He makes it more difficult, like I'm riding a bike uphill with the brakes on. It sucks."

"Caroline mentioned she'll go visit Ben this morning while we're busy. I gave her the keys to the Escalade. He might tell her." Josh flipped the left turn signal on.

"She doesn't know. I didn't mention it to her. So she won't ask him about it, and I'm sure he won't volunteer anything." She grabbed her phone to check for more messages from Bill.

"When you said you wanted to call her, I thought that was weird, but she fits right in. I must say, I get on with her well enough." Josh sped up into the flow of traffic.

"Yeah, she's okay, but don't change the subject. Besides, I'm worried Ben has designs on her virtue."

"Designs on her virtue?" he mimicked.

"Would you rather I said he wants to get in her pants?"

"At least it wouldn't sound like the eighteen nineties."

"Give me a break. She's way too good for him. If he hurts her in any way, you'll both pay."

"How?"

"I know you and Ben both think you're big-shot Hollywood stars and nothing can happen to mess up your world. I've got news for you. Shit can happen and often does, especially with murder. I live there most of the time. I know what a murder case does to families. It's never good."

His expression sobered. The traffic got heavier and took his attention, so she returned a text message to Sonya. She'd like to know more about what Tom McCall did after Ben left. Maybe he'd been the reason for the double homicide.

The phone rang. She talked with Sonya longer than she should have. When she disconnected, Josh parked their vehicle.

The Faded Pea didn't stand out from any other business on the block. The green décor seemed uninspired. She opened her car door and paused. "I need to go in alone. Give me fifteen minutes before you come in."

"A lot can happen in fifteen minutes."

"If you're gonna give me grief every time I need to do something, you're staying at home. I can take care of myself. Give me fifteen minutes." She slammed the door behind her.

A man in his forties stood two feet from the entrance. He didn't appear to threaten, but he didn't invite conversation either. She smiled at him, nodded, and went inside. He made no effort to help her. *So much for being a gentleman.*

A long mahogany bar ran the length of one side of the interior. Twenty tables filled the center of the room, but no customers sat at any of the tables. She saw a man who occupied a stool at the bar toward the end. Cigarette butts filled his green ashtray. Various papers lay scattered in front of him. He glanced up as she approached.

"You must be lost, but what a nice mistake for me. Who are you looking for?" He leered at her. His dark hair and fair complexion made her think of Ben. They could pass for brothers.

"Mark Bader. You're him, right?" She encouraged him with her smile.

"Could be. I don't believe I know you." His expression tightened.

"I'd like to ask a few questions about Tom McCall. I heard he did business with you."

"And you would be?"

"I'm sorry. I'm Paige Stone." She offered her hand to him. He took it in his, but he didn't shake it. Instead he examined it like it contained secrets.

"Hey, I might charge you rent if you keep that up much longer." She attempted to pull it away.

"I always think you can tell a lot about a person by their hands. Your knuckles are red and swollen. You worked the bag hard without gloves. Do you want me to back you for a career in fighting? Or do I smell a pig?" He hiked one brow.

"In this case, somewhere in between. I'm here to chase down leads on a murder case. Right now, I'd like to verify that Tom McCall owed you money and why."

"So you're a cop?" He took on a guarded expression.

"Not technically here, but in Tulsa, yeah."

"So I don't have to tell you shit."

"No. I suppose not. But if I found you, the locals will. If I clear you before they get here, you may not need to worry with them."

"I'll deal with it when the time comes. You can head on back to your little house on the prairie. Find a nice guy to keep you and leave the heavy lifting to the big guns."

She wanted to punch him big time. "The prairie is on the other side of the state. What difference can it make to verify he owed you money? Besides, loan sharks don't usually kill someone before they get part of their money back."

"So far, I ain't seen any of mine. He took me for a nice wad, and now you tell me he's dead. You can't collect from a corpse." He attempted to control his expression once he realized McCall was dead, but she sensed he didn't know before her visit.

"My point exactly. Why did he need the ten grand?"

"Ten? I wish. More like twenty-five. He lost too many dollars in a card game to someone he shouldn't."

"Do you know who ran the game?"

"He didn't say." He took a cigarette from his pocket and tapped it on the bar.

"So do you have any idea? You heard anything about who it might be?"

"I don't deal in rumors. Especially if they could get a person messed up for life. But I do know games in town that will get you dead real quick. It could've been one of those."

"I'm not from around here, so point me in the right direction."

"You don't want to find them. Didn't you hear me mention they could get you killed?"

"I'm afraid death's what I deal with on a daily basis. Where were you on Tuesday night? I only ask to clear you."

"Indisposed. I'm not a man to kiss and tell."

"Did you hang with your main squeeze or someone she doesn't know about?"

"It's time for you to go. I've been more than patient with you."

"I thought we were getting along great together. Surely, an alibi isn't too difficult to come up with. You had to be somewhere."

"Good day, Miss Stone." He nodded his head, and the man she'd seen outside walked toward her.

"Aren't we a little touchy?" She walked to the door and left. He'd given her more than she expected he would.

She stepped from the curb, walked to the Carrera, and climbed in.

"Did you find out anything?" Josh put his hand to the ignition, but didn't start the car.

"He verified Tom McCall owed him money and how much. He seemed startled to hear our vic turned up dead, but he didn't want to give an alibi. Probably doing something illegal."

"So you don't think he's guilty." Josh finally started the car and pulled out into traffic.

"Oh, he's guilty, but probably not of this murder. One detail of interest though, he looks a lot like Ben. We need to verify a lot more before we rule him out. Something else he said that made sense, he wouldn't kill McCall without getting most of his money back. He claimed he didn't get any back."

"You're not thinking Ben's guilty again." Concern etched his features.

"How the hell should I know when he keeps lying to me? But we need to check out every lead. In police work, you keep ruling details out as not important until you find what is. Right now, several possibilities exist, and not much of that is significant. We keep following rabbit trails until we find the correct one." She glanced in the side mirror. A silver Corolla three cars back caught her attention. If she wasn't mistaken, she'd seen one like it while she talked to Sonya on their way to The Faded Pea. She didn't think about it at the time. "Make a right at the next corner, then a quick left."

"Why?"

"Nothing. Just do it."

He followed her directions.

"Now go two blocks and right again."

"Okay." He stared into his rearview mirror. "Silver Toyota, right?"

"Yeah, he's still back there. No one knew where we were going. Or else Curtis Sampson *is* worried about his case. I can't think of anyone else who'd go to the trouble, can you?" Her thoughts drifted to the perp from last night, but the county detective wouldn't break into Josh's house. Surely not. Her phone rang. Bill's name appeared on the screen. She hoped he had something good for her.

12

———

en's morning started like the previous ones did. His greatest fear had always been that his father would find him. But he'd believed his father's return to his life would bring a paparazzi frenzy for several months, not the old man's death, nor the frame for his murder.

All of his life, his old man haunted him and lurked somewhere in his future. The bastard still reached out with his claws of terror from the grave. Now this. Paige found another reason not to believe him.

He heard Jerry Taylor's footsteps approach down the hall. He'd already learned to recognize the sound his gait produced. He'd finished breakfast. A ray of hope emerged. Caroline might be here to see him. She acted different from any other woman he'd ever known. She saw right through his bullshit and didn't appear to want anything from him. He longed to earn her respect. Her approval wouldn't come easy, either. The sound of his guard got closer, and he didn't want it to be anyone but her. The thought scared him.

"Hey, you got the hot-looking redhead here, again. What gives?" Jerry motioned for his hands.

"She's a preacher. She wants to save me." He heard how hollow his voice sounded.

Jerry nodded like it made sense. "Well, she's the most beautiful one I've ever seen. If I were you, I'd take my time. She might not come any more if you give in too quickly. Might figure she's got her job done. Know what I mean?"

"The idea never occurred to me, but she is a sight." He lifted his hands for the cuffs Jerry put on him and waited while his guard unlocked the cell.

By the time their conversation ended, they'd arrived at the visiting room. Jerry locked him safely inside and left. He heard Jerry's footsteps retreat down the hall. When he glanced over, Caroline sat and waited for him. He didn't want to analyze how glad he was she'd come here, but he couldn't keep the grin off his face. For the first time in many years, he felt shy with a woman.

"What are you doing here? Did Paige send you?"

"No. I planned to come this morning. Why?"

"She's not happy with me again. I figured she talked to you about it."

"No, but it's not the only reason I came to see you. I try to do the Lord's work, and you are a part. Besides, I want you to know someone cares about you and what happens to you."

He watched her closely for several moments. Her gaze never wavered. "I see."

"Do you?" She hesitated. "So what's your favorite hobby? What do you do besides make movies?"

"Before this I worked with the film editor on the *Liberty Valance* project. It's been a real learning experience for me. I found out I hold an interest in more than acting." He didn't expect her to ask about anything but his relationship with God.

"Yeah, but that's not what I asked you. Editing a movie has to do with your work. What do you do for fun?

"A lot of things you don't tell a preacher about."

She laughed. "Surely, you're not *that* one dimensional. Don't you ride horses, read, sail, do something?"

"Not often. The kids I grew up with didn't do any of those activities." He liked her. She stared him in the eye without flirting. It'd been a long time since a hot chick acted in such a manner.

"You should explore more. When I was growing up, my parents always made sure I tried a variety of lessons and classes, but I thought they were terrible pastimes. They used them to keep me busy and out of their way. I'm the typical rebellious daughter. I wanted their love and time, not their indifference."

"I didn't see that coming."

"I got sidetracked. What I started out to say was, I wished I'd paid more attention to the piano and ballet lessons. I think I could enjoy several of them now. I did find I do love to read. What about you? Do you read anything other than scripts?"

"Not much. I'm more popular now as an actor, and my agent sends me a lot of scripts to read. So it's basically work too. You need to pick the right projects and directors, or you wind up with sloppy work. Then you can't buy a role in this town."

"I see your point. What about surfing or something to do with the ocean? You live on the beach. I found I love to snorkel. Have you done any scuba diving?"

"I never go in the ocean. I prefer my pool."

"But your pool doesn't include marine life. You should see the fish around here. They look like they've been hand painted and with such brilliant colors. A few are iridescent. I fell in love watching them go by. I relax and float along. Oklahoma has lots of lakes, but they don't have the beautiful fish like in the sea."

"You make it sound wonderful." Her animated face kept his attention.

"It is. After you get out of here, we'll go so I can show you what I love about it."

"You've got yourself a deal." His smile sobered. "Do you mean it? You'll take me snorkeling?"

"Of course I mean it. We'll have fun. You wait and see." She met his eyes with her own. "I support an orphanage on an island off the coast of South America. It's warm there year round. You can visit the compound down there, but I need to warn you those kids steal your heart in an instant. The times I'm there, I never want to leave."

"I don't know if I would fit in down there. It's way out of my comfort zone," he said.

"Are you telling me you're a coward? These children will love you unconditionally. I couldn't live with myself if I didn't allow you to experience such joy. It's unbelievable."

"But I wouldn't know what to say to them. How to act around them."

"You could be yourself. Kids see through the superficial facades adults throw up to conceal who they really are. Children never hide anything."

"I think that's what I'm afraid of."

"Challenge accepted. I'm taking you, kicking and screaming if I must." Her grin became infectious.

They talked until Jerry came to get him. While she got ready to leave, he told her where to find his mother's Bible, and asked her to bring it to him on her next visit.

"I arranged a meeting tonight. I'm scheduled to teach at a local church. We start our conference tomorrow, but I'll try to work in a visit every day during my stay here. When you get out, you must come hear me at one of my sessions."

"You think I'll get out?"

"Of course. Paige is a great detective. The Lord's on your side. I know you're innocent. He'll help her find a way." She watched him for several moments. He suspected she could see the uncertainty in his eyes.

"It works this way. I can pray for you and share my faith with you, but you must trust in Him too. That's your part in the job. Believe me, He will do what he says He'll do. Once I bring the Bible, read it."

He nodded. She left, and he found a renewed hope. She believed in him. She thought he could get out of this mess.

AFTER HE WIPED IT CLEAN, Pete Goad dumped the pickup he'd stolen the day before at a convenience store and walked a mile into the housing addition. It might slow the cops down a little. If he rented cars during his work, it left a trail. Hot ones kept too long caused the same problem. Never leave a pattern, and they won't know where to hunt next.

Daylight would come in a half hour. The trail on his target ran cold, so he would track Stuart and the gal again.

An older model Toyota gleamed silver in the street light as he rounded the corner. It would do. In LA, people left early for work, but this was Sunday. He lifted a Slim Jim from his backpack. In less than two minutes, he fired up the car and drove away.

He turned several lefts and floored it for a block or two. It purred like a sleeping kitten. The Corolla suited his purposes. He cruised his way out o the neighborhood and turned onto the I-5 headed north. He needed to hurry and hoped traffic on the PCH remained light.

He caught the I-10 west, which turned into the Pacific Coast Highway near the Santa Monica Pier. The sun rose higher as he traveled north. He hoped Josh Stuart didn't rise early. The salt air drifted in his window, and he spotted a lone jogger with his dog making their way toward the rides at the end of the wharf.

He curved right onto the PCH and watched the gulls bob and weave in search of food. The journey along the coast reminded him how beautiful and deceiving the whole place was. Only the rich could afford beachfront homes. It usually meant Hollywood and the ego crowd they produced. He smirked and considered how quickly he could take any one of them down, but he had other plans.

When he got to Stuart's street, he turned right and moved up the foothill past the location he'd prowled the night before. He'd been surprised by the girl. She'd been tougher than he expected, but not a match for him. He wasn't foolish enough to underestimate her again. That was how plans fell apart.

He made a U-turn a quarter mile past their house and found a secluded place to observe the landscape. He could survey much of the area below him where the mini mansion sat. His car remained hidden by a small bush. He hated waiting, but nothing happened for nearly an hour.

The garage door opened, and the Porsche backed out. He lifted the binoculars and saw them both inside. The wires for the Toyota stayed in his hand until they turned left at the bottom of the hill. He started the vehicle and pulled out from his hiding place. He followed behind them at a leisurely pace but didn't get too close.

They pulled to the side of the road in front of the men's county jail. The woman he'd seen with the actor the day before got out, and Stuart came around to the driver seat. The woman went inside, and the vehicle took off. He drove around the block the opposite direction and hunted for a place to watch the front of the building. Close to thirty minutes later she came out, and the Carrera picked her up.

After several turns, they got back on the freeway and went south. They exited several miles later, and turned down various streets. He saw them park in front of a green restaurant, but only the chick got out.

She dressed like a cop and acted like one. Last night she moved like she'd been trained, and she carried a gun. If she didn't work as one now, she'd been a former police officer, most likely a detective. What the hell was the deal with that?

He turned left at the corner, made a U-turn, and nudged the car forward where he could see the front of the café. Less than fifteen minutes later the girl came out and got into their vehicle.

He remained where he lurked until they pulled away, then he eased out. A half mile later, they started maneuvers he recognized. They'd made him. He had to give it up and went right in the opposite direction from their second turn. He wandered away from the main road back to Malibu. They might have his plate number.

A few miles later he parked the Toyota in an alley, took a flannel rag from his backpack, and wiped it down. Once he finished, he took a Sunday stroll attitude and moved away from his previous ride. A mile and a half later, he eyed a black metallic Mustang. He knew better, but couldn't resist. He figured he wouldn't keep it long, so it shouldn't matter.

Within three minutes he cruised the I-10 back toward the PCH in his new wheels. He might give the Porsche another go, but something inside urged him to check out Ben McCall's house one more time. The pickup he actually wanted could turn up around there. He turned right and drove up the hill. Stuart's Porsche sat in the driveway.

He circled around and intended to park where he had

before, but the gut feeling wouldn't let go. So he passed the home and moved on down the hill. This time he turned right and proceeded to the other residence. He passed Ben McCall's gate and saw the old pickup going in the opposite direction. The next corner, he turned around and followed the truck. It didn't take long to ease up behind him and then back off enough to not be noticeable.

This time he wouldn't lose his mark. He would study the target long enough to learn what he needed. When he found his weakness, the hunt would stop, and he could return home to his island in the Pacific.

BY THE TIME Buck arrived at the crime scene, he felt frustrated, worn out, and pissed off. He wanted to put a bullet in the son of a bitch and retire. This perp didn't deserve to walk the streets. He hadn't felt this way ever. They needed to capture him quick.

Vern glanced over at him. "This one'll be fresher. The last one laid there a while. I know what you're thinking, but somebody has to do this. Don't get hinky on me now."

"I'm all right. I just want to strangle the asshole."

"I know what you mean, but I don't want him to go out easy. He deserves far worse."

He nodded, climbed out of the Dodge Nitro, and walked toward the crime scene tape. Two patrol cars parked nearby. Their colored lights strobed the area. The lot appeared empty.

"He's not particular about where he leaves them the way we first believed. The other places are a bit more civilized."

"This victim is a tall one. I might've seen her the night we canvassed." Vern stooped down. "Underwear's intact. I'd guess she's last night's pro." He stood back up.

"Has the ME cleared her?"

"I don't think he's arrived yet," Vern said.

"The way these ladies are dropping, he's busy, too. I guess we could canvass the area with SIDs until he shows up. All I gotta say is a person's head should never be in that position." He studied the body, which lay stomach down. The head faced up. Of the gore he'd seen on the job, this one seemed one weird too many. Her left forearm exposed bone midway to her elbow. Blood painted abstract patterns on the grass and weeds. How did a normal person make sense of it?

When he looked up, Gene Shaw was pulling the utility vehicle beside their crime scene tape. His assistant unloaded a gurney and rolled it toward the body. The ME set his case down on the ground, took a thermometer out, and shoved it into her liver. After he checked his watch and pulled the probe out, he noted the temperature on his electronic tablet. The medical examiner inspected the body and made several other notations before he raised his head to speak to the lead detective.

"Some time last night, estimated TOD between nine and midnight. Not official, but broken neck most likely cause."

Buck nodded.

"You can move the body now. I'm through until I get her on my table."

Paige turned into the self-parking area, and the valets on Grove Drive gave her a dirty look. She understood the Porsche screamed money, but Josh wasn't with her to foot the bill. Besides, she didn't have time to mess with them. It could take forever to check the stores in this area for Ben's pictures from Tuesday evening, and she wanted to hit the poker games tonight. She needed to hurry, or they wouldn't have time to make the drive.

If she worked on the force here, she would know where the big ones were located, but she didn't. So she left Josh at his house to phone his friends and connections to get information on the private games where a person could lose big time.

She entered the mall between an Italian restaurant and a steak house. The Cheesecake Factory stood across and a little to the left. The sunshine lit it up, and its yellow façade gave off a cheerful vibe. She noticed a Barnes and Noble close by. Hopefully, someone in the area used cameras.

When she got closer, she saw that the ground floor contained several smaller stores sandwiched between the two. Surely those businesses caught him on film. The eating establishment was crowded this close to lunchtime on a Sunday. The customers waited and formed a line out the door. So she went next door to Maxwell's. The women's clothing store held a few items that caught her eye, but she turned her attention from the merchandise. Instead she searched for cameras and the places they might hide them.

Ben wouldn't shop inside for female clothing so she moved back to the entrance and searched there. Finally, a shop assistant came to help her.

"I saw you give those sandals the eye. Want to try on a pair?" The girl was thin like a Paris model, and pretty too. Her name tag read Carla.

"They look comfortable, but I could use your help. I need to find camera locations. My friend walked through this area Tuesday evening. I'd like to check film to prove his location here and the time. Do you keep your recordings that long?"

"You'll like those shoes. They're wonderful on your feet. Normally, we only keep our tapes for two days." Carla stared down at her feet. "Those are your size. Try them on while I ask." She moved toward the back of the store.

The flat sandals more than tempted her, but she didn't try them. To hear Bill tell it, two feet of snow awaited her back home. Where would she wear them until summer?

A few minutes later the sales clerk returned. "We have Tuesday from four on. Would it help you?"

"Yes. Would you please make a copy for me?" She handed the shop assistant a flash drive. "I only need the cameras in the front. I don't think the male in question came inside."

The young woman nodded and left. Carla returned a few minutes later. She dropped the thumb drive into her hand.

"I can't tempt you on the shoes?"

"I wish I had time, but I've got a bunch more places to stop. Thanks so much for your help."

After she left the shop, she wandered next door to the restaurant in question. The customer line dwindled to only a few. The maître d' stood and waited to seat the next guests so she walked straight up to him.

"I want to talk to someone about the cameras on Tuesday evening. One of your customers' needs to verify his presence here. I'd like to speak with the person who could help me."

The man was about her age. He finally brought his eyes up. "I'm sorry. What did you say again?"

"I need to speak with someone about the security cameras here. Tuesday evening a man came into your restaurant. I need to verify he ate here. Can you help me?"

"We're busy. Come back later."

"I'm sorry, but I'm also busy. Perhaps I could speak with the manager."

"I am the manager. We're shorthanded. Give me half an hour. Seating should slow down by that time."

She decided not to push it. She nodded and left. Once she

came out of the building, she turned to the right toward The Grove Theater. Curtis Sampson and his sidekick exited the movie building. Sonny Harmon had a CD in his hand. They'd already gotten a copy of Ben's visit to the area from the theater. They could only know about Ben eating at the Cheesecake Factory if he told them. Why would he blab to them and wouldn't open his mouth to her?

Frustrated, she got video from several other stores. She collected her footage from the restaurant and moved toward the parking area to drive the Porsche home.

13

———————

Pete Goad studied the back of the vehicle like it held secrets. From his perspective, he couldn't see who sat inside, but he didn't need to. The face of his enemy was etched in his brain.

He picked up the fishing magazine he'd bought the night before and settled in for the wait. The house where the other death took place was only a few blocks away so he didn't want to kill the asshole in this area. No one needed to tie the two events together.

Ten minutes later the truck took off from the drive-in restaurant where his target ate. He waited a second or two, then followed. The afternoon shadows elongated and day transformed into night while he drove the PCH toward LA center. By the time they reached the Santa Monica Pier, colorful lights outlined the rides. He noted life often took on a magical quality when death lurked in his heart.

But as a person trained in such skills, you found dark humor where you could. Otherwise, nothing ever brightened your life. He hadn't remembered for a long time he once fancied himself an artist. The old memory leaped at him like a stop sign in the middle of the interstate. Something changed inside him after his daughter's death. A year ago, he'd never give place to such a notion. Maybe it was the finite quality of his life. Nothing of himself would live on. The bastard in the vehicle ahead stole his daughter's life. For this reason, the piece of shit wouldn't breathe much longer.

The pickup slowed and eventually found parking close to the Sunset Strip. He drove by the truck and went around the corner. A couple more right turns, and he squeezed in several spaces behind his mark. He grabbed the binoculars and examined the subject. The guy sat and smoked a cigarette. It looked like he checked out the streetwalkers on the corner before him.

His guy light up one right after another constantly for thirty minutes, then edged his Ford toward the girls. Their negotiation took only a moment. A dark-haired girl climbed in the old Ford.

He followed two cars behind for more than five miles and saw them turn into a shabby motel. Several buildings down he found a place to observe from across the road. The woman walked into the office and paid for their room. A few minutes later, they both entered twenty-nine.

He finished his magazine, grew bored, and flipped the switch on the radio. Immediately, he turned the sound down to zero and increased the volume slowly. Once he could barely hear the static, he stopped. His fingers turned the dial and hunted for a clear station to help pass the time. Finally, Toby Keith sang the last half of "How Do You Like Me Now."

Not much later, his guy came out and threw a bat into his truck. It seemed strange, but when it came to sex, people had weird appetites. The pro didn't come out of the motel room with him. Since his daughter's killer took off without her, he needed to stay with his target. He figured the hooker wanted to clean up and get dressed.

The news came on a few minutes later, and he heard something that changed his plans a little. The announcer said someone had killed several prostitutes. The description of the murdered girls fit the streetwalker he'd seen enter the motel room with his intended quarry. *Son of a bitch.*

No doubt in his mind. His prey murdered her. The sooner he got the scumbag off the street, the better. The gal favored his Selena in coloring.

PAIGE DROVE the red Porsche onto the dock by the huge warehouse marked twenty-seven. The man by the overhead door stopped to check them. His barrel chest and ham-sized biceps were offset by a nose ring exactly like the ones seen on bulls. She couldn't help but wonder who led such a man around by the contraption.

Josh let the window down and said the password, which he'd received from a friend. What buddy he knew who would attend such a place remained a mystery, but if you had big bucks to gamble, this place had the game. The whole area appeared deserted. Not a vehicle in sight, but the smell of fish and brine overwhelmed.

After he peered in each window and the trunk, the man nodded in the direction toward the overhead door. Seconds later, it opened. Inside she saw over a hundred cars. She pulled in and circled around until she found a place to park. A huge sign in the back hung over a red door and read *Chance.* They made their way toward it.

"Harry James," Josh gave the next password.

They entered a massive room setup much like a casino. Ray

Charles sang "You Don't Know Me" softly in the background. It reminded her of Hank. He liked the oldies.

Josh supplied the money for the evening, but they didn't know which bets Tom McCall preferred to place. They split up and roamed between tables. Josh played roulette for a short time. She gave blackjack about ten minutes, then moved on to Texas Hold'em. A popular game now, Hank sometimes watched it on TV. It seemed a logical choice for a trucker.

Half an hour later, she won several thousand dollars. She'd lived around cops most of her life and became adept at card games. The last few years everyone wanted to play Hold'em. Not her favorite, but she played it well enough.

The deuce of clubs, the ace of hearts, and the jack of diamonds sat in the flop. The pot held twenty-five hundred. She lifted the corner of her hole cards. The ace of diamonds and a two of spades. Aces over deuces. She put a five hundred chip beside the pot. A man with a naked lady tattoo on his forearm sat on the opposite side of the table. He raised to a thousand. The three others folded. Once the bet returned to her, she called.

The dealer burned a card and flipped another ace in the turn. She didn't flinch. Anyone who played much poker could spot a tell. She'd worked to never display one. A full boat meant a great hand. She intended to bet it easy so she didn't form a pattern. She pushed a hundred-dollar chip to the center on the green felt table. She believed her opponent held aces over jacks and didn't want to scare him off. He placed a five-hundred-dollar chip in the pot. She frowned a bit, but she called him.

The dealer burned another card and tossed the ace of clubs on the river. She wanted to go all in, but she wasn't here to win big. The need to go slow and get more information was more important.

She pushed another thousand to the center of the table.

The tattooed man placed two grand into the pot and smiled. He must have a boat or trip aces with king high. When she called, he turned over another jack, which gave him aces full over jacks. He grabbed for the pot. She turned over her ace, and the smile on his face froze. His hands paused. "Son of a bitch," he breathed. She dragged the chips toward her stacks.

She folded the next hand to the thug with the tats and let him take the pot. Her cards were decent for another hour, and her chips steadily built. She'd been there long enough to get friendly with the people around her and asked if anyone had seen Tom McCall tonight. "I met him several months ago. He told me about this game. I haven't seen him this evening. I didn't know if he hung out here or not."

No one answered. Her eyes surveyed the table. She assumed she wouldn't get any takers. Eventually, the tattooed man's gaze fell on her. "I never seen him here, but I played him a couple times at Ooh-rah's."

"He owes me a little. I figured I'd find him while I'm in town. I'm not familiar with the place."

"Closer to San Diego. Marine hangout. Similar to this one, but Pier eleven, warehouse seven."

"I might check it out, if I have time. Thanks."

She played another thirty minutes until she'd given them a chance to recover part of their losses. Once she felt comfortable with the extra time she'd spent, she asked to cash in and tossed the dealer two hundred-dollar chips. She took her winnings and hunted for Josh. He played at the dice table.

"I'm ready to leave, honey." She cozied up next to him.

"After this roll. I already placed my bet." He stared at her for a few seconds.

Fifteen minutes later they left the warehouse behind. She glanced over at Josh as he counted the money. "How much do we have left?"

"You won over twenty thousand so we're ten ahead," Josh said.

"You lost ten grand. What the hell? Go slower next time. We don't want anyone to break our legs."

"I've got you to cover my losses. Besides, we're through, aren't we?"

"No. We're headed to Ooh-rah's. Supposed to be near San Diego. You ever hear of it?"

"No."

"This time we know he plays Hold'em. I talked to a guy who played with him there."

"Do you know what the place is like?"

"No. He said Marines hang out there. He gave me a pier and a warehouse number. We'll be fine. I'm the police. Remember?" She smiled and batted her eyes.

He didn't act too convinced.

She followed the road out to I-5 and turned to the south. Half an hour later she drove down Harbor Drive and searched for signs to the correct place. Ten minutes passed before she pulled up to another warehouse with the correct numbers.

"This place looks a lot tougher. We should pass on this." Josh wore a frown when he gazed over at her.

"Come on, we've got worse places than this in Tulsa." They didn't, but he didn't need to know that. Busted windows lined the top row. Paint peeled from every sheet of tin, and gang graffiti covered the rest. She tried to tell herself the dinginess came from the salty air while muted music floated in the distance.

Here, the overhead door was open. She drove inside and checked the cars out as she circled for parking. The *Ooh-rah* sign lit in bright red letters close to the back rested over the main entrance.

She parked near the open doorway and slid from the

Porsche. Josh followed. "I don't trust this place. Here, we stay together." He raised his arm and put it around her shoulder.

She leaned into him. They walked closer to the main door in the back of the huge warehouse. "We can play this young, in love, and drunk. Not sloppy drunk, only a little."

He nodded.

At the door, a huge bouncer frisked them, but didn't require a password. They made it inside. She assessed the setup and spotted the Texas Hold'em tables. She counted six. Josh moved toward the players, but she held him back. "It's better to watch a little bit. See which table you want to play and how they bet."

A waitress walked by with drinks. They both took one. At least they would smell like they drank. She dipped her finger in the drink and applied it like perfume.

After ten minutes or so, she decided which table she wanted to play. Josh went to buy their chips. He came back, and she moved toward the one farthest away. They placed larger bets, and the players appeared rougher. Of the tables that played Hold'em, the group at this one seemed more the type to know a trucker like Tom McCall.

When she sat down, she bumped the guy on the left next to her. He drew his arm back to belt her one, until he gazed up at her.

"Oh, I'm so sorry. I didn't mean to hit you," she said.

He gave her the once over and smiled like he'd won the lottery.

"It's okay. No problem." He had a crooked nose, broad shoulders, and a Marine emblem tattooed on his upper arm.

She offered him a demure smile in return and placed her chips on the table. This time she spoke casually to the players, put on her innocent face, and stayed a little above even. Soon the man next to her was her best friend.

"I heard a guy who owes me money might play here. Tom McCall. About fifty, dark hair. You know who I'm talking about?" she asked.

He stayed quiet for a few seconds. "I know who you mean. He lost big here several weeks ago. I think the house spotted him money."

"How much did he go down for?"

"I'm not sure, but I saw him lose over twenty grand on two pair. He left after he lost, pissed as hell. If you ain't got it to lose, don't bet it. Right?"

"It's what they always told me." She played an hour and slowly built her winnings.

Finally, she stacked her chips and asked to cash out. She studied her new friend for a moment. "I gotta go home and get the kids off to school. Nice talking to you."

He stared back and nodded.

Josh got up from the small bar where he'd observed her. He stayed thirty feet behind her while she walked to the Porsche. When she got even with a dark Navigator, a man jumped out and attempted to slug her. She ducked and ran around the other side to the next vehicle, keeping it between her and the stranger.

By this time, Josh had caught up with them. He wrapped an arm around the guy's neck and held it long enough to put him out. He walked over to her and grabbed the key fob from her hand.

"We're going home."

"Hey, I only came out here to discuss how we want to play the next part. How did you learn to take a guy down with a choke hold?" She moved around from behind the Lincoln, rolled the man over, pulled his wallet from his pants pocket, and read the driver's license.

Josh hesitated a moment.

"I started out with stunt work. The other guys taught me a few moves. I picked it up."

She didn't know if she believed him or not. A choke hold was a tricky maneuver. People wound up dead, if you didn't know what you were doing. She decided not to call him on it. The man in front of her came around.

"Hey, moron, you think it's smart to steal money off a cop?" She flashed her badge. He didn't need to know the shield came from Tulsa.

He peered up at her, still groggy, shook his head, and rubbed his face.

"I wasn't going to steal your money."

"Then what were you doing? Trying to boost a Navigator? You jumped out at me like you were up to no good."

He licked his lips, but didn't say a word.

"Larry Godfrey, I got your name. I got your address. You'd better live like a monk. Otherwise, I'll come after you. Now, get out of here." She threw his wallet and license down at him.

He got up, grabbed his identification, and scampered away.

She turned back to Josh. "Now what we need to do is figure out how to talk to the people who run this joint. Why make a second trip, when we're already here?"

"I don't like it. Did you look at the place?" He spread his arms to encompass the area.

"Yeah, it won't be any better tomorrow."

"I suppose not. You got an idea?"

"We could go back in and act like they shorted me on my cash out, but it might not get us where we want to go. Or I could ask for a job playing for the house."

"Let's try, we go in and ask to speak to the owners. I might want to invest money in the business." Josh nodded toward the main door like he'd already decided.

"It could work. I'll play your devoted lady, I suppose."

"You suppose right. I'm doing this for you. You like the thrill of the place. That's why I want to buy a piece of this establishment."

"Okay, but don't make me out too dumb. I could never sell it."

Josh's smirk came out like a snort. He put his arm around her and walked back toward the entrance.

The gambling den didn't seem any better the second time they entered. They moved to the pit area where a blonde showed her bleached white teeth. She saw Josh read her name badge.

"Darleen, I'd like to speak to the owners. My sweetheart loves to play here. She thinks it's a great investment idea. Can you hook me up?"

"I don't know. No one's ever asked about this before. Let me call someone who might know." She turned and walked to a phone on the back counter. After a brief conversation, she returned. "Someone will come to talk to you shortly."

Josh stared down at her and nuzzled near her mouth. "It worked."

She pretended to kiss his neck. "We'll see."

"Can I help you?" A Hispanic man, missing a chunk from his left nostril, stood behind them.

Josh turned and gave him his hand to shake. "I'm Josh Stuart. She wants me to buy her a stake in this place." He gazed down at her like he was crazy in love with her. "I promised her I'd try. Is it possible?"

"I'm not in a position to make those decisions."

"Who is? I want to talk to them."

"It's not that simple." The man frowned.

"Sure it is. I got money to invest. From what I see"—he shrugged and gestured with his head—"this place could use it."

The man excused himself and took out his phone. He took

several steps away from them and talked into the mobile device. He appeared to argue for a moment, nodded his head, and disconnected the phone. "If you'll follow me, I'll take you to see someone who can help you."

Josh grinned at her and walked behind him. The Hispanic man opened a side door and climbed a flight of stairs. They entered an open room that looked down on the gambling floor. Three men sipped coffee and snacked on various pastries. They invited Josh to sit, but left her standing. The eldest of the three, with four teardrops tattooed high on his cheek, gave the orders. His eyes were empty and old, though she figured he was only in his mid to late thirties.

"What foolishness is this? You cannot buy my club. Are you so"—he motioned with his hand like he searched for the right word—"ignorant you don't know who I am?"

"I'm sorry to offend you, but no. I don't know who you are. I live in Malibu."

She stopped them both. "We came here to find someone who might owe you money. We heard you loaned him cash a week ago or so. Tom McCall. Late fifties, dark hair. Lost big at Texas Hold'em. Do you know where we can find him?"

"He paid me back two days later. So I don't care where he is." His disdain for women showed in his cold stare directed at her.

"Has he been back to play since?" She held his threatening eyes with her own.

"I haven't seen him. Has he done something wrong?"

"We're not sure. He owes me, too, and I'd like to find him."

"I noticed you do pretty good at the tables. The very one he lost at two weeks ago."

She lifted her brows.

"I ain't seen him around. If you need to find him, go else-where. I don't care for bimbos getting my attention with bullshit lies. Now get the hell out." He motioned toward the door. The man with the scarred nose accompanied them. They descended the stairs, and got in the Porsche. Only when they started the engine and drove to the exit, did their escort finally walked away.

"Did they have anything to do with it? I think they seemed right for the part." Josh turned his head to study her as he maneuvered the vehicle from the dock area.

"They weren't nervous enough. I don't think they know he's dead. If they did it, we wouldn't have gotten away so easily."

"Are you sure? They acted deadly to me."

"They verified they got their money. Unless they had another motive, they wouldn't care about McCall enough to kill him. We know Bader gave him the money, and we know he paid the loan. He didn't use the cash for something else. It leaves this rabbit trail a dead end."

"What do you mean, dead end?"

"It means we ran out of motives. We need to go in another direction. Or Ben killed his father. He has a much better reason."

"I thought you believed in his innocence."

"I believe in evidence and facts. They always hold true." She saw his disappointment. "We're both tired. It's been a long day. Let's go home."

He pulled onto the I-5 and floored it. The Porsche ate up the miles while the sun lightened the eastern sky.

14

Paige dropped her clothes and let them land in chaos on the floor. She didn't care. Fatigue gnawed at her body. She crawled beneath the sheets, punched her pillow, and laid her head down. She turned on her back. Her eyes popped open. She stared at the dark ceiling. She turned on her left side. Finally, she grabbed the remote and flipped on the TV.

She turned the sound down before she saw the two cops she'd seen the other day on the news and turned it back up. The young female reporter asked several uninspired questions until one grabbed Paige's interest.

"An inside source claimed the women were beaten with a pipe or a baseball bat. Can you confirm that for me?" the pretty blonde asked.

"We don't give out that type of information with an ongoing case. Care to name your inside source?" The older man looked upset with the reporter.

"You know I can't do that."

"We can't discuss an ongoing case." The detective turned to leave.

The news anchor came on and announced they were looking for anyone who might have witnessed the dead prostitutes in the last few days. The woman gave the telephone number to call if someone had information.

She reached for her cell and dialed the number.

After several rings, a man's voice answered, gruff and tired. For a second she went blank. *This is a terrible idea.* She hung up.

A few seconds later, her phone rang. She answered it.

"What the hell do you want? And don't hang up. If you're afraid—" the same voice from before said.

"I'm not afraid. More like, I realized this is a stupid idea," she interrupted.

"Look, I haven't got time for games. Do you know something about the case or not?"

"I don't, but the one I'm working on has a similar MO. I questioned whether they're related in some way."

"And how's that?" he said

"My guy uses a bat," she said.

"Who the hell are you, and what case are you working?"

"I'm Detective Paige Stone from Tulsa PD. I'm out here to consult on a case where the victim was clubbed with a bat. It's a long story, but I figured we could benefit if we meet and compare notes. Are you opposed to such an idea?"

"Why does your name sound familiar, and why would you consult with the police on a case out here?"

Shit.

"You might have heard about me, but not because I did anything special. I helped to take down Grant Windsor a few months back, and I need to be honest with you. I don't work with the police department on this case. It's a favor for a friend." She waited for his reaction.

"I don't know many open cases where the perp used a bat or pipe to beat someone to death. I only know about one and the victim is male. My guy's only interested in female prostitutes."

"I understand, but if I could see your photos of the victims —" She decided to back pedal. "I don't know, it seemed strange to me within twenty-four hours of my murder, your guy started. It appeared a little too coincidental not to have a connection. Remember, I started by saying this is a stupid idea."

The line stayed quiet for several seconds. "You know I'm more intrigued by your whiskey voice than the idea our cases are related, but what the hell. I'll spare you twenty minutes. How about sometime today?"

"Sounds good to me."

She ignored the comment about her voice. They arranged a time and place to meet. She'd been told enough times in the last six months how awesome her voice sounded, but she hated it. The voice didn't belong to her, and it always reminded her about the monster she'd failed to completely destroy. Six months later, she suspected she would sound this way forever.

James Silsby stopped at a convenience store to stock up on nonperishable food and grabbed a small chest, which he filled with ice, water, and sodas. He stared at the liquor section a long time, picked up a Bud six-pack, and pretended to read the label. He breathed heavily, his heart rate spiking. Finally, he put the beer back into the refrigerated display case and moved away.

He brought everything to the front of the store and motioned behind the man at the register. The cashier pulled a Marlboro carton off the shelf and placed them by his other purchases. After he paid, he drove to the location of the trucking company near the docks. A half dozen trucks with the Con-Haul logo on the side waited like children scattered on a playground.

He got out of his car and walked up to the loading area, which ran twelve bays long. The loud horn blast signaled the beginning of a new shift of employees. Two men came out through the side door. One lit a cigarette and grinned. "You know old truckers never die. They just get a new Peterbilt."

He'd heard the joke many times before, but pretended to laugh as he fell in step with them. Once he found an opening, he asked, "Anyone know a black-haired guy over six feet? I'm not sure about his age, but he looks young. I heard he drives here, or he could own a private rig who hires out for runs from here to LA. I forgot his first name. Didn't know his last."

They watched him suspiciously, waved him away, and walked on.

The next person to wander out kept his head down and studied his cell phone. He attempted to get the man's attention. The guy ignored him and continued to walk with his eyes still fixed on the gadget in his hand.

A few minutes later, a mass exodus departed the building, and he couldn't get anyone's attention. He got ready to tap someone on the shoulder. He'd come too far not to ask.

A latecomer who seemed troubled straggled through the door. He hated to approach him, but he needed to know if the guy he was after worked here. He walked up to the man and tapped his sleeve. "Can I ask you a question? I could use your help."

The guy finally glanced up at him. Below the Con-Haul logo, the front of his shirt read Harry. The man's ruddy complexion covered a full round face. He carried considerable weight on his short frame.

"Look, Harry, I need to know if a man works here and how I can find him. He's tall and under thirty. Black hair. He's supposed to haul between here and LA. I'm not sure if he drives one of yours or if he contracts out on a rig he owns. They told me he works with this company. Does that sound like anyone you might know around here?"

Harry gazed up like he couldn't comprehend what he asked about.

"His friend passed away. I came to tell him the bad news. Someone said he worked here or ran trips out of here. He looks better than average. Does great with the ladies, I'd guess. I only saw him one time."

"It sounds like Brady, but we got one hell of a bunch who run through this place. The guy I'm thinking about has his trailer painted with the silhouette of a woman on both sides. They're bright red. Boss only uses him if he's hard up. He usually gets a run at least once a day." He went to walk away.

"Hey, are you all right?" he asked. The man looked as if he'd received a blow to the solar plexus.

"I don't know. My wife called, and our fifteen-year-old daughter is pregnant. Damn it to hell." He moved away and dragged his worries with him.

"At least she's not dead," he mumbled. After he turned to leave, he wished he hadn't added the last comment. That could make the guy remember him.

He went back to his car and decided the food he'd shopped for earlier in the day would come in handy. Who knew when the truck would show up. Once he saw the guy, he planned to follow him until his chance for a confrontation came. Soon the constant craving started, but he'd promised himself he wouldn't touch tequila again until he'd killed this bastard. He was so close. He needed a clear mind and a steady hand.

He drove the area several times until he found a place to park that didn't look too obvious. One where he could still keep the parking area of Con-Haul in view. Eight long hours later, he'd emptied two and a half packs from his carton, and he still hadn't seen a truck with red silhouettes on it. By midnight, his eyes drooped, and he drifted into sleep.

Paige's cell sounded Bill's ringtone. "Hey, what's up?"

"I think I filled at least one space in Tom McCall's timeline."

"How so?" She motioned to Josh so he'd turn the radio down.

"I got a match on facial recognition in Arizona two years ago. He drove under the name Tom Jameson. Worked for ZYX Trucking. Moved freight cross country. Stayed there for about a year, and disappeared. I'm still checking related news stories, but it takes time. I'll give you a call back after I know more."

"Keep the facial rec going. See if we can't find him in other states and fill in more blanks. Once I get home, I'll work the computer on the related news stories. If you find anything more about him let me know, ASAP. How far are you on the murder book?"

"Will do on the recognition program. I'll get the book tonight I hope, but no promises."

"Thanks. You still got snow?" she asked.

"Up to my knees. Gotta run. I see Underwood headed this way, and he never visits this building."

"Okay." Her phone went dead.

She turned to look at Josh. "So how much farther is it?"

"A couple miles, I think. I'm not familiar with this part of town."

They rode in silence for a short while. She couldn't help but wonder why Ben's father changed his name unless he was up to no good. The obvious choice, he hauled contraband on the side. What if his boss got wise and didn't want the publicity? Or he could have killed another female. With so many holes in his timeline, something of significance went on over a long time span.

Josh wasn't happy they were working with the police, even if they weren't the ones on Ben's case.

She tried to start a conversation. "So where're you from?"

He gave her a pointed look and raised his brow. "Around."

"I know you don't want to do this, but cops often use their gut feelings to solve crimes. Anyway, I still need to check this out. You're pouting, so you can wait in the car again."

By this time, they'd arrived outside the bar. She climbed out and closed the door softly. "Guys," she muttered.

When she opened the door to the bar, familiar smells and sounds awaited her. Eight cops lined the bar and talked smack back and forth. A couple played pool at the table. The stale scent of beer consumed the place. She fit right in. These were her peers. For the first time since she'd arrived in this town, she felt at ease.

Two older cops sat at a back booth. One was the same one she'd seen before on the television. When they saw her, they nodded. She moved in their direction. Once she sat down, the more grizzled one ask what brand of beer she wanted.

"Pepsi, please. I hate beer."

"What the hell type of police department do they run in Tulsa? I'm Buck Tillman. We talked on the phone." He seemed about Hank's age. A few pounds thinner, but the years on the force showed.

"As you know, I'm Paige Stone. This must be your partner."

"I'm sorry. This is Vern Dowdy. We've been together more years than I'd like to admit."

She put her hand out to shake Vern's, leaned back, and got more comfortable next to Buck.

"How long have you two worked together?"

"Around thirty years give or take a few. He can finish my stories, and I can his. If you can get him to talk at all." Buck motioned toward his partner.

Vern smiled and nodded.

"We've helped a lot of dumbass people, believe me. Too many to count." Buck rubbed his finger over a chip on his cup's handle.

She listened to them share stories about their time together. Like most cops, they told several crazy ones. Gently, she urged them back to the case at hand.

"So what can you tell me about your latest killer? I'd like to see the crime scene photos if possible."

"He's a psycho, like so many before him." Vern looked like a toothpick in a suit and tie. She figure his type never sat still long. He burned up energy by breathing. His face showed he cared more than he should, but she didn't think he'd eat his gun, either.

"Anything significant about his MO?"

"He likes to use women's heads as a ball for his bat," Buck said.

"Are any beaten beyond recognition?"

"Some show more signs than others, but none were beaten that badly. He doesn't molest them sexually that we can tell." Buck took a long drink from his coffee.

He pulled a folder from the seat beside him and dropped it on the table. "Here, take a look. We found two more bodies yesterday. He seems to take one female a night."

Before she could open the folder, the waitress slid a Pepsi in front of her.

After the server left, she lifted the first page. The top photo showed a woman prone in a grassy area, her head positioned in an awkward angle. Blood matted her hair and face, but you could see the blows were powerful. There'd been no hesitation. Exposed bone in several places attested to the excessive overkill.

She glanced through several other pictures. They assured her the same perp killed each of the victims. If he'd killed Tom McCall too, the built-up rage was much more personal and explosive in nature. He hadn't been able to stop with McCall, but in these he'd needed only a few blows to abate his inner demons.

It gave her more to think about, but she still didn't rule the man out. If he switched from a male to female victims, most detectives would. She possessed knowledge the others didn't. Ben's father killed his mother. He might have killed other women, too. So a slight chance existed for a connection.

"Is there any way I can get a copy of these? I'd like to take the time to examine them for a while."

"They're yours. I figured you'd want to take a better look. Don't say where you got them. I don't need to get my ass chewed at this point in my life," Buck said.

"Gotcha. I've never seen them. Do you have any leads so far?"

"Nada. We contemplated using a female police officer for a decoy. It could flush him out, but it's risky. It takes too much man power to cover them. You know how tight budgets are these days." Buck took another swallow of his coffee.

"Don't I know you from somewhere?" Vern leaned in closer.

She hated to talk about it, but he would figure it out eventually. "I was involved with the Celebrity Strangler case last summer. It got a little news attention. Don't believe everything you read."

"Yeah, your picture ran in the papers out here. And on the news. Heather Balentine was a big deal in the movie industry," Buck said.

"I know."

"So now you're interested in our serial killer." Vern leaned back and crossed his arms.

"No. Only as it might pertain to my case. If I never see another perp like Windsor, I'll be completely content. In fact, I hope the murders aren't related. I don't need the aggravation."

"We agree on that. I'm ready to retire and this case falls into our lap. What crappy luck is that?" Buck shook his head.

She nodded. "If I give you my phone number, will you call me out to the next crime scene? I'd like to make sure he's not my man. It always helps to see the real deal. By then I can study these photos more closely. I'd love to rule him out."

"We'll give you a call, but if any higher ups show . . ." Buck answered.

"I'll disappear. Promise."

When she walked back outside the bar, Josh stood leaned against the Porsche. She climbed in without a word. He didn't look happy, but he'd have to get over it.

"We've discussed this before. Wheels. Nondescript vehicle. I want to come and go as I please. I've been here long enough to get around. I could use a GPS, but those are no problem for you. You're too well known and attract attention. Besides I might get a call to leave in the middle of the night or something," she said.

"What the hell? You talk to them for an hour, and you want to leave me in the dust."

"I want to go to their next crime scene, and I can't drag you along. Your car sticks out like you do. I can't drive the Porsche to a crime scene. I told you the other day—brown, dark blue, nondescript, blend-in type vehicle. Anything not conspicuous."

"What about the Lincoln? It's black." Josh flipped on his turn signal.

"Caroline needs it. Her meetings start tonight or tomorrow. If she stays here, which is inconvenient for her to do, she'll need to use the Escalade. What car does Ben drive? Or Tony, who's out of town?"

"Their cars are similar to mine. I think Ben still has his black Escalade. They're exactly alike. Will it do?"

"I guess, but it's a little fancier than I'd like. He won't mind, will he?"

"No. I don't think he's driven it since we got back."

"Why?"

"Bad memories, I guess. The three of us bought matching black Escalades before we came to Oklahoma. We drove mine out and to the airport for our flight home. They sent three guys out to drive them back for us. I think it's still sitting in his garage."

"How many cars does he own?" she asked.

"That and the Lamborghini, but he mostly rides his Harley."

"Do you have a key for it? We could go pick it up now."

Josh nodded, but a frown furrowed his brow.

15

———

Paige figured she should go with Caroline to her meeting. They hadn't spent much together since she'd arrived. She needed to study the crime scene photos, compare them to the ones from Ben's case, and search through the footage from The Grove. Caroline would understand.

She put on her workout clothes, gathered both sets of photos, and examined the details from the various crime scenes. The work progressed slowly. An hour in, her eyes ached. She stretched, inserted the flash drive, and sat down again.

Once she pulled the footage up from different stores, she located Ben without any trouble. He passed a few stores and spent plenty of time in the restaurant. Each time, he wore the same designer shirt and brown slacks. If Bill could get her a copy of the murder book, she could verify the clothes he wore when the police arrested him.

She went back to study the crime scene pictures for another thirty minutes. Afterward, she made her way down the stairs into the gym.

Josh got there first. He'd built up a fine sheen of perspiration over his body. His muscles rippled while he continued to punch the bag she'd worked the day before. She ignored him and climbed on the rowing machine. She began her own sweat-building program.

She watched him throw punches for twenty minutes or so. He walked to the mat and dropped to start doing pushups. She lost count somewhere around fifty-three, but he continued. By then, she'd quit the rowing machine and gone on to weights.

Fatigue screamed in her biceps as she did another rep. His hand gently repositioned her arm.

"It'll do more good if you hold it like this."

She jumped.

"I didn't mean to startle you." His voice was low.

"I know. I came down to stir myself up a little. The photos wore me out." She turned into him, her eyes questioning.

"That sounds absurd."

"Yes, but it's tedious work. Each one tells you a story about what happened there. Sometimes you study them for hours before you see something you didn't notice before. A new detail can change your whole perspective."

"Did you find anything helpful?" He stood so close, his eyes penetrating.

"Not much. The crimes seem like they're committed by the same person, but I've found nothing definitive yet."

Before she knew what was happening, he leaned down and kissed her.

She told herself to move, to pull away, but his lips found her cheek and traveled to her neck. Her breath caught. His head came back up and captured her mouth. The kiss didn't feel like Bobby's, but it stirred a kindling low in her belly. Something she shouldn't be feeling. Not for this guy. Josh belonged in another world far away from her home. She could never leave Tulsa and Hank.

She pushed away from him and stepped back. "I can't. I'm sorry." She climbed the stairs without peeking back at him and fled through the door to her room.

She stripped and made her way to the shower before Josh used the hot water. He probably owned a huge water tank, but she wouldn't take any chances. The heat relaxed her muscles. She couldn't stop thinking about the kiss.

She dried off and slid into her gray T. Her computer sat on the table so she turned it on. She donned a pair of her white underwear, grinned, and thought of Josh's reaction the morning before. She'd considered fancier lingerie, but why bother? Men weren't worth the effort. A memory of Bobby flashed. He had been worth it. She'd bought several lacy pair before he and Chrissy died. She'd never worn the lingerie. It remained tucked in the back of her dresser at home.

The computer dinged and she typed in her password. She waited for the laptop to boot up and flipped through the file folder. ZYX Trucking, Arizona, produced a long list of possibilities. She worked her way back by date until she found articles from two years ago. Her search led through dozens of stories around the same time McCall disappeared. If she wanted to know why he left, it seemed the best starting place.

She scanned for local news articles along the same time period. More than an hour later, she found the beating death of a local girl. A color photograph showed the victim, Selena Goad. A beautiful female with long dark hair stared back at her. She had the same physical description as the prostitutes.

Dusk had fallen before Pete Goad followed the old pickup as it left behind the tractor trailer with the red ladies on it. He figured the asshole lived in the big rig. Probably cleaned up at truck stops when he needed to. But he wanted to catch the guy in a motel with a dead woman he'd bludgeoned. It would leave the police with positive proof he was their killer. They might not care too much who'd stopped him. It should give him enough time to get across the Pacific before the cops attempted to track him.

From his position up the block, he could see the street light focused on the brunette. She looked similar to the young woman from the evening before. He saw the young man smoke one cigarette after another while he waited. She sauntered a short path back and forth near the corner. Forty-five minutes passed before the pickup pulled up alongside and the woman got in.

He stayed back a fair distance and tracked the pair about eight miles to an ancient motel shabbier than the one used the night before. He had put a device on the old Ford pickup while the kid drove his big rig for the day. He wouldn't lose the asshole again.

The girl went in to the office to pay for the room. Once she came out, she motioned for her john to follow. She walked about halfway down the row, unlocked the door, and went inside. His target grabbed a bat from behind the seat in his pickup and followed her.

He glanced at his wrist for his timepiece. It took him four minutes to get turned around and parked in a secluded place. The night before, his prey didn't stay in the room more than fifteen minutes total. He waited six more minutes to give the kid time to get his business done. Allison Moorer sang "A Soft Place to Fall" quietly on the radio. He listened to the end before he turned the motor off, opened his car door, and slid from the seat.

He studied his watch. Thirteen minutes had passed before he approached their room. Without a sound, he tested the handle. Locked. He pulled the Glock from his waist, backed up a step, and planned to kick it in. But just as he lifted one leg, the door opened and threw him off balance. He fell forward into the room. Pain exploded through his neck.

I PUT the bat down and dragged the body into the room. The door shut behind me. I felt for a pulse but didn't find one. The black Mustang had followed me all day. When he didn't follow me in the Mack, I didn't know what the man planned to do. The guy wasn't a cop so why wait until now to make his move? The bastard had breathed his last breath, so I'd never know.

I rolled the body over and went through his pockets for keys but didn't find any. The gun fell loose from the dead man's grip. I paced. Who the hell was he? I barely parted the curtains and watched the street for any people who might be prowling about. I spotted the Mustang parked close by.

After I left the motel room to get the vehicle, I still didn't see anyone hanging around. I hunted on the floor and in the ashtray for a key fob. Then I spotted the way the car started. It only took a few moments to touch the wires together and fire it up. I backed it in beside my pickup. The body felt heavy as I lifted it into the trunk. I drove the dead man half a mile away and hoofed it back to my pickup. Who was this dude who stole a car and carried a gun? Probably intended to kill me. The biggest question: Why? I didn't think I'd ever seen the man before.

I still wondered why the hell the guy was after me while I

grabbed my bat and picked up the Glock. I got in my wheels and left the hooker behind. For a reason I didn't understand, I couldn't leave the man's body in the motel room with her. It shouldn't matter, but it did.

HER LEGS ACHED. She'd run so far. Paige felt shame at her nakedness. Where did she put her clothes? Goosebumps raced across her skin. She strained to run faster, but her muscles gave out. His hot breath fanned her ear. She sensed air move across her shoulder as his arm reached out to grab her. Fear seized her. Panic. Oh my God. His hand gripped her throat and fiery needles shot through it. Her fingers pulled at the constriction that suffocated her. I can't breathe. I can't breathe. She struggled to loosen his hold from her throbbing neck. Next she floated out from her body and felt herself move toward the black void.

When the sound from her cell finally stirred her, sweat drenched her T-shirt. Darkness cloaked the room. The small light flickered with each ring and cast eerie shadows. Still half asleep, she reached for her phone.

"We've got another prostitute. If you want to see the scene, you'd better hurry. I got the call a minute ago." Buck Tillman's voice finally woke her.

"I just need to change, and I'm on my way." She wrote down the address and thanked him.

She got up, ran a brush through her hair, and stuffed it in a ponytail. Jeans and a clean T-shirt came next. She hurried to the bathroom. The door to her room closed behind her less than ten minutes since the phone roused her from the nightmare.

She arrived on scene. Klieg lights flooded the open doorway. Her eyes searched for Buck or Vern. After a minute or so, she saw an old burgundy Impala pull up. Buck crawled out.

She endeavored not to draw attention to herself and made her way toward him.

He looked haggard. She knew cases ruined your sleep patterns. Especially if they didn't turn up any leads.

"I see you found it okay," he said.

"Thanks to GPS."

"Let's see what we've got." He walked closer toward the crime scene.

She followed but kept quiet. Once he got to the yellow tape, he signed in and nodded for her to do the same. They ducked under the barrier and approached the motel.

She entered the derelict room where blood spatter and gray matter covered the female's black hair. Fear still etched her face, though her eyes saw nothing. From the position of the head, she could tell a broken neck caused the death. Exposed bone protruded from her left arm where she'd attempted to protect herself from a blow. The pieces of shattered ulna lay mixed with muscle tissue about three inches above the wrist.

Noise drew her attention away from the vic. She watched Vern approach.

"Glad you could finally make it," Buck said.

Vern shrugged. "What have we got? Anything different on this one?"

"Nothing I can tell yet." Buck turned his focus back to the deceased.

She continued to examine the crime scene. One purple stiletto lay discarded two feet away from the body. Did she lose the shoe running away, or did he knock her out of the pump? The perp must be powerfully built to smash an arm the way he did hers.

Vern lifted the victim's short leather skirt. "Her underwear's still intact. Same as the others. Do we know the identity?"

"We only got here a few minutes ago. I don't know." Buck motioned to one of the patrol officers. The young man approached. "Did anyone find an ID?"

"Yeah. Her purse is on the other side behind the bed. I think she threw it at the perp when he attacked her. It's open and the contents spread out." The officer pointed in the general direction where the black bag lay under the bed's edge.

The scattered debris seemed about normal for a working girl. Red nail polish, a brush with black strands of hair, a lipstick tube, several condoms, and a wallet lay among the items on the ground.

She studied the surrounding area for anything that might help her. She moved back toward the victim to scrutinize her again. Blood from the broken arm puddled beneath the body. Most of it soaked into the filthy gray carpet. In a few places, the red liquid smeared across her face. From the mouth, another small pool gathered in the hollow near her clavicle.

Her heart skipped a beat. She recognized a pattern in the blood. She'd seen the same repetitive design in one of the other crime scene photos.

"What did you find?" Buck watched her for a second.

"Not much. The blood in this pool contains an imprinted pattern. See the repetitive design?" She took her phone out from her pocket and peeked up at Buck. "Do you mind if I snap a quick one for comparison? I'd like to check it against the photos you gave me." Certain she'd seen a similar pattern before, she couldn't remember if she saw it in McCall's pictures or those of the other females. Since she didn't want to mention the other case, she didn't reveal anything further.

Buck nodded. She snapped two and quickly slipped the phone back into her pocket.

After she finished, Buck asked the photographer to come over and take multiple shots for their official records. She followed him to the purse and its contents. He asked if they'd finished with their pictures and picked up the wallet. Inside he found the driver's license. "Tisha Johnson, Rapid City, South Dakota, twenty-six," he read. He lifted his head. "Shit. She's too damned young to be dead. We gotta catch this son of a bitch." He glanced up at her and continued. "I hate when we got one on the loose with nothing to go on."

She nodded but didn't add a word. When he motioned for her to join them, she examined the area with the men and the SID unit for another hour. No one found anything else that appeared significant.

Daylight edged the sky with a rosy glow when she pulled Ben's Escalade into the drive. She moved toward her room and didn't notice Josh follow her inside until she turned on the light. She jumped and glared at him.

"Where have you been?" he asked.

"How did you know I left?"

"I saw Ben's car gone and checked it out. I wish you'd tell me when you're going to leave."

"I didn't know I needed to. Besides you understood it's why I wanted the extra car. Buck called. The perp killed another one tonight. Why aren't you asleep?" She walked over and sat down on the bed. She placed one foot up on her knee and pulled off her shoe. Then started on her sock.

"You're not the only one who has difficulty sleeping. Especially now that Ben's in jail."

"I never asked for a babysitter."

"I feel responsible for you. I brought you here. You're staying in my home. I care what happens to you." He walked over and sat on the chair.

"Thanks, but I can take care of myself. Can I catch a little sleep before we start our day?"

"What did you find out?"

"Not much. Someone beat her to death. A twenty-six-year-old woman, not much older than I am, proved once again life is fleeting." She didn't fully comprehend, and yet, she felt the reason had everything to do with what happened last summer. "It just makes me so mad. Who does this guy think he is? One minute this woman was alive and well, now she's on a metal table in the morgue. And we can't stop him. Sorry. I'm not good company right now."

"I'm sorry I pushed you."

"It's okay, but I need to get some sleep." She nodded toward the door.

He hesitated and looked back at her, the scowl slowly faded. Regret etched his face as he closed the door behind him. His footsteps grew faint.

She got up and went for her phone to download the two photos to her laptop. Comparison would be much easier on her computer screen.

The stack of prostitutes' pictures still lay on the floor by her chair. She went through the photographs of the female victims, then examined the prints from Ben's case. Partway through his pile, she found the one she'd searched for. The repetitious shapes looked like the new shots she'd taken. *Ben might be innocent after all.*

She used an app on the computer and marked the area of interest. She typed an e-mail and sent it to Bill's private account.

I need to know what made this pattern. I think it's a glove used for construction or heavy labor. If so, I need to know what type made the distinctive depressions in the blood. Get back to me ASAP.

She attached the pictures and clicked SEND.

As she contemplated sleep, she heard a loud bang in the garage.

JOSH GRABBED the door handle and gripped it tight to work past his frustration. He wanted to slam it hard enough the house shook, but he couldn't let her know she'd got to him. She pushed him away and thought she didn't need him, but he knew better. He'd learned to trust his gut completely, and it shouted danger concerning Paige. No one could protect her better than he would.

If he could only explain to her that he was equipped and trained better than anyone, but it meant he'd open a subject he refused to discuss. Their relationship would change. It's why he never told anyone, but the compulsion to protect her over-whelmed him.

He moved silently through the house to his room, crept inside, and flipped on the light. The brightness hurt his eyes for a split second before he found the bed and sat down. Paige would give him hell if she ever found out what he contem-plated, but anything could happen to her on the streets in LA, especially in the wee hours. She was a trained cop so she figured she had immunity to danger, but she came from Tulsa. What the hell did she know? LA was a lot tougher.

He sat up straighter and stared at the door. She often went to the gym late at night. If he found her there, he'd fake an excuse. Maybe he could even kiss her again. She had said the distance couldn't work, not that she didn't like him. He could find a way, if she wanted him.

But not if she got herself killed before they solved this case. He got up and left his room. Not a sound escaped while he made his way to the basement door. When he opened it, only darkness awaited him. Disappointment raced through him as he reached for the wall switch and closed the door quietly behind him.

His gym felt empty without her. How had she become such a familiar part of his life in so few days? All the more reason he needed to do this, even if it would infuriate her if she ever found out. In the southeast corner, he lifted the edge of the weight set and moved it over three inches. He placed his left index finger over the scanner emitting a beam of red light from the floor. The adjacent wall slid back and revealed his collection. Tools he used proficiently.

He walked over to the drawers fitted below the guns. His hand opened the top one from the middle column. His eyes stared down at the array of gadgets in the tray before him and found the tracking device he wanted. He dialed the combination to unlock the drawer below. It sprang forward and revealed a computer he kept for this purpose. Once he closed the hidden wall and replaced the weights, he took both items with him. He retraced his steps up the stairs.

As he entered the garage, he glanced to the side and saw light under Paige's door. *Shit. Didn't she ever sleep?* By the driver's side door of Ben's Escalade, he placed the laptop on the cement and got a flashlight off the shelf near the kitchen door. He bumped a small hammer, which dropped to the floor. The sound echoed through the garage like an explosion. He hid behind the vehicle and dropped down instantly.

The door to her room opened, and Paige stuck her head out and looked around. She switched on the garage light and blinded him. She moved toward the tool. He squat-walked down the far side next to the Escalade that she drove. He saw her reach for the ball peen from where he hunkered behind the Escalade. He stuck the Maglite in his pocket and picked up the computer. What the hell could he say if she saw him? He heard her walking toward the end of the SUV.

He scooted back near the engine and strained to keep quiet. She held perfectly still for several minutes, then walked to the shelf and placed the hammer back where it rested before. She stood there, listened, and examined the garage again. Finally, she hit the light switch and closed the door.

After his eyes adjusted to the darkness, he opened the driver's door and finished his job. It took only a few minutes to plant the emitter under the dash. He synchronized the computer with the tracking device and returned to his room.

16

P aige started back through the photos one more time. Her head felt sluggish. Concentration eluded her. Finally, she got up from the chair and went into the kitchen.

The hammer that fell last night still bothered her. Did the prowler from the other night return? Should she mention it to Josh?

She opened the refrigerator, grabbed a Pepsi, and stared at her options. Nothing tempted her. She decided she wanted a hot breakfast, took the key fob from her pocket, and moved toward the door to the garage. When she got there, Josh leaned against the Escalade.

"Why are you out here?" she asked.

"I can't stand waiting at home, not knowing what you're doing. I figured if I didn't watch for you, you'd take off without me."

"Climb in. I want something hot. Let's go out for breakfast."

"I've got plenty to cook in the fridge."

"I saw the food, but I don't cook. Hank never taught me how. I can boil water and that's about it."

"I cook. What would you like?"

"Anything hot and filling. I'm hungry." She turned and moved back toward the kitchen.

"What kept you up last night? Before you ask, I saw your light. It's visible from my room." He followed her.

"I didn't know you watched my every action. Do I need to move into Ben or Tony's place? Or would you still spy on me there?"

"I'm not spying. I notice details." He pulled a skillet from the bottom cabinets. He walked over to the fridge and grabbed the bacon and eggs. "I've got canned biscuits. Are you interested?"

"Sounds great." She noted the way he phrased his sentence. Police were trained to discern specifics. It made her wonder where he'd received his training. In her peripheral vision, she saw Caroline come into the room.

"Good morning. The coffee smells lifesaving. I stayed out late." Her friend sauntered over and poured herself a cup. "I like a man who knows his way around the kitchen. What are you fixing?"

"Bacon and eggs. Maybe biscuits." Josh pulled another strip from the package and placed it in the skillet.

"Ooooh, I could go for those. I'll make gravy to go with the biscuits if you want," Caroline said.

"I want," she said.

With everything done and on the table, Caroline blessed it. They got busy and ate.

"This is all excellent, Josh. You're almost as good a cook as Hank." She popped the last bite of biscuit into her mouth.

"Paige went out on a case for a bit last night. They've found another prostitute," Josh said.

"Do you think it's connected to Ben's case?" Caroline asked.

"I think it might be."

Josh and Caroline studied her like they waited for more information.

Finally, she glanced up and saw them. "I'm working on it. A murder case can turn tricky. Ya'll can't know every little facet. We need to let the sequence of events unfold. If the case goes to court, the prosecution could subpoena you to testify. The less you know, the better."

They both stared at her like she didn't trust them.

"I won't put you in a place where you would need to lie under oath. Especially not you, Caroline. Now, I must get to work, but you can't come along for reasons I already stated. I will say the case has progressed, but we didn't prove his innocence, yet."

"But you do think you can," Caroline said.

"I've got an idea I'm going to pursue. You must trust me on this."

"Hello, Ben." Paige hesitated. "I've got more questions."

"Okay." He frowned.

"Have you decided to explain why they found your prints at the scene of a double homicide?" She studied him to see if he lied.

He shrugged and stared at his hands. She waited, but he didn't look up.

"I don't hear an answer. You did know they'd run your prints after they took them."

"I figured they might."

"It's one of the reasons they take them, to see if you've been implicated in other crimes."

He didn't move and kept his eyes down. The silence stretched longer.

"I saw the detectives on your case, canvassing around The Grove when I went there to do the same. Did you speak to them about your clothes? You don't share with me like you should, but you told them about your trip to The Grove. Why?"

"I didn't talk to them about it. Why would I?" Ben finally glared up at her.

"I don't know why you would. They obviously found out. They came from the theater with a CD in Harmon's hand. You didn't mention it to them?"

"No. I didn't tell them anything. They probably found the doggie bag I brought home with me and figured it out. I don't know how else they would know."

"Did you use a credit card? It could also account for the situation."

He nodded.

"About the other, I won't beg you to explain. I'll find out eventually. Let's hope it's not too late by then to do you any good." She paused again and hoped he'd reconsider, but he remained quiet. She decided to try a different approach.

"In the years you lived with your father after your mother's death, did he ever live with another woman? Do you know if he ever had other children besides you?"

"No. Not to my knowledge. He messed with other women sure, but he never married again or anything."

"He didn't need to marry one. Did he ever live with a woman? Maybe she got pregnant?"

"If he got another woman pregnant, I didn't know about it. I'm sorry. I wish I could help you." He appeared troubled for a moment. "You mean you think I might have a brother or sister out there somewhere?"

"I wish I could say. It's an idea. Someone filled with rage killed your father. It means they had a powerful motive. More than likely, it's something else, but we haven't found the reason yet."

"I wish I could help you, but I can't think of anything close to what you suggested. I was young. He could have, and I didn't know. I never considered it before."

"If you really wished you could help me, you would. Why were you at the scene of those other murders?" She stood and intended to go. He stared at her but never said another word. Even when she gave up and left without speaking again.

Twenty years earlier

Ben McCall left the motel at ten fifty-five. Five minutes to check-out time. He didn't know when he could afford another room. Not certain how to pick up a woman, he entertained a few ideas from the way Cathy Crowder had swindled him. During the time he wasn't asleep, his mind worked on it the rest of the night. He needed to learn quickly. His survival depended upon it.

He walked away and wondered if his father still hunted for him. The old man's thick head couldn't be hurt too badly. If he got the chance, he'd keep an eye on the news.

After several miles, he saw a park off to the side of the road with towering palm trees. Hot and thirsty, he decided a break from the sun and some rest was a good plan. His backpack held the water bottle from McDonald's. He saw a fountain and hoped it worked so he could refill it.

He turned the handle, took a large drink, wiped his face, and filled the container. A picnic bench covered by a shelter offered shade. He strolled over, sat, and leaned back against the table. When he felt rested, he returned to the fountain, drank his fill, and walked back the way he'd come.

As he neared the street, he moved north away from his old man's place. He needed to get farther away before he found a job or a place to stay. If he ran into his father by accident, he'd wind up dead. Period.

He estimated the distance he'd traveled from home at fifteen miles. If he walked steadily, he could make another twenty today, but would it take him far enough? He had a bus pass in his wallet. The one he used to travel for grocery shopping. No need for it now. He might get to La Jolla with his ticket. He remembered his fourth grade teacher said Dr. Seuss lived there. He didn't know anything else about the area, but he remembered he'd once loved to read *Green Eggs and Ham*.

He continued to watch for the nearest stop and walked in the general direction toward his new goal. If he could get close to the town, he might stay there for a while. His father never caught a load for the ocean-side community that he could remember. He plodded on for five more blocks before he saw a transit sign.

After numerous transfers, he finally reached La Jolla. The sunlight faded toward dusk as he stepped off the bus. If he got lucky, he might find a diner who needed a dishwasher. He could use a free meal this evening. He'd grabbed a hamburger earlier, but his stomach ached with hunger again.

He needed a job to replenish the cash that he knew would dwindle quickly. In a town boasting mansions and mini mansions on the ocean's edge, where nice shops lined the streets, surely he could get a piece of the wealth these residents had accumulated.

He checked with five different businesses before he walked into the El Casa Restaurant. His blue eyes and fair complexion looked out of place, but his black hair fit in nicely. A fifty-ish Hispanic man came from the kitchen with a tray of frosted glasses. He placed them in a cooler and made his way over.

"Do you need any kitchen help? I need a job." Ben's stomach growled.

"No. No need help kitchen." The man shook his head but stared at him for a moment.

His gut made another strange noise.

"You speak good English. Yes?"

"I speak English." He nodded.

"You how old?"

"Eighteen."

"Where you live?"

"Close by."

"How close by?"

He stayed silent and searched for an answer.

"You trouble with law?"

"No. No trouble with the law." He shook his head and chewed a hangnail on his thumb. He remembered he wanted a job handling food and pulled it away from his mouth. "I'll wash dishes for a meal. If I work hard, maybe tomorrow you can use me again. I need a job."

After a long pause, the older man finally spoke. "I speak not so good English. You work front. Take money. Help customers?"

"Yes, I can do that."

"You no cheat me. I give you chance."

"Thank you. I won't cheat you. I promise."

The man nodded again.

"You help me get better to speak at customers. Yes?"

"I will." He nodded.

The man's name was Cicero De Palma. His wife, Bonita, cooked in the back. She didn't speak any English. With much pointing, she gave him a bowl with rice, peppers, and chicken. It tasted wonderful, and his belly quit hurting.

Ten minutes later, the man turned the lights up and opened the door to place an OPEN sign outside. While they waited for diners to come in, the man showed him how to operate the cash register. The old clunker didn't contain any type of computer. When the store closed for the night, over two hundred bucks rested inside the machine.

Cicero took the money into the back rooms behind the kitchen. He tucked it safely in a hole in the wall.

The place was shabby, but it kept the rain off at night. By this time, he figured the De Palmas came here illegally, and they needed him as badly as he did them. He taught them better English, and they gave him a room in back.

For the next seven months, he worked, cleaned, and painted. The De Palmas grew their business and improved the building. Soon the few hundred doubled each night, and they managed to pay him a little. Bonita washed his clothes by hand until he finally taught her enough English to explain about laundromats. They bathed in a tub they kept by the back door. He missed his showers, but he kept clean. They got by.

As the evenings grew longer, the customers drank more, spent more, and laughed more. His work brought him satisfaction and a secureness he'd never felt before. The De Palmas treated him more like a son than his own father.

On the last Friday in May, a young girl showed up at the back door. Her split lip accompanied a black eye, with a ring of bruises surrounding her neck. Her waist swollen, he guessed her pregnancy was advanced. She looked Hispanic, like many of the people in this area. He glanced at Bonita.

She spoke fluently in Spanish. He could pick out only a

few words, but he felt she didn't tell the truth. He sensed Bonita also recognized she lied.

"Go to get ointment, bandages." Bonita nodded toward the backdoor.

He left by the rear entrance and sensed she wanted to talk to the girl alone. At the drug store, the busy pharmacist filled orders. With no other help, it took a long time to pay for his purchases. By the time he returned, forty-five minutes had passed.

He stepped through the entrance to their home, spooked by the silence. He inched around the door into the kitchen. Bonita lay on the floor, her throat gaping open. He wanted to run to her, but he was sure she was dead. Blood ran down past her feet, pooling into a large puddle against the wall, and her open eyes lacked focus.

He crept into the next room where her husband lay over the counter. Multiple stab wounds pierced his back. He rolled Cicero over and the older man's body fell to the floor.

He turned around, searching for the girl. She wasn't in sight. He searched every room, but she was gone.

He didn't know what to do, but he couldn't stay here. The cops would come and they'd send him back to his father. The old man would kill him if he brought the police to his door. *Son of a bitch.*

He went to the room where he slept, grabbed the backpack he came with, and filled it with his belongings. In the kitchen, he took what money they'd stashed in the wall and left by the back entrance. He hated to leave them there like they didn't count because they mattered to him. Tears ran uncheck down both cheeks.

With a ball cap pulled low, he rushed through the streets in La Jolla and promised himself he'd never return. When he got to the I-5, he took the ramp north. Hitchhiking scared him, but his father and the lifeless bodies of the De Palmas terrified him.

He couldn't explain about the De Palmas to Paige, how he'd gone off and just left them there. They'd treated him better than anyone besides his mother, and just like her, they'd been murdered. Why did everyone who cared about him end up dead?

~

James Silsby awoke and slowly remembered why he'd fallen asleep in his car. He hadn't slept overnight in his Chevy since he'd quit drinking. He stretched the crick in his neck, then got out of the car to find a bathroom.

The big rig he'd been watching for was there, parked a hundred yards away from him. He worried he'd been seen, but his bladder hurt so badly he couldn't wait. He moved behind his vehicle and relieved himself. He slid back in his car, eyes on the trailer, watching for the driver. What he'd give for a single shot of tequila.

He opened a package of crackers to munch and chugged a half bottle of soda instead. It didn't help his craving but eased his empty stomach a little. From his T-shirt sleeve, he grabbed the cigarettes he kept rolled there. He lit up, took a long drag, and enjoyed a few moments of relief.

Thirty-seven minutes later the huge truck fired up and moved toward the loading bays. The eighteen-wheeler backed into number four. A man got out and went inside the building. *Son of a bitch.* He'd found him. Without a doubt this was the bastard who had left with Marcia. He'd finally caught up with the scumbag who killed her, and if he got his way, the coward would die before this night finished.

He finished his cigarette while watching the workers load

the trailer. The guy was huge, ripped like a bodybuilder. Marcia never stood a chance against this animal. He lowered the binoculars and rubbed his eyes.

When the semi departed, he waited until the truck turned onto the next street before he pulled out from his hiding space.

He followed the big hauler while it worked its way toward Harbor Drive. Six miles later, they turned left on Civic Center Drive. His target dropped multiple boxes off at various companies. They wound their way back toward the I-5 and entered the northbound ramp. Next, the guy exited on La Jolla Village Drive and stopped at the University of California at San Diego.

He let the Chevy fall back a bit, worried he might be spotted. The traffic was lighter on the campus, offering less cover. He crept behind the truck as it made its way toward the back of the college, then idled nearby while it unloaded.

When the eighteen-wheeler passed by on the way out, the driver stared directly at him. He grabbed a magazine from the floor and pretended to read. The guy scowled, and the rig took off onto Voigt Drive, leaving the university behind.

He followed farther back and hoped to stay away from his target's sight. The truck drove back toward the I-5, and everything quickly went to hell. A bar dropped in front of him, and signals flashed. Moments later, a train crossed the tracks in front of him. Twenty minutes later, he knew there was no point continuing. The red ladies were gone.

Only one option remained. Go back to Con-Haul and wait for Brady to show up again. The SOB saw him. He'd need a better place to hide. No telling how long until the asshole showed himself.

17

Sonya's ringtone sounded as Paige pulled onto the Pacific Coast Highway. "Hey, Goob, what's happening?"

"I'm sick of snow. How do they do this in Canada? I haven't left the house since Sunday. I'm almost praying for school to begin again."

"Really? Has it come to that?" She grinned, and Sonya moaned.

"Sure, make fun. You're the one in LA where it's sunny and seventy-five degrees every day."

"Not every day. Sometimes it's only seventy-two."

"Oh, if I could reach you, I'd hit you." Sonya giggled.

"You can't assault a police officer. I'd have to lock you up. Then you'd never get back to school."

"You are so full of it today. Did you solve the case yet?"

"No. Some girl calls me every ten minutes so I can't get any work done. Now I'll probably need to stay until it thaws out in Tulsa."

"That's so low. At the rate it's going here, we won't get above freezing before July."

"Exaggeration. You're the queen of it. Seriously, traffic is a mess. Tell me what you need. I gotta run." She flipped the turn signal on.

"Nothing, I wanted to whine a little. I got cabin fever. Please hurry home."

"I promise, I will. Tell your mom I said hi."

"Okay. Call me if you get a chance."

"Promise."

She opened the door to Jacob Carston's law firm. She didn't find anyone in the small front office, so she knocked on his inner door. It opened a few seconds later. Jacob instantly smiled when he saw who came through the entry.

"And how are you this fine morning?"

She closed the outer door and moved toward his office.

"I survived the LA traffic to get here." She shrugged.

"So you're acclimated?"

"A little. I wanted to come by and talk for a few minutes. Update you. I want your opinion on something." She closed his office door and followed him to a seat across from his desk.

"What's up?"

"I saw on the news they found our client's fingerprints at the scene of a double homicide. I assume you've heard the same news by now."

"Yes. I did. It's unsubstantiated, but where there's smoke. You know the saying." He picked up his cigar.

"Ben said you came to see him. He told you who the victim is?"

He nodded.

"I talked to him this morning. He still won't discuss the prints at the double homicide. I don't know if it's someone his father killed or what. I doubt it. He gave up his father for killing his mother when he told Caroline the victim's identity. You got any idea what happened?"

"Nope. He hasn't told me any more than he has you."

"How long until we get discovery? Did you hear anything?"

"No. They're still stalling. We'll get it before the trial, early enough to meet legal requirements and not before."

"I know. We do the same if one of ours goes to trial back home, but we need to get it soon. My boss won't let me stay out here forever."

"Now you get to see it from the other side. We drag our feet when we give ours in return." He rolled the unlit cigar between his thumb and index finger.

"I found one piece of good news. I verified what Ben wore earlier in the evening at The Grove. He claims they're the same top and trousers he described to me after he got arrested. I know from the detectives on the case that they didn't find any blood or tissue on his clothing when they booked him. It should help some. Whoever killed the victim must have been covered in both."

"Good. There's our reasonable doubt, but we need more."

"We're still in the process on the victim, but Ben has motive to want him dead. Josh and I chased down numerous trails that led nowhere. Then I stumbled onto something promising. I need your feedback."

He picked up his cigar from the ashtray, leaned back in his chair, and nodded for her to continue.

"You've heard about the prostitutes bludgeoned here in LA."

He nodded again. "But what could their cases possibly have to do with ours?"

"As it turns out, I suspect they're related. I called the detectives on the case. Buck and Vern are the good kind of cops who aren't so territorial. They gave me access to their files and photos. I figured the cases needed a check. The guy killed the first sex worker within twenty-four hours from the death of our victim, and the females were bludgeoned in a similar manner to Ben's father."

The lawyer looked at her without much interest.

"Last night I visited the crime scene for the latest fatality. I spotted a pattern in the blood. I didn't mention it to them, but I remembered I saw a similar pattern before in the crime scene photos. Once I got home, I checked to see which one, but the only one I found was in Tom McCall's crime scene photos."

"Really?" Jacob Carston sat up straighter in his chair. "How did you get copies? I didn't."

"Don't ask. It isn't exactly legal, but I have my ways."

He bit the side of his lip for several seconds. "It could add more doubt," he said.

"It could give us a whole lot more, if I can get him to confess. If we get a DNA match on the weapon this killer used, it would be even better."

"Sounds good, but unlikely. He's dangerous as hell. He won't roll over and give up so easily. I can't see a way to make it happen." He took the cigar from his mouth and rolled it between his thumb and index finger. Finally, he placed it in the ashtray.

"When did you go to see Ben?" she asked.

"You called to tell me Tom McCall is the victim. I went later that day. Ben wasn't forthcoming, but we talked some."

"Did he mention anything helpful?"

"He didn't know much about his father after he ran away. He wouldn't talk to me about the motive you say he has. What did he tell you?" Jacob said.

"At twelve, before he ran away, his father beat his mother to death. It took over two years before he managed to escape. I wonder why he wouldn't tell you."

"Hell, I'm used to clients who leave information out or lie to me. More do that than tell the truth. Also a lot are asshole killers, but you think Ben is innocent. You understand, it doesn't matter to me one way or the other. I haven't believed in a long time. I get paid to give the best defense possible." He chewed on the cigar he'd picked up again. "Damned habit," he mumbled.

"I'm glad I don't do your job. It would suck to get a murderer off."

"It's not like Perry Mason, you know. I experienced trouble at first, but now it pays the bills like any other job."

"I suppose, but I'm still glad I don't do it."

"You're young yet."

She could tell he seemed more haggard than the last time she saw him.

"I will help the police try to catch this perp until another avenue breaks loose. Or something could come from the samples Josh and I gathered. Who knows? Until I get other evidence to work with, I'll stick with this."

"If it can get Ben off, I'm for it." He sat back in his chair and relaxed.

"Do you want anything else checked out?"

"Now you know who the victim is, did you research his father's past life?" he asked.

"My genius with computers continues to check into it. So far, not too much. His timeline contains huge gaps not accounted for. Ben said he drove trucks and worked on docks some. My guy's still in the process on his background. We assume he used aliases."

"What other details did you track down?"

"Josh and I chased down Tom McCall's money man. Mark Bader verified McCall borrowed twenty-five grand to repay a poker debt. Which we later verified. He did repay the debt. It's the same amount he tried to extort from Ben."

At the mention of Mark Bader's name, he raised his eyebrows. "So it led nowhere?"

"I'd say so. I mean, you could try to pin it on Mark Bader. He favors Ben a little. You might be able to use him to discredit their witness, but I don't think he's our guy. "

"You know we don't have to find the guilty party. We only need to raise reasonable doubt, and I'd rather not tangle with Mark Bader if I don't have to."

"And you forget, I catch bad guys for a living. I hate to see one get away." She raised her eyebrow.

"I could use a good detective full time around here. You sure you don't want to come and work for me? You'd make a lot more money than you do now, and I'd get more time to court you." He smiled and winked.

"It would never work. I don't date your type."

"And what type is that?"

"Lecherous." She grinned.

"A little harsh, aren't we?" He burst out laughing.

"I call them like I see them. Besides I want to live in Tulsa. Hank's there."

"Should I be jealous of Hank?"

"Not so much. He's like a father to me."

He stared at her for several moments and smiled.

"I've got work I need to do. I can't stay around here and joke with you." She got up.

"The dream was great while it lasted."

She rolled her eyes, shook her head, and closed the door behind her.

⁓

Trin picked up the file the researchers threw together. Another victim added this morning caught his attention. With a twenty-four-hour interim, the number of victims would grow at an alarming rate. He'd brought his go bag with him. By this afternoon, he should arrive in LA. He just needed his supervisor's permission.

He perused the file and expected the phone call any minute. The unsub had experienced a powerful stressor. A major event must have set him off. Serial killers rarely started with a kill per day.

The phone on his desk rang. His boss confirmed his assignment. He put on his jacket and picked up the files from his desk. He surveyed the room for anything he'd missed. He grabbed his garbage, turned off the light, and closed the door.

Paige got in the Escalade and called Buck to see if she could tag along. She figured he would grill her about the pattern found in the blood. The only two samples she'd found were in the photos from Tom McCall's case and the ones from last night's victim. She would evade him on the issue, but the information from these cases might tie to hers. She needed their help.

"Would you like company? I'm fresh out of leads over here. I figured I'd watch two veterans in action. I'm out here, I might as well learn from LA's finest."

"I thought you were working another case."

"Technically, I still am, but I've hit a brick wall. A day away from the case might knock something loose. You know what I mean. You're the only two cops who've been cordial out here. So I wanted to spend time with friendlies."

She could hear Buck talk with Vern for a minute, then his voice came back on the line.

"Sure. Why don't you leave your wheels at the bar where we met yesterday?" He paused for a few moments. "Listen, we got a call from a couple of detectives in our division. The officers found a male victim in a stolen black Mustang. They assume someone used a bat on him. We need to check it out. If you want to meet us there, I can give you the address."

"Sure. I'm downtown anyway. See you in a few."

Within fifteen minutes, she climbed out of the Cadillac. Her colleagues stood across the street. She walked up to the scene, and Buck motioned her through. She signed the log.

"Is it our guy?" She glanced at Buck for conformation.

"I can't say for sure. Our perp's only been interested in women so I doubt it."

"He appears fairly fresh. When did it happen?" She squatted to better examine the bruises on the neck.

"ME said last night after eight but before ten."

"Who is he?" She stood back up and looked at Buck.

"Don't know. No ID on him. The backpack has weird contents inside, but nothing to identify him. A few clothes with every label removed. A flannel cloth, Three in One oil, Slim Jim, and wire strippers. A carjacker maybe? The owners reported this car stolen Sunday a little past noon. If he is, it's a long time to keep the vehicle without cashing in."

"They found a box of nine millimeters under the front seat. No gun." Vern walked up.

"What about an assassin? Any victims who fit the description?" she asked.

"We didn't find any reported, but if he didn't finish the job yet, we wouldn't. Or the target could have got him first. Whatever he did, it was illegal," Buck said.

"You can bet on it, but nothing fits our cases. It ain't our guy," Vern said.

"Probably not. Why don't you leave your car at the bar? We'll pick you up there." Buck moved back toward their Nitro.

"Sounds like a plan." She got in her vehicle and closed the door. This crime scene certainly presented a strange combination. The broken neck appeared similar to their other cases, but no escalation or rage. The odd contents in the vehicle might signal an assassin, but no weapon. Her mind worked on the puzzle until she parked at the cop bar.

18

R elief swept through Ben as Caroline stepped into the visiting room with a smile on her face. She sat down and lifted the receiver.

"I got your mother's Bible and turned it in. They want to check the book out before they give it to you. Hopefully, it won't take long. Josh loaned me his key to get in your house."

"Thank you. It's great to see your lovely face. I'm so glad you came to see me. How is Josh?"

"He cooked breakfast for Paige and me this morning. He ever cook for you? He's great in the kitchen."

"Can't say as I ever did. More to tease him about after I get out of here." He grinned for a moment before he remembered he still sat in jail.

"Now, that's the way to think about your situation. By staying positive, I mean."

"If I can hold onto it. It comes and goes."

"They will bring you your Bible soon. Continue to read it. It will help take your mind off the negative events that go on around here."

"I remember my mother read it to me in the darkest times."

"It's an especially good time to read it. An even better time is once you're through that season. It can prevent a downward spiral. Now, how did you get started in the movie business?"

"I knew someone. They gave me a chance." Shame lingered. He'd lied to her by omission. Paige was right. Caroline was way too good for him. He needed to run her off before he contaminated her with his filth. "This whole mess will come out before it's over. You've been kind to me. You can do whatever you want with this information." He searched for the words to tell her the truth, but they wouldn't come to his lips. He didn't want to lose the goodness she brought to him each visit, but she deserved to know.

Her forehead creased, but she smiled again. "You can tell me anything."

"I ran away from my father when I turned fourteen. I survived because I pleasured women for money. It's a long, sordid story, but it is what it is. I can't change the past." He ran a hand through his hair. He couldn't bear to meet her eyes, so he stared at his hands. "Eventually, I got a small part in a movie. Only a few lines but enough to grab some attention. A year and a half later, I made enough from acting to support myself. I stopped the sex with married women and never went back. I'm not exactly your clean farm boy from Oklahoma."

Caroline sat quietly for a few moments. Her eyes didn't tell him much. "I never suspected you were. Everyone has something they're not proud of. I've done plenty of things I wish I could take back."

"Not like what I've done."

"Ben, you're a good person. You didn't stay there. You found another way. A chance came to get out, and you took it. Besides, the scripture stresses we're not to judge others. It's for them to judge themselves."

"What do you mean?"

"I mean everyone has done wrong in their life. We don't have the right to judge someone else."

He searched her eyes for any betrayal, but he only saw acceptance. "I guess I didn't know that part, about the not judging."

"If you read far enough, you'll find it's in there."

"I figured you'd surely walk out."

"I'm made from stronger principles than that." She grinned. "You didn't forget, did you? We plan to snorkel at the orphanage after you get out. You promised. The girls there will think it's awesome such a handsome man from the movies came to see them."

"I didn't forget. I already signed contracts on new film projects, but I'll find time. I'll make time. Assuming those jobs are still mine when I get out of here."

"You're a great actor. With this much exposure, everyone will want you. I've always heard there's no such thing as bad publicity."

An hour later Caroline left him. She told him she needed to get ready for her meeting. He wished he could hear her preach. Just another reason he had to get out of here.

Twenty years earlier

BEN CONTINUED NORTH ALONG I-5. Time drifted with no context. Miles separated him from the De Palmas. He'd cried until he had no tears left. He had to learn to survive on his own again.

He didn't know what happened back in La Jolla. He felt sure that whatever had happened, that young pregnant woman was involved. She'd lied, but about what? Bonita had been suspicious, too, but she still wanted to help. The killer surely took the girl with him. Was it the father of the baby? He hated not knowing what had happened. Hated that he'd run away even more.

He put one foot in front of another until he wanted to drop, but a breather on the interstate was impossible. In the distance he could make out an overpass. He could rest there and hide from the sun for a few minutes.

The sound of a vehicle slowing down got his attention. His first instinct was to run, but that would be impossible. Cars by the hundreds crowded the lanes. He turned to see a black limousine pull up next to him. Thank God. He'd thought for a second it was his father.

If they meant to harm him, plenty of people would witness it. The back window eased down, revealing a woman inside. Ear lobes covered in diamonds, she belonged in the limo. She seemed older than forty. When she smiled, crow's feet crinkled at the corners of her eyes.

"You're one handsome young man. Where are you headed?" The words sounded rehearsed. She'd made arrangements like this before. Her brown hair was highlighted with blonde streaks. When she lifted a hand to her cheek, he saw her perfectly manicured fingers, long false nails a brilliant red. The cream-colored suit fit as though tailor-made specifically for her.

"I'm between jobs right now. So I'm open to suggestions." The line sounded stupid, but he couldn't think of anything else to say.

"How old are you?"

"Eighteen." He figured he couldn't push it too much, or she'd never believe him.

She tilted her head and studied him for several seconds. "I think you'll do fine. Get in."

He should feel leery after Cathy, but this woman seemed different. And he couldn't resist the chance to ride in a limo, even though he was certain he knew what she wanted. For his next meal and a bed for the night, he'd gladly give it. He strolled around to the other side and scooted his butt across the seat.

"My name's Ben." He stuck his hand out to shake, but she ignored it.

"Call me Sweetness. Everyone does."

"Okay." Seemed like a stupid name to him, but whatever.

By this time, the limo traveled toward downtown LA. They sat in silence for the rest of the journey. When they past the Staples Center on I-10, he didn't know where they were headed and didn't want to ask. Wherever they went, he'd covered a lot of territory from La Jolla. Sweetness kept herself occupied by gazing out the window. She'd seemed attentive at first, but now she didn't seem interested.

Whatever happened, he would keep alert. At least they got him farther away from his old man. He didn't doubt his father meant to kill him, and nothing was worse than dead.

The vehicle turned off I-10 onto the 405. Once they exited on North Santa Monica Boulevard, he recognized the rich part of LA located nearby. He'd been there before with his father. They'd picked up a pregnant lady who worked as a maid in the area. He said someone paid him to give her a ride to the doctor, but his old man lied a lot. So who knew what the real story was.

They took a left on Rodeo Drive and arrived at the heart of Beverly Hills. Everyone understood what this meant. People with real money. He sat back and wondered if he'd turned a corner into something good.

The limo wound through a neighborhood of glitzy, monstrous homes, finally pulling into a driveway. Ben stared up at the glass and concrete mansion, all sharp angles and stark tones. This was a house, not a home, but it seethed wealth. He couldn't dream of owning such a place.

The chauffeur opened the door for Sweetness. She got out and went directly into the main entrance. She didn't indicate what she wanted him to do so he stayed put. The man got back in and drove them to a huge garage in the back. The guy still didn't say a word to him, so he got out and waited for directions. The old driver stared at him and moved toward a back entrance to the main structure.

He was starting to have second thoughts about this. Was anyone going to invite him in? "What should I do?"

"This way, please." The driver motioned with his head toward the doorway.

He followed him into an ultra-modern kitchen, huge and sterile, nothing like the De Palma's tiny, bustling kitchen that had always simmered with conversation and spices. His stomach growled. "Sorry," he mumbled. "My name's Ben. May I get yours? I don't know what to call you."

The old gentleman swung around. "I'm Charles."

He nodded.

"Are you hungry?"

"Yes, sir. Last I ate was early this morning."

"Sit down. Our cook will bring you something shortly."

He sat at a breakfast nook with his backpack. Charles left through a door to the far side of the room. In a few minutes, the man appeared with a short, thin woman in her fifties. His dad always said never to trust a skinny cook, but his old man hadn't been right about anything else. He smiled at the lady.

"My name's Myrna. Charles says you're hungry."

"Yes, ma'am."

"Dinner isn't served for several hours so how about a ham and Swiss cheese sandwich. That should hold you over."

"Sounds good. Do you know, will I stay for dinner?"

"More than likely. An attractive boy like yourself? She's been known to keep them for a long time."

He sighed with relief. A long time with a roof over his head and food in his stomach sounded great. He'd work hard at whatever the woman wanted.

After he finished his sandwich and a glass of milk, the cook took him up the back stairs to a room—a huge room with a queen bed and plush carpet in tones of beige. He ran a hand over the bed cover. *Was that silk?*

He glanced at Myrna. "When will I see Sweetness again?" He still didn't know for sure why he was here instead of on the streets.

"She'll come down for dinner. You'll see her then."

"How long until the evening meal? I mean, I need to know what time to come down."

"I put it on the table at seven sharp. Don't drag in late." She closed the door behind her.

"Yes, ma'am," he said to the empty room.

He explored and opened the two other doors in the room. One contained a large walk-in closet, the other a good size bathroom. He found the remote in the night stand, and flipped on the huge TV. In a few seconds the screen lit up with HD clarity.

He still worried a little about what she expected from him. He'd thought he understood, but now she didn't seem to want him for sex. So he didn't have a clue, unless she needed other jobs done that Charles couldn't handle anymore. He surfed the channels, found his favorite show, and watched an episode of *The X-Files* to pass the time.

He came down the back stairs ten minutes before seven. The cook was putting the last of the food into serving dishes.

"Need help?"

She peeked up. "Sure. Take the dressing caddy in and set it on the table."

He picked up the contraption she'd nodded toward and carried it to the huge dining table, wondering how rich you had to be to serve this many salad dressings on a table set for three guests. A table set with delicate china and silver, he noted. How did anyone keep all those forks and spoons straight? Maybe he should offer to eat at the breakfast nook by himself.

He returned to the kitchen and asked the cook, "What do I do with the extra silverware out there? We only used one fork, spoon, and sometimes a knife at home."

She laughed. "Use the one on the outside first and watch the others for the rest. You'll do fine. Besides, Sweetness loves to teach young men new tricks."

He didn't know how to take the last comment. That could mean anything. Damn, he wanted to get this over with. Surely by tomorrow he'd know what went on around here.

At seven, Sweetness entered the dining room with an older gentleman on her arm. The man stood small in stature, but so did she. They seemed to belong together. Both nodded at him as they took their seats. They'd barely sat down when Sweetness addressed her companion.

"Paul, this young man's come to stay with us for a time. I found him hitchhiking on the I-5 and thought I might keep him busy for a bit."

"I bet you can." The man grinned.

"What's your name? I didn't catch it before."

"Ben." He smiled.

She proceeded to ignore his presence for the rest of the evening.

Sweetness and Paul discussed many subjects during the meal. He learned Paul produced movies and sat on many boards to do with the film industry. Sweetness had her committees, too, but she didn't seem as busy as Paul. About halfway through the evening, a beautiful man in his late twenties came into the room and seated himself beside Sweetness.

"Gordon, this young man is Ben. He'll stay with us for a time," Sweetness said.

The dark-haired man nodded at him. "Understood."

"I'm so glad you got here in time to join us for dessert." Paul's expression softened.

"Always," Gordon answered.

The three finished the evening with talk about issues that held no interest for him. He wanted to excuse himself, but he hesitated to interrupt their conversation. By his manner with Paul, Gordon appeared gay, but he'd never paid attention to anyone who was. His father always called them horrid names. He'd never been around homosexual men before and didn't know what to say, but he understood he couldn't say what his father did.

Around ten thirty, the two men got up and left together. It didn't surprised him. He figured the evening might turn out this way. When Sweetness came to his side of the table and took his hand, he got up and went with her. This time they climbed the expensive stairs in the front of the house. They strolled down the hall to his room. After he opened the door, she went in and closed it behind them.

She sauntered over and sat on the bed. "Did you ever learn to please a woman?" She patted the place beside her.

He shook his head no and moved toward her.

"Do you think now would be a good time for a lesson?"

He knew the correct answer and gave it.

By the time he left Beverly Hills, two and a half years later, he equaled any expert in the field, but he got too old for Sweetness, so he had to go. While he stayed with her, she helped him get his GED, taught him how to use silverware, and set him up with an apartment. Her last gift was a list of women who'd gladly take her place.

A year later, on a whim, he walked into a casting call. Paul Malone stood in the outer foyer, and gave him a nervous glance when he recognized who he was. By then, he understood what a beard meant. Sweetness was Paul's. They'd been married for thirty-odd years. Everyone believed they lived as the perfect Hollywood couple, and they did. They loved each other, but not in a sexual way.

"Long time no see." Paul nodded.

"Yes. I hope Sweetness is well." He smiled cordially.

"She is. What part are you auditioning for?"

"I'm not sure. I saw the sign and wanted to give it a shot. Dumb idea, I guess." He shrugged.

"This movie has a small part with several lines, a character named Todd. Go study those lines for a few minutes. We'll give it a run through and see what happens. I can't do any better than this since you're new in the business. I'll come get you in a bit."

"Okay." He wandered back out into the common area and followed Paul's instructions.

He got the part, and they never mentioned why. He believed Paul feared not to, but he didn't intend to out him. He'd been as surprised to discover Paul there as Paul had been to see him.

After the break the producer gave him, more offers came his way, lengthier and more involved roles. Women loved him, and the camera did too. The first time he was asked to read for a lead in a film, complete shock accompanied the thrill. He told himself he'd earned this with hard work. But he never lost the shame of how he landed his first role.

19

Paige waited on a bench in the hallway for Buck and Vern to get through with their meeting. Her phone signaled Bill's ringtone. She hoped he finally got the murder book for her.

"Hi, gorgeous. Good news. I put the murder book on your computer a minute ago."

"Thank God. I need to find out where Ben McCall's fingerprints were found all those years ago and why. He still hasn't coughed up the truth about them."

"I didn't go through it. I've been busy on another case. That's why I took so long."

"It's okay. I'm glad I finally I got it. Now I can study it. I'll work on it tonight. At the present time, I'm waiting for friendly cops to come out of a meeting. Is Hank still doing okay?"

"I stayed there again last night. He's fine, unless you consider he doesn't leave his recliner except to go to the toilet."

"Thanks. I appreciate your help with him. When I get home, we'll tackle his liquor problem and sedentary lifestyle. You will help me, won't you?"

"Of course. He meant a lot to everyone on the job here. Besides he half-raised Bobby and me."

"I'll hold you to it."

"I need to go. My boss is headed my way." He disconnected.

She glanced up and saw a familiar face. His dark hair and tall stature would turn any woman's head, but he'd saved her life so she had an additional reason to like this guy. "Oh my God. They let anyone in here, don't they?" She got up to shake his hand, but he turned it into a hug.

"We're way past handshakes except in formal settings. So why are you here?" Trin's smile reached clear to his eyes.

"It's a long story, but I got caught up in this case. Once we have a few minutes, I'd like to get your take on it. They're expecting someone from the FBI. You, I guess. I'm not officially on the case. So I'm waiting out here."

"Who says you're not officially on the case?"

"Listen. Buck and Vern have been great. I don't want to make any waves. I'm reasonably sure their supervisor knows nothing about me. I can't prove anything, yet, but I think our cases are related. So I want to stay a little mouse who hears any small detail that could help me."

"Yes, but unlike the last time, I won't let you out of my sight. Why don't you come in? We'll let them assume you're with me."

"You think it'll work? I don't want to get anybody in trouble. I want their help."

"It'll be fine. If the detectives in charge of the case shared with you, you might know more than I do. Besides, you know how these cases go between police and the FBI. They won't divulge any piece of information they can hold back."

She grinned. "It's the way we usually play it, but this time I'm not officially the police."

"You mean you don't work for TPD on this."

"In a way, but not technically."

"Cryptic, are we?" Trin raised his brows.

The squad room door opened. Buck stuck his head out.

"We wondered what took so long. Figured you might've gotten lost in the maze."

"I met an old friend along the way. We worked a case together last summer," Trin said.

"I see." Buck nodded.

"Any chance we could get her on the case with us? I found her helpful last year."

"We can run it by LT. Vern and I got no problem with it."

"I told him I came to observe, but he seemed to think I could help. You sure? I don't want to butt in." She paused for a moment to watch Buck's response. "I'll do what I can to assist. We need to get this guy off the streets."

"You're the one who recognized the pattern in the blood. I got no problem if you give us a hand. I don't think LT will either, but we gotta ask. Hell, I'm retired once we solve this case. What do I care?"

The three moved through the door. Eight individuals had gathered in the room. She spotted one other woman in the group plus a tech who searched through videos.

Buck walked up to speak with a handsome black man who looked twenty years younger than the detective. She assumed he was their lieutenant. After they spoke for a short while, he glanced over at her for two or three seconds. Then he nodded at Buck. She took a seat by the door and hoped it meant she belonged for the present time.

Trin strolled up to the same man and offered his hand in greeting. They talked quietly for several minutes. A few nods later, the African American took center stage behind a podium.

"Most of you know I'm Tillman and Dowdy's supervisor,

but everyone calls me LT. Last name's Bennett for those who don't know me. They drew rotation on the first female discovered who was actually the second victim. We've increased the number involved to five detectives from Robbery Homicide. The FBI agreed to send us Special Agent Jordan Trinity, and our guest detective from Tulsa, Paige Stone. She worked the Celebrity Strangler case last summer. Successfully, I might add. She will join us for the time being."

He shifted back and forth multiple times. Eventually, he leaned on the lectern. "As you know, our perp has been busy. He's managed to kill a prostitute a night without any regard for our increased police surveillance. We think he might drive a pickup truck, but we don't know the make or model. Thanks to Detective Stone, we believe he wore a certain type of leather gloves. He hasn't left any other discernible evidence so far. For today, Special Agent Trinity will need help to view the various crime scenes. Give him your complete cooperation. The sooner everyone gets up to date on the pertinent details, the better we can form a plan to catch this SOB. Give Special Agent Trinity access to anything he asks for. I want everyone to get acquainted with each other. From today on we eat, sleep, and dream this case together. We need to use each detective's strong points to move this case forward."

LT motioned Trin to follow him into an office. She watched them through the glass partition to see if she could tell how Trin's request was received. The LT seemed a little too accommodating for most departments. She'd always felt Hank latched on to Trin so easily last summer because his health was deteriorating. It made her wonder if the LA supervisor had a hidden agenda.

The dark-haired woman moved up beside her. "I'm Grace Helston. Robbery and Homicide. Welcome to LA."

"You seem young to be on the task force. You must've done something right."

"I think it has less to do with my job performance and more to do with my coloring."

"You do match the perp's type. You think they plan to use you for a decoy?"

"Bait's more like it." Grace leaned against the desk across from her.

"It could work. You ever play a prostitute before?"

"Yeah, I worked vice for three years. You might say I'm a prime candidate."

The woman appeared nervous. She couldn't blame her. Their killer was one sick pervert.

"I went straight from patrol to homicide. The strangler last summer was my first case as a detective. You learn a lot on these high profile types. Hang in there. You'll do fine."

"We've got coffee in the back, if you'd like some."

"I'm not a coffee drinker, but thanks."

"Me either, but I usually take one to fit in." She shrugged. "It's easier when you're the new girl. They never notice I don't drink it."

"See, you're one step ahead of me. Great idea. Less explaining." Both grinned, but she watched Trin walk out of the office. She wanted to talk to him alone to see if her theory was valid or impossible.

He moved back toward Buck and Vern. Then he motioned with his head for her to join them.

"Trin wants me. Nice to meet you. I'm sure I'll see you later."

Once she came close enough, he said, "I'm headed to visit the crime scenes. You interested?"

"Sure." She nodded. They exited the squad room.

"We'll take you to the motel where we discovered the first

victim. We found her second, but he killed her first." Buck turned toward Trin.

"That's what I need. Do we have any photos from the scene with us? It would help me to compare them."

"I brought a file we copied." Buck handed it to Trin.

"Thanks. I'll study it on the way. The research department from my office gave me one, but their folder's incomplete. This one's much more detailed. I always prefer actual photographs."

By this time, they'd arrived at the same car she'd ridden in before with Buck and Vern. She got in the back and Trin joined her, his nose stuck in the folder.

SON OF A BITCH. Josh waited over two hours for her to return. The GPS tracker in the Escalade didn't work after Paige dumped the vehicle outside the cop bar. His idea to watch over her didn't go as planned. He needed to find something to plant on her, a device he knew she would keep on her at all times.

She didn't wear jewelry. He'd seen her put the purse or backpack that she carried in a hidden compartment in the Cadillac. He considered her gun and holster, but she'd find the bug too easily in there.

He sat, stared at the black SUV, and drilled his brain for another idea. The device he intended to use wouldn't come loose, but Paige would never stand for it. This could make for a tricky situation.

For certain, he wouldn't leave her unprotected. He'd been waiting over thirty years to find his "one." Now he'd found her, he refused to lose her. Not an option. He started the Porsche, put it into gear, and released the clutch. Besides, he felt responsible for her since he brought her out here.

Paige got a better perspective when Vern drove them to every place the killer left a body. She longed to get Trin alone for a discussion about her ideas, but so far it hadn't happened. He studied the photos from the individual crime scenes and examined the locations themselves. Occasionally, he asked a question, but not many.

Hank taught her to always follow the evidence. He studied by himself and made his own theories about what went down. Often times, other detectives would get off on the wrong track and take everyone else along with them. Hank stayed grounded until he discovered enough evidence that lined up to make a more accurate premise.

"We know he picks up prostitutes. Do we know the range of his territory?" Trin's attention finally came up from the file.

"So far, he's been sporadic. He grabbed a couple off Sunset, but they were several miles apart. We've posted all his locations we're certain about on a map, but we didn't find a pattern yet." Buck sat half turned in his seat and peered over the back at Trin.

"If we try to trap him, which is probably the only way we stop him, we need to know where he hunts and the circumference of the area included," Trin said.

"We reasoned along the same lines. In fact, we pulled one of our finest. She worked vice until a short time ago. We plan to use her for a decoy. Grace can strut her stuff with the best and her coloring matches his tastes. We'll put a wire on her and follow closely," Buck said.

"She wants to do this? The unsub is volatile at best. These are rage based killings. If you consider the fact he doesn't appear interested in them sexually, he probably doesn't keep them long. The time between when he picks up the victims until he explodes doesn't give us much time to catch him." Trin closed the folder and gazed up at Buck.

"It could make the sting operation difficult," the detective said.

"And deadly. We need to carefully plan for every conceivable situation that could arise. We can't send a woman to her death." Trin's expression became grim.

"Agreed." Buck turned back around, and the vehicle stayed silent.

When they arrived back at the PAB four hours later, they went straight to the room set aside for the task force. Trin studied the map marked with the abduction sites. He measured the two located farthest apart. Then he took a string apparatus from his pocket and quickly found the center from the two points. Next he drew a circle from the center that included every location.

"To start, we'll call this his range of territory. As we get more victims, we may need to adjust it."

Buck nodded agreement.

She watched the two. Someway, she needed to become the decoy. A confession seemed the only way to save Ben. Or she needed to get the murder weapon with traces of Tom McCall's DNA on it. Otherwise, she couldn't prove Ben didn't kill their victim.

"I want to volunteer for bait duty," she finally said.

"You're not his type. Grace is perfect. Besides, LT will never let an outsider do our job." Vern glared at her like she'd gone too far.

She nodded her head in agreement but intended to change their minds. She hoped Grace would refuse to go along with them.

Trin glanced at his watch. "It's late. I've been up for over twenty hours. I want to get a little rest and study these crime scene photos again. Let's meet early in the morning and form a plan to trap him. This could be the last decent night's sleep we get."

As they left the task force room, she walked beside Trin. She wanted to get his attention, but no one else's. Finally, when they neared the elevator, he looked at her.

"So what's the long story, and why would you volunteer to go undercover in so dangerous a case? Especially after the last time."

"I'll only talk once you and I are alone."

"Okay. I'll give you a ride to your car. Where did you park?"

"At a bar three miles from here." She gave him the name of the business.

They got in his rental car, and he found it on the GPS.

"So we're alone. What gives?"

"Last Wednesday night I got a call from Josh Stuart. He wanted me to come to LA. The police arrested Ben McCall. He threatened a lawsuit because of last summer so the captain encouraged me to come out here with him. Long story short, I figure this perp murdered the victim in my case, and that kill is the stressor that set him off on the prostitutes. You've studied these creeps and know more than I do. Is what I suspect possible?"

"Who's your victim?"

"An older male. I'm not sure if the police know the identity yet." She didn't want to lie to him, but she'd landed in a tricky situation. "The perp killed him with a bat. The killer scattered his brains everywhere. Definitely rage induced. The bludgeoned prostitutes started the next night."

"What else?"

She hesitated.

"I found a pattern in the blood from one of the last victims.

I felt certain I'd seen it before. At first, I figured it matched another prostitute's photos, but it didn't. The imprint in the blood resembled what I found in the photos from my male victim."

"I assume you didn't tell the LAPD."

"No, I couldn't. They would never let me near these cases if they figured out what I was up to."

"So you've used Vern and Buck."

"I had to. The idea started with an outside shot. Only a guess the cases were connected. The killer's MO seemed similar, but the more I got involved, the more convinced I was. Originally, I figured Ben more than likely killed the guy, but now I think it's possible he's innocent. I can't let him rot in jail for something he didn't do."

"You mean the Ben McCall case. What do you want from me?" Trin asked.

"To know if my idea is possible. My victim's a middle-aged male. These victims are young women."

"It would depend on a lot of factors. The history from our killer and why he feels compelled to kill the prostitutes. Hell, anything's possible. I can't give you a definitive answer. Your suggestion is possible, I suppose."

They both sat quiet for a short time.

"So how has Hank adjusted to his retirement?" Trin glanced over at her.

"Not good at all. I'm worried about him. He drinks too much, and he knows he's not supposed to consume any alcohol. He only sits in his recliner and sips tea laced with bourbon. I've talked to him about it, but he ignores me."

"We need to find him a reason to feel useful again. Everyone needs a purpose in life."

"I provided opportunities to get him involved in a number

of my cases, but he saw right through it. I'm not sure what to try next."

"Give him a little more time. He probably hasn't recovered completely from his surgery."

"You mad at me since I got you involved in my messy case?"

"Naw. I could never get angry at you. We'll figure something out."

20

Paige drove up to Josh's dark house. The garage door was closed. Most likely, they were in bed. When she opened the overhead door, Caroline's Escalade sat inside beside the Porsche. She moved with stealth to her private entrance and let herself in.

Her laptop sat on the walnut end table beside the comfy brown chair. She lifted the lid and turned it on. The shoes came off next while she waited for the software to open. After a few tries, she found the correct file to download. She liked to start on the first page with the incident report and follow the murder book through to completion. Then she understood exactly what steps they took in what order, and often received insight into what the cops believed happened. This time, the lateness of the night and the particular information she wanted precluded her normal approach.

The file opened. Their MB setup appeared similar to what they used in Tulsa. She quickly skimmed through until she found where they ran his prints. Under the results, a case number came up from La Jolla, a little over twenty years ago.

Thank goodness, Bill had attached the appropriate file so she clicked on it. It showed a male and female, both Hispanic, the De Palmas. The female, COD, exsanguination. Her throat slit, she'd bled out. The male died from stab wounds.

They'd recovered a multitude of prints at the restaurant, but Ben's they found throughout the establishment and the residence in the back. Every other print, except for the victims, they found only in the front of the business, except they had one set of prints found only in the kitchen.

Ben's prints at the location weren't conclusive, but people showed up dead around him. Not a good situation.

Next she searched through information about the booking process. They took pictures of the clothes he wore and reported the tests done on them. The shirt and trousers matched the same he'd worn to The Grove, designer labels Armani and Polo. Once she had more time, she would comb through the murder book, but tonight she felt drained.

She walked to the bathroom and flipped the switch on. If Josh watched from his room, hopefully he wouldn't see her light. She changed into her workout clothes and tiptoed through the kitchen to the door that led to the gym. Exercise would help her sleep. Most nights the dream still haunted her. Only exhaustion took her under. Without it, she could never relax enough to doze off.

She started with the rowing machine. Although she'd never used one at home, it wore her out faster than the other methods.

When she heard footsteps, she jumped. But it was only Josh.

She yanked harder on the rowing machine. "You startled me. I assumed you were both asleep."

"Where the hell have you been? It's close to one o'clock," Josh said.

"Around. I'm working a case."

"Surely, not this late."

"I met an old friend from the FBI. We stopped to eat and catch up. You're not my father, so cut the crap."

"What's that supposed to mean? I'm concerned about you. You've been chasing a serial killer. You could call in once in a while."

"I didn't realize you'd elected yourself my keeper. I don't need one." She glowered at him.

He dropped down on the weight bench. "Damn, you make me sound like an old lady."

"Yes. You do. Last time I looked, I'm all grown up."

"Damned if you're not right." He produced a crooked smile.

"Don't think you can get out of this by flirting with me. It won't work. I'm immune."

"Oh really." He got up and walked purposely in her direction.

She stopped the rowing machine.

He stared down at her.

"So you're immune?"

"Yep." She grinned.

"You don't sound too sure. Let's see if it's true." He attempted to take her hand to pull her up.

"Oh no you don't. I won't fall for any devious tricks." She laughed, jerked away.

"You know, you're only delaying the inevitable." The expression in his eyes drew her, but she turned away. He grabbed her waist and easily lifted her over the rowing machine, near enough she felt the heat of his body.

His lips were so close. She wanted to experience nothing, but emotions stirred that she didn't want to acknowledge. Before she could think, she grabbed the back of his head and pulled him into a kiss.

He breathed deeply and pulled her closer, his soft mouth gentle. He trailed down her neck and back again. His breath on her cheek and the nip to her ear stimulated sensations in her center. She understood where this could go, and for a moment she wanted to journey there, too.

She turned her face to his and found his lips again. More firm this time, they coaxed and taunted her to go further. She drifted in the pleasure that drew her. Then she remembered Bobby and how she'd loved him. Guilt gnawed at her conscience and wiped her desire away.

"I can't." She pushed him away and stepped around him. "We can't . . ." She couldn't find the words to explain about Chrissy and Bobby. She didn't know when she'd get over it, but she wasn't yet. The memory remained too painful to let go.

"I need a shower and a little rest. Tomorrow's a long day." She attempted to walk by him, but he grabbed her hand and turned her back.

"What happened? I know you felt something." His eyes captured hers.

"It's too soon." She forced her hand free and climbed the stairs.

JOSH PACED HIS ROOM. He had to do it. How could he safeguard her if he didn't? The furniture's clean lines melted into the background as he continued to put off the unavoidable. If she woke up, he'd be in deep trouble. She came here to do him the favor.

He ran his fingers through his hair and sat on his bed only to get up again. If something happened to her, he wouldn't make it through this time. After those white panties fell out of her suitcase, her cheeks blushed, and he knew she was the one.

He never believed it would happen to him. No one ever came close.

She was more beautiful than any woman he'd ever seen. Smart. Athletic. She didn't know she brightened every room she entered. But her prickly ways and standoffish attitude wore him down.

His only hope remained she didn't wake up, but her sleep habits were worse than his. He moved over to his walk-in closet and opened the door. His old duffle bag lay in the back corner. He rummaged inside until he found the small case that contained what he needed. He hadn't used it in over a decade.

He took the syringe apart and went into the bathroom to get the rubbing alcohol, the ether, and a big gauze pad. The clock on his dresser showed the time. Now or never. She needed time for the drug to wear off before morning. Gauging the correct dosage was the tricky part.

He moved silently through the house to her door and placed his ear close. For several minutes he listened. No sound. He turned the handle, entered, and used the stealth he'd learned long ago. He pushed the curtains back and enough moonlight came into the room for him to finish what he started.

He took the lid off the ether, and tilted the metal container into the gauze pad. Quickly, he placed it over her mouth and nose. She coughed once while he counted the time in his head like he trained to do so many years before. Her body seemed to relax more as the fumes overtook her. After he thumped her shoulder with no response, he took the syringe and inserted the tracking device under her skin, right below her shoulder blade. She couldn't know about the chip he planted. If she ever did, she'd never forgive him, but he had to protect her.

She stirred and turned toward him. Her eyes slowly opened. "Bobby? Don't leave me." She dragged her tongue across her bottom lip, reached up to put her arms around him, and pulled him down to her. The movements were awkward because of the drug, but she still found her target. Their lips barely touched before she collapsed in his arms and slumber took her again.

Who the hell is Bobby? He wanted to hate him, but she'd spoken of losing him. He hoped the man no longer remained in her life.

He wanted more than anything to climb in bed beside her. If nothing else, to hold her through the night. But he knew if he ever got that close, he wouldn't be able to stop at simply holding her. He stood and watched her stillness in the faded moonlight.

As much as he wanted to stay, he left her sleeping. Longing accompanied him through the kitchen and down the hall. Emptiness overwhelmed him once he entered his solitary room. Exhaustion overtook him, and he crawled into his bed, knowing his own nightmares would visit before morning.

James Silsby's body jerked, startling him awake. He listened intently for whatever had woken him. He watched the Con-Haul parking lot. Only an old Ford truck and twelve Con-Haul rigs lined up in a row, not his guy. He glanced at his watch. Three thirty-five in the morning. He yawned. His man probably wouldn't show up until daylight.

He reached for a cigarette from his pack on the dash. He lit it, inhaled deeply, and sat a little longer. Uneasiness crept over him, but the urge to relieve himself pushed every other idea away. He opened the door and got out, shaking his tingling legs to get the feeling back.

"Why are you following me?" A voice from the dark spoke right before something slammed him in the stomach.

His vision blurred, and he doubled over. "What the hell!"

He went for the knife strapped to his ankle but heard his wrist crack. Excruciating pain followed. His sight cleared, only to shoot terror through his veins. His hand dangled from his arm, barely attached. He understood he was already a dead man, but his reflexes attempted to get him on his feet and away from the danger.

"Answer me," the voice commanded.

But James couldn't focus on anything but his sister and the agony that radiated from his wounds. He shook his head to bring about rational thought so he could talk.

"Hell, I don't care why anymore," the shadow said.

James smelled the fear in his sweat, saw the bat swing toward him, and heard the air swish before the pain exploded through his neck.

I HEARD air whoosh out of him, and he fell to the ground. *What the crap.* Two men followed me several days in a row. Nothing made sense, but I couldn't leave the body here across the street from Con-Haul. Eventually, the police would get involved. I didn't want them to snoop around this area.

The interior light fell across the dead man's face when I opened the passenger door to the old Chevy. I recognized the man as the brother of a young girl from Texas I picked up and brought to my old man.

The bastard had trained me well. I could always pick 'em for him. He taught me exactly what he liked in a female. Early on I learned no one argued with him. While I served him, I found young beautiful women for him to rape and kill.

I shook the notion away and looked inside the car to see if there was anything that might tell me why this guy had been following me. I didn't understand why I'd become so popular with white men. At least this guy wouldn't follow me anymore.

I took my gloves off and dug through the piles made from food wrappers. Nothing pointed in my direction. I grabbed an old sack and stuffed the loose papers inside it. The prints on the bag would go with me once I left.

I put my pigskin gloves back on, unlocked the trunk, and shoved the body inside. I hunted for anything else that might leave the cops a trail. I went through the dash and found only his registration for the car and a flashlight. I checked again to make sure. Nothing.

This time I drove a mile and a half before I pulled into a parking lot. In the past, I'd bought groceries here and knew this place didn't have working cameras. I left the key in the ignition and walked away in the opposite direction from Con-Haul. After two blocks, I changed my course. The long stretch back to my truck would take time, but I'd walked farther.

21

Paige started the morning early and went to see Ben. She told Ben what she'd uncovered about the De Palmas. He was less than cooperative but eventually explained his part in the business and how they'd helped him survive—and why he hadn't reported the crime. The state would've return him to Tom McCall.

She could see his point, but the explanation wouldn't help with the murder case. If anything, it made the motive stronger. Since the beating presented so savagely, he couldn't get by with self-defense. The overkill factor ruled it out. That and the purchase of the bat.

She parked the Escalade and entered the PAB before eight. As she walked in the door, she spied Curtis Sampson move toward the elevator. She slowed her pace and hoped he didn't see her. After he entered the lift and turned around, she quickly stepped out before the doors closed.

She searched for a bathroom, any place to disappear but didn't see one handy.

"What the hell are you doing sniffing around here?" Curtis demanded.

"I made an appointment. I don't believe you personally own the building."

"You know I'll find out where you go. Who you see. You're not about to screw up my case. It's airtight. We have Ben McCall, whether you like it or not."

"If you do, I couldn't possibly impact your case." She stared at him.

"I don't trust you. Your kind is always up to something."

"My kind? What kind am I?"

"A female who trades on her good looks to get exactly what she wants. You may have had Sonny eating from your hand, but not me. I know you're up to something. I intend to find out what."

She nodded in agreement. "Well, I certainly know I can't fool you. Don't want to be late for my appointment." She walked to the elevators, caught the door before it closed, and got off on the third floor. She pushed the door to the stairs open and went two flights down. When another lift came, she rode up to the correct level.

As she exited, she saw Grace holding a cup of coffee. The aroma smelled wonderful. Too bad she couldn't stand the taste of the stuff. "You're up bright and early."

"Yeah. I couldn't sleep. I know what they plan to do. I'm a little uneasy about it."

"You know you don't need to do it. No one would think less of you if you refused." She saw the dark circles under Grace's eyes.

"But I would. More women would die. I don't think I could live with that either." The detective gave a halfhearted smile, took a sip from her beverage, and grimaced.

"Listen. Don't do it unless they devise a foolproof way to protect you. It's not worth it."

"I know, but . . ." She shrugged.

They entered the task force room and let the door close. LT and Trin talked in the small office attached to the main room. Buck walked their way, but she didn't see Vern. She figured he always arrived late.

They came out from the office and glanced around. The door to the hall opened and two stragglers joined them. One was Vern. LT moved to the front and prepared to talk to the group.

"If our guy keeps to his schedule, we could receive a report on a new victim sometime this morning. Tillman, Dowdy, Stone. I want you on it once the call comes in. Continue to fill in the murder book and work the leads. The rest of us will prepare and plan for tonight."

She glanced at Vern and Buck, who tipped their heads in return.

"Helston, I'm sure you've figured out why we chose you for the team. You're the perp's type. I hope you'll agree to walk the streets once again. We need to lure him out so we can catch the bastard."

She nodded.

"Thanks. I figured I could depend on you. Men, this brave woman is counting on us to have her six. We need to safeguard every contingency. It's our job to think of every possibility and cover it. Don't miss anything. If you have a question of any kind, voice it. Everyone here will work to bring her home unscathed tonight and every night until we catch this sicko."

~

PAIGE READ the murder book through on the first two victims. She studied the crime scene photos again. She'd pulled up the third MB, when the call came in. Someone had discovered the latest dead prostitute.

"We expected this call to come. Let's go." Vern got up from his computer and grabbed his jacket.

Trin went with them, and it surprised her. The four of them hurried out the door. They waited for the elevator, and she motioned to Trin. "I figured you'd stay and help the others on the task force."

"I want to study the fresh crime scenes. I think my time is better served this way. I need to keep up with the changes while they occur because he will evolve." The elevator dinged. They stepped inside and began the downward journey.

When they arrived at the crime scene, the deceased lay face down in a shallow ditch two blocks off Laurel Canyon Boulevard. Only a single muscle attached the head to the torso. The exposed bone from the spinal column crawled with blow flies. Coagulated blood covered the surrounding area.

A purse lay three feet away, covered with blood spatter. SIDs took photos, and Vern pulled the driver's license from it. "Sylvia Striker, twenty-nine. She's a local." He handed the identification to the crime scene tech, who added it to the plastic bag she held out.

"Shit. I spoke to her the night we canvassed. She must have worn a wig. Her hair was bright red then."

She glanced at Buck for a moment and continued to search the scene for anything that might give them additional information on the perp. She stepped closer to Trin. "His rage continues to grow."

"Yeah. He has exploded out of control. It'll only get worse until we stop him."

"I figured as much. I could go out there, too. We need to

take him down." She walked over to Buck. "I want to go out on the street. A friend can get me a wig and clothes from where he works. We need to stop this guy tonight. With two of us out there, we can cover a lot more territory."

Buck finally looked up from the crime scene at her. "I figured you'd want in on the action. I already asked. LT said no way. Ain't gonna happen."

She chewed her bottom lip, biting back the argument she wanted to make. Grace shouldn't have to face this alone. But for now, she didn't have a choice.

She wandered away from the group, turning over possible ways to convince them she should go out tonight. She spotted a cigarette butt thrown into the ditch. "Buck, I need a tech over here with a sample bag."

"What have you got?" Buck asked.

"A cigarette butt. Appears fresh. It's a Camel."

"Son of a bitch. DNA, if it's his." Vern turned toward Buck and grinned.

The tech brought a camera with him, laid down a marker, and snapped off several shots. He picked up the evidence with his gloved hand and bagged it.

She continued to sweep the area for anything additional and considered the amount of force needed to take a person's head off. He must have massive muscles. A longshoreman or a construction worker who lifted heavy objects. The coastline of California must have millions of workers that are powerful from hard labor. To weed through them would take too long. The DNA, if the stub contained any, might give them a hit.

Trin walked up beside her. "Great find."

"Not so much. The techs didn't search the area I worked. It doesn't matter. I'm glad we found it."

"If the DNA gives us a match or produces a family member, everything could change quickly."

"Yeah, it could. I'm thinking a dock worker or someone who does a lot of physical labor. He about took the head off with one blow. Not everyone's that strong. What do you think?"

"You're probably right. A job with hard manual lifting is logical. California has many ports. Doesn't narrow it down too much, but it's a good place to start." Trin yawned and rubbed his jaw. "Lost too much sleep lately."

He walked beside her as they moved back closer to the street. They strolled along the asphalt and hunted for brake fluid, a leaky transmission, skid marks, but found nothing.

"His anger gets so intense, you'd think he would mess up and leave trace," she said.

"If we ever find his vehicle, it will contain plenty, but I don't think he's with them long once he gets them outside of it."

"Do you know why he kills them? Or does he need a reason?" She stopped to stare at him.

"In his mind there's a reason. We may never know what his motive is. The way he's escalated, it may take death to stop him."

"Suicide by cop."

Trin nodded.

They left the uniforms to canvass the neighborhood for any witnesses. Finding someone who'd seen anything would be a long shot, but they had to try. The four detectives regathered and decided to go back to the office and work what evidence they had.

Grace walked up to the desk where she sat. "Anything different at the new scene?"

"We found a cigarette butt and hope for DNA. You know how it goes. Wait for results and see."

"The way I hear it, you found the evidence."

"Dumb luck I guess. Besides, someone else might have left it there at any time. Who knows if it's the perp's."

"You're way too nice for a detective. Why did you come out here to work this case?"

"I don't want to bore you. It's a long story. I want to keep a low profile so they don't run me off, but it revolves around my captain who asked a favor. We have to do what they want." She shrugged. "What happened while we were out?"

"Not much. They found me a slutty outfit with shoes to match. You know, show everything for the team."

"I can't say I do know what you mean. I went straight from patrol to homicide. I never dressed like a pro. I'm not sure I would know how. Hank protected me from the time I was young."

"Who's Hank?"

"He raised me from ten years old. My mom passed away the year before from cancer. My father died the next year in a shootout. Hank was his partner. He saved me from the system."

"You must love him a lot."

"Oh yeah. He's the type it's difficult to come out and say it to. But definitely."

"Yeah. My old man's the same way. He's on the job, too. Look at me, I pretend I'm the son he never had."

"Not exactly the same, but I know how you the feel. So what time do we go out tonight?"

"Everybody should be in place by seven. I enter the scene by seven thirty. You're part of my back up?" Grace said.

"If LT doesn't say no. I wish I was on the street with you, but he won't let me do that. Buck already asked."

"The paperwork would take forever if anything happened to you. I can see why he wouldn't, but I appreciate the offer."

"Did you eat anything? I haven't since breakfast."

Grace shook her head.

"Let's go see what we can find." She turned to leave and remembered today was Wednesday. The first time she'd missed her weekly visit to the cabin after she died there. She stopped for a few seconds and gazed out the window while the sun shot tangerine streaks into the sky. Several clouds burned a brilliant fuchsia. Her breath caught as she realized how glad she was to be here to see it. Whatever happened tonight, she wanted to be around to see plenty more sunsets.

PAIGE LIFTED her phone to read the text Sonya sent her. The kid was still bored. She pushed three and hit enter. Eric Burdon's guttural voice sang *When I Was Young* on her phone as she waited for Sonya to pick up. She smiled. If the girl found out, she wouldn't leave her alone about the music ringtone that matched her number. The kid was an early diva in the making. Somehow, the little pot smoker wormed her way in. Sonya gave up the weed in the process, which was the whole point in the first place.

"Oh, thank God. Mom's about to drive me crazy. She won't let me play my iPod with the speakers because she can't stand my music. She claims the earbuds will make me go deaf. I'm grounded from the computer. She saw me watching a YouTube video she claimed would poison my mind. I swear, I'm looking forward to returning to school. I never thought I'd say it, but I don't want any more snow days."

"Okay. That's an ear full. I can't referee you two from here. Did the sun come out yet? It's your best hope with the snow."

"No. It's still cloudy and ten below for the overnight. That's not with the wind chill factored in, either."

"I don't know what to tell you. You're stuck until June at least." She chuckled. The snow would melt way before then.

"You don't understand," Sonya said.

"I'm not that old. I remember. But you'll find out in a few

years. Stuck at home from school isn't the worst thing in the world. Hang in there."

"It's so easy for you to say."

"Yeah. I would rub it in about the sunshine here, but I'm trippin' over dead bodies everywhere. I think you and a little snow is *not* so bad after all."

"I suppose. How long until you come home? I miss running together."

"I do too. Can't you find a way to do pushups, sit ups, or jumping jacks? You need to burn off a little energy."

"I guess, but it's not the same without you griping at me."

"I know. I'm the world's best. Listen, I've got to go. We leave for our stakeout in a few, and I want to call Caroline real quick. Talk at you tomorrow."

"Okay. Miss you."

"Miss you, too."

She disconnected and punched in Caroline's number.

"Paige. Where are you?"

"I'm downtown at the Police Administration Building. Trin and I leave soon to take our female detective out on the street. I thought I'd let you know, I won't be back until late this evening. Josh worried about me last night so pass the message on to him."

"I will, but you're not the one out on the street are you?"

"No. They picked one of their own for the bait."

"Be careful out there. I'll be praying for you but don't do anything—"

"Listen, we're about to leave."

"I know. I'll tell Josh, but use wisdom. You're not the only one on the force. Sometimes I think you forget that."

"No. I don't. Trin's here. I forgot to tell you that, and the rest of the team has been great to me."

"I'm glad he's there, and of course, the other officers would be. You're excellent at your job. I'll pray for you. You'll come home safe. Paige, you're not still angry with Ben are you, about the fingerprints? He couldn't even tell me about it."

A discord struck in her mind. Caroline sounded too involved.

"Are you developing feelings for him?"

"I don't know, but I do think he's innocent. He's scared. He cared for those people who helped him, but his father would have killed him if he saw him again. He assumed the police would send him back. He was only fourteen."

"At that age, they usually do return them home. I see his point a little, but still—"

"Don't stay mad at him."

"I'm more concerned about you. Ben's an attractive guy, but his morals equal a tomcat's. Take care of your heart around him."

"I will. But I must confess, I do like him."

"Oh, Caroline."

"I know."

"Thanks for the prayers. I have to go. I'll see you tonight or in the morning." She disconnected and walked out to the elevators with the others. She probably needed to pray for Caroline and her heart, but she wasn't sure where to begin.

22

———

Sue Perry's mother committed suicide the day after her ninth birthday. She often wondered why her mother waited for that day. It left her alone with her father. What difference did the extra day make?

She'd known for a year her mother was a coward. By the expression on her mama's face the day after her eighth birthday, she understood no help would come from her.

Dreams of her new Brat doll and dark chocolate cake swam through her head while she danced to the tune "Happy Birthday." She heard footsteps. They sounded like her father's. Half asleep, she smiled at the comfort his presence brought. He'd come to check on her. She drifted back to sleep, but the door opened and let the hall light fall across her eyes.

"Daddy," she whispered.

He raised his index finger to his lips, walked over, and sat on the edge of the bed. He gently brushed the hair at her temples and placed soft kisses on her cheek. She snuggled close to him. Her father loved her. She counted on him. He stood so tall and strong. He often laughed and lifted her high over his head as he twirled her round and around. Sometimes she turned into his sack of potatoes, but mostly she was his precious princess. She enjoyed the latter more.

When he rubbed his hand over her private parts, she didn't understand what had changed. She only knew something did, and goosebumps raised on her arms. She didn't feel sleepy anymore. She hoped that had been an accident.

He undressed, slid under the covers, smelling like liquor and cigarettes. His hand covered her mouth, and she turned her head to attempt to shake it off. Something unfamiliar dragged across her leg, and she felt anxiety toward her father for the first time.

It turned out she had every reason to fear him. In the morning her mother could no longer look her in the eye. She endured the next year in silence along with guilt and shame.

PAIGE SAT with Trin in an old Chevy parked half a block from where Grace strolled with a cocky gait and waited for a customer. He relaxed in the driver's seat while she held a pair of binoculars in her lap and twisted the strap.

"So how are you after last summer? Do you sleep at night?"

She turned toward him, her eyes questioned. "What brought that on?"

"I'm a psych major. They taught me a few lessons about how it works. So do you sleep or not?"

"Not much." Her hand tightened on the leather.

"At least you didn't lie to me. That's a start. You did try to prevaricate."

"Well, I trust you more than most people. You saved my life." She chewed her bottom lip and kept her eyes averted.

"So why try to evade my question?"

"I'm still embarrassed I let the memory have any hold over me, but I work on it."

"Oh. How's that?"

"I try to face my fears. I know that's the only way I'll ever get over it." She picked up the field glasses and wrote down the license number from the car stopped by Grace. They settled on a price, and Grace got into the vehicle. Once the target drove off, they eased from their spot and followed.

SUE WAS sixteen before she finally escaped from her father. The last two years she endured by listening to Kenny Chesney sing about "California," the place filled with sunshine. She could only save a little at a time from the grocery money he gave her. She carried a backpack and three hundred dollars. It took her five days to thumb her way to Los Angeles.

A few of her rides seemed nice and bought her a meal, but others expected the same favors she wanted to escape. She'd been left stranded by the roadside twice. The last leg of the trip she spent part of her precious stash on a bus ticket.

Then she met Terrell at the bus stop the day she arrived. He treated her better than anyone had since she turned eight years old. For a week he never touched her. He fed her and gave her a place to stay. He bought her special presents and made her feel he cared what happened to her.

He taught her to make tequila sunrises. Before the night ended, he taught her new delights about herself and sex. He made it fun and thrilling. She'd finally found someone to love her and treat her good. For another week she held onto the belief things were better.

"Baby, I got a new name for you. You're sweeter than

cherry pie. So that's what we're gonna call you. Cherry Pie. You like it?"

"But my name's Sue."

"I know that." Terrell looked at her like she was stupid.

In a moment he changed. She understood she'd been trapped. Like her father, he intended to use her. In the same second she felt dumb, and recognized she'd never get free.

"I got you a date with Harold. He's an old friend. You give him a real good time like I showed you. He's gonna give you money. You better bring every dime to me. Do you hear? 'Cause if you don't, I'll sell you to these men I know. They'll ship you out to places people don't come back from. They won't treat you nice like I do."

Shame burned in her cheeks. He didn't want her for herself. He only wanted the money he would receive because she turned tricks for him. This time she didn't cry. She couldn't. She could only harden her resolve to never trust anyone ever again.

PAIGE RODE in the passenger's seat while Trin drove their vehicle and followed Grace with her customer. They stopped at a small motel. The john sent Grace in with cash to rent a room. The officer came out and they drove to room 125. After the detective and her trick went inside, she and Trin walked up to their car and peered through the windows. No bat. No pipe. They didn't see the man carry the weapon when the light from the open doorway fell on him.

"I don't think it's him. Do you?" She searched Trin's eyes for confirmation.

He shook his head no.

They backed off the car as a second unmarked vehicle pulled into the parking lot. Several minutes later, Grace came out with the perp in handcuffs. They searched his car, but found no weapon that matched their killer.

The unmarked cars carefully set up in a location about two blocks from their original site. Grace put her hips into her walk, and they started the process over again. Three more customers turned into false alarms. By two, the task force called it a night. They had to be at work by eight in the morning.

SUE TOOK the black wig from Terrell's hand and went into the bathroom. She placed the long dark waves on her head and attempted to tuck her short blonde hair beneath it. With every push of her curls she cursed him. She hated him more than her father.

She didn't know why he wanted her to wear the hair piece, but figured it had something to do with her dead associates. Why put a nice name on it? They were whores like she was. She studied herself in the mirror and swore to kill Terrell if she ever got the chance, but doubted if she'd get enough courage to complete her vow. Before this, she hadn't.

"Hey, bitch. Hurry your ass up. We got business to take care of." He walked through the door.

She continued to work on her hair but didn't say a word.

"He likes red lipstick, so borrow one and wear it. Cover your eyebrows with dark pencil. We need to make him think you're a brunette."

She rummaged through his other girl's makeup that sat around the sink and picked up a tube marked *Stunning Red* and slathered it on.

After she finished, he grabbed her wrist and lifted it up. He placed something on the underside of her T-shirt sleeve. When she put her limb down, it fit into her armpit. The snug black top displayed bold red letters. *Come Play with the Pros.*

Within ten minutes he made her walk the street. She hated to put herself on display, but he'd only beat her if she didn't. She'd gone that route before. It always ended the same. She provided sex the hard way, with broken ribs and a busted lip.

She saw his other hookers snort cocaine to ease the pain from their soulless lives. She'd seen a few burn crack. At least, that's what she thought they called it. They stayed in a world so horribly depraved they acted like zombies most of the time. She only knew she couldn't crawl into the hellhole with them. One night he'd encouraged her to try drugs, but she was certain she would only hate herself more.

Her feet ached. She wanted to give up and get a soft drink. A pickup truck stopped to check her out.

"How much for a ride?" the stranger asked.

When she glanced in the window, she attempted a smile. He was handsome. This time she would lie to herself and pretend he cared. This time wouldn't be so bad. "A hundred fifty."

"Are you worth it?"

"Yes."

"Get in and we'll see."

She strolled around to the other side of the truck and climbed in. He handed her the money, and they took off.

Paige gathered her items together as Trin pulled the Chevy back into the parking space at the police department.

"This night dragged by. It may take a while to catch our unsub." Trin grabbed the door handle and glanced at her.

"I hope not. Hank once told me, someone has to die for them to call us out. He reprimanded me for my impatience the first week I started homicide. It changed my mindset in a hurry. I've never been restless for a call out again." She wrapped the strap around the binoculars and put them in their case.

"Hank's a smart man, and he's right. LA is a huge city with a large population of pros. It may take time for Grace to get his attention. Whatever we do, we must protect her. He's volatile and driven. We can't underestimate him."

"I know you're right, but in the morning we will still find the next prostitute dead."

"Yes, but we'll get him eventually."

She knew his answer wouldn't comfort this night's victim.

Sue looked over at the john. He hesitated before he got out.

"I need you to walk. Like you did back there."

She hopped out of the pickup and sauntered to an area where she had more room to move about. Everyone had their own fantasy that got them off. She shrugged. This was the first guy to hire her to do the hooker strut, but what the hell did it matter. He would get down to business soon enough.

When she turned on her third trip back to him, he had the strangest expression on his face, like he couldn't figure something out. She continued the pace while her mind toyed with the idea that she'd become a toilet for men's sperm. They used her to relieve themselves and threw her away.

It happened in a split second. So quick she barely had time to act. From the corner of her eye, she spotted Terrell lifting his gun. She saw her john swing a bat and recognized she could end her own torment. If she moved now, she would hold the power over her own life for the first time. Nothing could be worse than the hell she lived in now. She threw herself between the bullet and the bat, hoping for sweet relief. Death swooped low and carried her away.

23

————

Paige spotted something wrong with the crime scene immediately—a huge crimson stain some distance away from the victim. She asked the medical examiner to lift the deceased to see where the blood pooled on the body. Postmortem lividity gave no indication someone had moved the corpse after death.

She contemplated the importance of this new bit of information. The ME pointed at the bullet wound in the latest dead prostitute. She glanced up at Trin and could tell he was analyzing the same differences she'd noticed. Something had happened here that hadn't at the other crime scenes. She waited a beat, thinking about the possible explanations.

"Can we type the blood from the victim and the pool over there?" DNA testing often got backlogged and was expensive. If the types were different, they'd know if they had two victims or possibly just one.

A blonde tech took samples from each and carried them to her vehicle.

"What's your theory for this change?" she asked Trin.

"Definitely a bigger struggle, but the victim isn't large. With the bullet hole in her, the dynamics on this one changed drastically. If the blood pool belongs to the killer, we finally caught a break."

"Could we get so lucky? If he's wounded, it might make him easier to catch. The bad news, I don't see the gun. If he has a new toy to play with, it makes him more dangerous," she said.

"Firearms are easy to get. If our unsub wanted one, he'd already carry one. Still, it's not a good situation."

She stepped away from him and started a more detailed search of the area. Buck studied the footprints in the leaves. She'd noticed they didn't have dirt here—not like in Oklahoma anyway. Only grainy sand covered in grass or other plants. She wandered over beside Buck.

Non-soil aside, it appeared a real fight took place here. How would a slip of a girl hold her own with a powerful man who killed so ferociously? It didn't make sense. Could someone else have been at the scene? If so, who? Why didn't they report it? Surely, they attempted to help the young woman. Nothing added up here. She shook her head.

Her ringtone sounded. She peeked at the caller ID display. Bill Graywolf. He might give her good news. "Hey. What's up?"

"I ran the blood patterns by Hank. He said it's pigskin leather. Usually used in work gloves. Does that help you any?"

"I don't know yet, but it could. This perp's so strong he virtually took the head off the victim with a single blow. We were thinking someone who loads on docks or works heavy physical construction. It would fit the theory. Of course, it could also be a body builder on 'roid rage." She hesitated for a moment. "What about Hank? You get anywhere with him?"

"The last two nights I slept in your old bed. Talk about strange. I felt it." She heard him laugh.

"Okay, knock it off. I know it still looks like I'm ten years old, but we had more important business than to update my old room."

"I never said a word." He chuckled again. "But Barbie or whatever she is stared at me all night. I figured you'd at least own one G.I. Joe, but no. Not a one."

"If it makes you feel the least bit better, I never played with her except when Chrissy came over. She loved to play with dolls, not me."

"I'll bet she did. Gotta run. Boss walked in." He chuckled, and the phone went silent.

She slipped her phone in her jacket pocket. A smile still lingered as Buck walked up.

"Anything important?" he asked.

"Not sure. A friend of mine called. Hank said the pattern we found is pigskin, probably work gloves."

"Hank?"

"Yeah, he's retired Tulsa PD. He raised me. My mentor you might say. Damned good homicide detective. We clear upwards of ninety percent of our homicide cases."

Buck tipped his head. "So Tulsa's not a good place to murder someone?"

She grinned. "Not really. I mentioned yesterday to Trin a possible dock or construction worker because of the strength involved in these deaths. What do you think? The glove could match that vocation."

"It could." Buck squatted to move a blade of grass. He stood and shook his head. He didn't find anything.

"California has a huge coastline. It doesn't rule out enough people." She gazed down at the large pool of blood, but nothing stood out.

"Spot on. But if we could find something else to help narrow it down . . ."

"We've got someone who carries a bat, we think drives a truck, and prefers pigskin gloves. We've canvassed with less in Tulsa. How many docks you got in southern California where they load enough product by hand to make someone powerful and strong?"

"Unfortunately, too damned many. Not to mention other men who work loading and unloading from manufacturing plants in the area. You're right we added to our list. I'll get someone to check and see if it's difficult to find pigskin gloves, and who manufactures them."

She started to turn away to hunt for other evidence. The SID tech walked back toward Buck.

He stopped and stared at the tech. "What did you find?"

"We've got two different types. The blood pool does not belong to our victim."

"Son of a bitch. Now it's getting interesting. Good call, Stone. We've got two victims. Makes you wonder if the other one is still alive. The blood pool covers a huge area. Someone lost a lot."

Did they have a witness or not? If the person who produced the blood pool didn't die, they needed to find them.

Trin walked over beside them and nodded. He stuck his right hand in his pocket and rubbed something inside with his thumb. She observed he often did when he endeavored to unravel what troubled his thoughts.

"If our unsub is the other victim and lost so much blood, will he come out to play tonight? *That* is the question. And will it affect the rules of his game?" Trin said.

"Good question. Like always, we'll have to wait and see." Would the perp splinter even more? If Tom McCall's death caused him to kill prostitutes, what would happen after someone attempted to stop him with a gun?

～

Paige watched Grace prepare for her job as bait. "Okay. I have to ask. How do you walk in those?" She pointed at the five-inch heels that laid on the floor.

"It takes a while to get used to, but women have done worse to get attention from men. Didn't you ever wear any before?" Grace shrugged and replaced her slacks with shorts that barely covered her ass.

"Never. Hank raised me. He and my father were partners on the job. It about did Hank in to buy me my first bra."

"You don't still live with him, do you?"

"No, but I probably should. He went through open-heart surgery a few months ago. He doesn't do well with his restrictions. They made him retire at the same time."

"Man, that's harsh."

"Yeah."

"You need to explore your feminine side. Here, put these on. I'll show you the finer side of a hooker's life." Grace handed her the stilettos.

"I don't know. I'm not much for frilly paraphernalia."

"It's okay to feel sexy sometimes. Parents don't need to know everything." Grace nudged the shoes closer with her bare foot. Her nails sported ruby lacquer.

She stared at the pumps. Eventually, she picked them up, examining the leather and the tip of the heel. "These could make a good murder weapon."

"Before you try to club someone, put them on. Your foot looks about the same size as mine." Grace moved in front of the mirror to gaze at her backside.

She slipped off her Nikes and stuck her foot inside. It felt weird. She put the other one on and struggled to stand. "Oh my God. I don't dare to walk."

"It's not difficult. Here. Grab my arm."

She took her first step. Wobbled. Took another. Several minutes later, Grace let go.

"I think you've got it. Practice until you gain some confidence. When you walk in high heels it's all about self-assurance."

"You know, I asked them to let me go out, too, but whoever has influence around here wouldn't let me."

"I know. Sway your hips a little. Not too much, but you need to roll them when you're in heels. Keep your confidence up. A man has to see you know exactly what he wants and how to deliver it. Visuals. It's totally about visuals." Grace dragged mascara over her eyelashes.

She tottered around the room feeling foolish but determined to master it. Still, she couldn't work up the courage to swing her hips in the process.

"If you want to get any takers, you need to shake that ass." Grace added more blush to her cheeks.

"Give me a minute. I still need to figure out how to get each different part to work at the same time. You sure guys are worth it?" Her heel caught on a snag in the carpet, and she stumbled.

"If they weren't, why would we put ourselves through this much bullshit? Here, give them to me."

She took them off and handed them over. When Grace put them on and stood, she converted into a professional working girl. Her strides were perfectly timed with the sway of her hips, and the expression on her face told everyone she understood exactly what to do.

"You sure you don't moonlight on the streets?" She didn't know if she could ever act so accomplished.

"Hell, no. Who wants an old fart to slobber and sweat on you while he gets his business done? No thanks."

"You could be missing out on a fortune."

"Yeah, you know any wealthy streetwalkers? Their pimps keep the cash." Grace tugged her shorts out of her crack.

"I guess you're right. It doesn't sound like a dream job." She sat down in a chair and motioned for the heels back. After she got up, she attempted to mimic what Grace had shown her. This time her movements more closely matched Grace's.

A few moments later, she took one shoe off and gazed at it. "Do you ever get afraid? I mean like tonight. This psycho is out there, and he could call your number at any time."

"Hell, yeah. I couldn't sleep last night." Grace pushed her hand through her hair.

"Most nights, my dreams are nightmares. You know last summer I helped take down the Celebrity Strangler. He killed me. I know that sounds strange, but he did. If Trin hadn't resuscitated me, I'd be six feet under. I still see myself in dreams at night. Grant grabbed me by the throat and dangled me in midair. I can't seem to get past it. I hovered close to the ceiling and saw my empty body. I recognized I was dead, and I didn't care."

"For real?" Grace stared over at her with a grave expression.

"Trin came in and shot the SOB. Once he killed Grant Windsor, he worked on my body until I returned to it. I've attempted to face my fears, to work through it. Still, what happened haunts me. I can't explain. It's like I've lost a part of me. I don't feel so invincible anymore." She sat and looked down at the stiletto in her hand.

"You can't give up. We'll catch this asshole. Eventually, you'll get past what happened last summer. Time will help fade the painful memories. Hey, no one is invincible. Not one of us."

"You stay careful out there. Though I know you don't cease to exist when you die, I don't want you to come close to it the way I did. It changed me somehow. I continue to work, and I intend to find my way back. But it is a challenge." She glanced up at Grace and saw raw fear for a split second before the woman chased it away.

"It's about time to go. You'll need these." She handed Grace the shoes.

24

———————

Within an hour, Paige sat with Trin and kept Grace in view. He sat behind the steering wheel, and she held the binoculars in her lap.

"I walked in those heels. It's an art. I practiced for thirty minutes, but still couldn't pull it off the way Grace does. Wait, we have a taker." She lifted the field glasses to her eyes and wrote down the license plate number.

After Grace got into the SUV, Trin eased their vehicle out onto the street. They followed for a little over three miles. The Mercury turned into a small motel, and Trin drove on by. Half a block up the street, he stopped and waited for three minutes. He turned the vehicle around and drove back to the motor inn. The door closed on a room next to where their target parked.

Trin pulled up behind to block the automobile. He got out, and Buck did the same from his Dodge. They both moved up to the Mountaineer, peered inside, and shook their heads. She figured they didn't see a weapon.

Less than a minute later, Grace walked out with the perp in tow. They checked the vehicle from bumper to bumper. No bat or pipe. Once Buck warned the man, they let him leave. She guessed another long night lay ahead.

Close to eleven, an older model pickup pulled up to the curb next to Grace. The angle wasn't right for her to get a license number. She observed a dark-haired man inside but not well enough to make out his face. "I don't like it. I can't see his plate number. Can you read it from your vantage point?"

"No." Trin said.

The sound on the wire squawked with static. Grace came around the passenger side and climbed in. As the truck pulled away, a car wedged in front of them, cutting Trin off. The light turned red. An Aveo stopped, which blocked their vehicle. The dodge couldn't squeeze around the Chevy. Trin called to Buck and Vern in a car up the street to follow the pickup truck, but they didn't receive any answer. The radio stayed dead.

"Son of a bitch. What the hell happened?" Trin yelled and slammed his fist against the dash. The light finally changed. When the small car took off, he floored it, shoving her back into her seat.

She dialed Buck's number. "They're in a pickup truck headed your way. Go. Follow them. We got separated in traffic. It's an old brown Ford. Do you see it?"

"No, they didn't pass us. We parked farther away than last time. What's the plate number?"

"He parked where we couldn't get it. We've got nothing. He has dark hair. It's the only detail I could see. They must have turned at the next intersection. You go left, we'll take right. Get everyone available in the area on the hunt for her. We've got to find her." She heard the panic in her voice, but she didn't care.

They drove up and down street after street, but the truck had vanished. "What do we do now?" She ran a hand over her hair and rubbed the back of her neck. "This absolutely cannot happen."

Trin didn't say a word. He continued to drive in a grid pattern and explored every street and alley. His knuckles stayed white around the steering wheel, and he constantly chewed his bottom lip.

~

PAIGE CLIMBED out from the Escalade while the overhead lowered. She trudged to her bedroom door and opened it. Eyes burning and nose stuffy, she shouldn't be able to produce another tear, but they continued to spill every time she thought about Grace. *Son of a bitch.* She lay down on her bed, but her head throbbed. She got up and set out for the bathroom to get a wet wash cloth, but Josh sat in the chair by the corner. The light awakened him. He yawned.

"You scared the life out of me." She glared at him.

"I wanted—You've been crying. What happened?"

"We lost Grace. The whole force was out, but we never found her."

Josh got up and sat beside her on the bed. "What do you mean you lost her?"

"Her tracking device came off when she got in his pickup. We never saw her again. Trin and I drove through the night, searching for her. She never called us on her phone. We've heard nothing from her in hours." She rubbed her forehead to ease the pain. "They closed ranks and sent me home to rest. I'm not LAPD. I couldn't argue, but who can rest?" She got up to pace, walked into the bathroom, and glanced in the mirror. *Shit. My eyes are redder than a stop sign.*

She grabbed a washcloth and turned the hot water on.

Once the water heated enough, she wet the terrycloth, wrung it out, and pressed it to her eyes.

"What will they do?" Josh asked.

"Continue to comb the streets and motels until they find her. Every cop in the city will explore every avenue for any sign of her." She sat back down with the cloth still over her eyes.

"Why don't you lie down and get a little sleep? You need to get in better shape before the morning."

"I can't sleep. I can't do anything but weep. I feel so stupid with all these tears. I know they don't help anything." She shook her head as she spoke.

"Anyone would cry, Paige. It's only normal. Try to calm down. You'll think more clearly."

"I can't. My nerves are gone, and Grace is out there alone . . . and . . . and I'm afraid she's dead. There, I said it. I know she has to be, and I feel so helpless and like such a failure."

"You gotta calm down. You can't help anyone like this. They'll need you tomorrow." He took her hand in his and gently massaged the top.

She pushed his hand away. "I can't. I don't want to sleep."

"Let's go in the kitchen. I'll fix us something to eat. You have to force yourself not to think about it. Focus on what's next."

"I know, but my mind won't let go. Grace is a good guy. She was so scared. She only wanted to make her father proud. I know how she felt." Her eyes met his, and she shook her head. "I don't think I could eat anything." Her tone softened.

"Yeah. I could, but I won't leave you alone."

"Let me reheat my cloth, and I'll come join you."

Josh left through the door that led to the kitchen while she walked into the bathroom. She put the hot cloth on her eyes until they felt a little better. By the time she got to the kitchen, she smelled coffee brewing. A few minutes later Caroline came in.

"I'm craving my caffeine fix. Thank goodness Josh is addicted, too. Paige, what's wrong? You look—"

"I know, awful. I look awful."

"Not my choice of words, but I can tell you're upset. What happened?" Caroline moved over and sat beside her at the table.

"Our decoy police detective went missing. We fear she's dead." She put the warm cloth to her eyes again. "Her name's Grace."

"I'm sorry." Caroline grabbed her hand and squeezed it.

Josh slid a ham and cheese omelet in front of her. She picked up the fork and put a piece in her mouth. It gave her hands something to do. Although she finished every bit, she never tasted a bite. She rubbed the fork tines over her plate in a design only she could see.

"There. It wasn't so bad, was it?"

She stared at Josh like she didn't know what he was talking about.

"You said you couldn't eat, but you finished your meal."

She attempted to smile, but the gesture felt lame. "Thank you for the effort."

"It's the least I could do. I hate that I got you into this mess. You think this is tied to Ben's case?" Josh took the silverware from her hand and placed the dirty dishes in the sink.

"I'm too tired to know anything at the present time." She yawned and tucked her hair behind her ear.

Caroline stood and pulled her up too. "Let's get you to bed. Several hours rest can't hurt. The police will need you strong and ready in the morning. I'll stay with you."

In the bedroom, Caroline helped her undress and put on her gray T-shirt. Her friend plumped the pillows, turned off the lights, left the kitchen door open, and helped her climb in. A soft glow eased the darkness from the room.

"I know you'll get through this. Sometimes life can seem difficult, but you must never give up. You have more courage than most. The rest of us who don't, need you. The world requires people like you."

The dark shadow felt thick with his scent. She could feel his moist breath on her neck like the whisper from the death to come. His huge hand seized her throat and cut off her air supply. She clawed at the constriction, but to no avail. She bucked and kicked at his feet, but she couldn't breathe. Her hand stabbed him with the scalpel. She jabbed him again and again. Blood ran down her fist. Was it his? Was it hers? Her body searched for oxygen, but she found none. Oh, for just one lungful.

Soon the black void consumed her, and it didn't matter anymore. She floated away from herself and knew she'd died, but she didn't care. As she glanced down, she saw the empty red eyes which were her own. Time drifted away, and she felt herself glide up. She hovered near the ceiling. Such absolute freedom.

She gazed down. The body sprawled below her, brains scattered everywhere. Blood drenched and pooled in the matted carpet. She observed exposed bones from the beating. Tears flowed from the eyes while the head lay separated from the body, but the face which stared up and pleaded for help was not her own. It belonged to Grace.

Her body quaked, and her eyes popped open. She came fully awake. Sweat drenched her T-shirt. She fought with the covers until she finally got loose. Unsettled and shaken, she sat up and grabbed her head. Once she could, she stood up and walked to the bathroom.

She climbed into the shower turned the spray to hot. No matter how hard she scrubbed, she couldn't wash away the images. She didn't believe in visions, but the dream rattled her.

Whether it proved to be a premonition or simply her brain working through its worst fears, somehow she knew they'd find Grace dead.

~

By eight the next morning, Paige and the rest of the team gathered at the PAB. No one had heard a word from Grace. Jokes didn't fly around the room. The quiet felt like a tomb. They wanted to hope for the best, but everyone knew they'd find her dead. Her GPS tracker apparently came loose while she got in with the perp. They found the device in the street where she'd walked.

She felt such rage build inside her, she didn't know how to deal with it. She could only think about the day before, when Grace taught her to walk in those damned shoes, and how they'd talked about invincibility. How could she face the detective in a grotesque death scene?

She yearned to pound her fist against the wall, but like everyone present, she sat in desperate silence and longed for the phone to ring. They waited to do the job they'd been unable to do the night before. Find Grace and protect her.

When Trin sat down beside her, she whispered, "What about her cell phone? Did they locate a signal?"

"We've got nothing."

His expression remained stern. She struggled with frustration and fear for her friend while she forced herself to remain motionless. Unable to hold it together, she got up and left the room to pace in the hallway outside the door. Several tears slowly made their way down her cheek. She quickly wiped them away. Her hand went to her mouth, and she bit her knuckle until it bled. Still she couldn't find the release she craved.

She glanced up and saw Curtis Sampson get off the elevator. *Son of a bitch.* She needed to disappear fast before he saw her and figured out which case she was working. With their female detective gone, she couldn't get thrown off. She must avenge Grace, even if she went around the police to do it.

She scooted into the restroom and hoped he hadn't noticed her before she escaped inside. She cracked the door and peered through to scan the hallway.

Sampson looked around as if he'd lost something. *Shit.* He'd seen her. He'd know where to hunt for her in the future. She closed the door and put her back to it. He'd found the floor where she kept herself busy. It wouldn't take him long to track her down.

She waited a few more seconds and made another sliver to peek through. She didn't see him. She maneuvered herself and created a wider gap. He'd left.

She waited another beat or two and attempted to walk back into the hall. When she glimpsed a silhouette move, she retreated, this time into a stall. She sat down and put her feet up on the toilet paper dispenser. She heard the door and held her breath. A moment later, she heard Curtis shout from the hallway.

"Hey, Tulsa. I know you're in here, and I intend to find out why the hell I continue to see you in this building."

A woman's voice answered. "Are you losin' it? Ain't nobody in here but me." Water turned on, then off. Someone dried their hands and closed the door.

She didn't know who the strange woman was, but she wanted to hug her after the lady covered for her.

She waited in silence for several more minutes before she finally took her post back by the door. Once she came out, she discovered Trin searching for her. She saw the mass exodus from their task force room.

"What happened to you?" he asked.

"I got caught up in something. What's going on?"

"They found Officer Helston." His somber expression confirmed what they'd found.

"Oh my God." *Oh my God.* Her hands went to her face. She sobbed and shook her head no. She had fully expected they'd find her dead, but some part of her had still hoped for a miracle. And they didn't get one.

Trin moved her gently to a place down the corridor away from the others. "Are you able to go to the crime scene?"

She nodded.

"Then we both need to pull it together. She'd want us to stay strong no matter how difficult the job."

"You're right. I know. But I just talked to her last night. How can she be gone? Just like that."

"I don't know. I've relived those few minutes many times. Five minutes sooner and Grace would still be alive. What matters is we must stop him before he gets another one. It's the only way to come close to redemption for our failure."

She wiped her eyes and grabbed his hand. "I'm ready. Let's go."

Paige and the guys pulled into the parking lot for the Slumber Inn. Paint peeled on the ancient blue motel. The last sight Grace saw was this dreary place, and she hated that. She dreaded getting out and going inside. But she grabbed the handle and threw her shoulder against the car door. She would stop this asshole. That would be the ultimate justice for Grace.

She saw the stiletto first. The shoe lay inside the door, near the end of the bed. She remembered Grace strutting around the room, teaching her to walk in them. As she entered the room, Grace's foot appeared in her line of vision. Two more steps, and she saw the full view. Thank God, the woman lay face down, but the entire back of her head was a mess. A chunk of her skull was missing, and gray matter mixed with her hair. Bone protruded from the left arm in several places.

Others started into the room, and she glanced over at Buck. "You need to keep them out. Grace would hate for her fellow officers to see her this way. How about Trin, you, and me? I know one crime tech and the ME are required, but we should respect her privacy."

"You don't need to see this, guys. She looks bad. Let one tech in and the ME when he gets here." Buck stared at her and nodded.

"Thank you. It's bad enough we have to see her this way. I know you all will need to testify. If you don't want me here, I understand. I want to do whatever I can. Does her father know, yet? She told me he works on the job."

"I don't know. LT will handle it, but her father does have connections. He may already know. He'll go ballistic. She's his only child." Buck wiped at his nose and pulled his latex gloves on.

A tall brunette with a badge that read "Hailey" carried a case into the room. A camera hung from her neck. She set the container on the untouched bed and photographed the body and the room's contents. The female technician lifted finger-prints, took blood samples, and did everything SID should do. The silence in the room suffocated.

She got Hailey's attention and pointed to a bone fragment over by the wall and cigarette ashes close to Grace's body. The tech retrieved the samples, but no one spoke unless strictly necessary.

After the other woman left, she hunted for excuses to stay until the ME examined the body and moved it to the morgue.

She felt the need to stay close by and protect Grace. She didn't want to let curious eye see her at her worst. Once they bagged the body, she knew what she had to do. No one would like it, but if nothing else, she'd get Josh to help her. They wouldn't stop her this time.

She felt certain she could recognize the pickup. The old Ford was branded in her memory, and she knew the perp had dark hair. He wouldn't come to the same corner tonight, but she could work another one. Josh worked with makeup people who could turn others into monsters. Thanks to Grace, she could walk like a pro.

As they followed the body to the ME's transport, she took out her phone and dialed.

"Who are you calling?" Trin walked up beside her.

"Josh Stuart. He'll know the best makeup artists in the business."

"What do you think you need them for? You're not going out there, Paige."

"I'm free to spend my time however I see fit. I know the truck. He won't catch me unaware like he did Grace, and the bottom line is you can't legally stop me."

"The last time you pulled this shit, Hank damned near died. Listen to me, you cannot do this." Trin's face turned red.

"Hey, Josh. I need a favor." She turned and walked away from Trin to talk in private. "Do you know someone to make me over? I need them to turn me into a brunette with red lips. I need to work as a hooker for the evening."

"Damn it. When do you get back on Ben's case? I've let you go off on your own for days. What about him?" Josh's voice raised in anger.

"Don't you understand? This *is* about Ben's case. It's the only conclusion that makes sense. Whoever killed these women murdered our victim. It's the only detail I can tell you, and I want your help."

She walked back over to Trin and got in his SUV. He scowled at her. She'd never seen him mad before. This wasn't good. She needed his support and the resources the FBI could bring to the case.

"Please don't be mad at me. I will go out there tonight whether anyone goes with me or not, and I won't stop until I get him. I'd prefer to take him in, but if it comes down to it, I'll kill the son of a bitch. I will not let him slaughter another woman. I won't." She stared up at him.

Trin didn't answer. He started the vehicle and pulled out onto the street. His knuckles turned white on the steering wheel while he drove them back to the PAB.

25

The sun reflected from the red Porsche that waited by the curve when Paige arrived back at the Police Administration Building. She saw Josh standing beside it, his face flushed with anger.

Trin looked from Josh to her and started in again. "Is that him? How will he protect you from yourself? I'm telling you, you can't go out there without back up, and you can't go with him. He's an actor for God's sake."

"Then back me up. I trust you. We won't catch this freak if we don't trap him, and you know it." She searched his expression hoping to see the answer she wanted.

"I know a lot of things, but it doesn't change the fact you're not experienced in this type of operation. You're outside your jurisdiction. If Hank finds out . . . well, I can't even think about that discussion. Assuming you survive this hair-brained idea of yours, Hank would kill us both."

"Hank knows you do what you gotta do. You protect the public. I can recognize the truck. Only you and I saw it. You're the wrong sex to bait the trap. I need to go, and you know it.

End of discussion. I'm going." She climbed out of the car and moved toward Josh.

"Damn you, Paige. You put me in the worst situations," Trin called to her.

She turned and walked back toward him. "So, will you help?"

He nodded.

She leaned in the window of the passenger side. "What time shall I meet you to get wired and go over the specifics?"

"We have to let the LAPD in on it. I'll talk to LT. If they won't agree, I'll call the FBI team. Unless I call you, let's meet back here with the task force. We'll go from there. Come back by six. We want time to prep. Nothing can go wrong. I'll have Hank to deal with if it does, not to mention my superiors."

"Bring in whoever you want." She glanced down for a moment. "I need to do this. I couldn't live with myself if I don't. I have to get him for Grace. I have to."

She turned and walked back to Josh. They both climbed into the Porsche and peeled out. At the light, Josh applied the brakes and turned to her. "Will you tell me what the hell has happened?"

"We lost our police detective last night. Our perp got her. I'm gonna kill this bastard. I need to go out there to get close to him. He likes brunettes with shoulder length hair, red lips, and trashy clothes. Know anyone who can help this afternoon?"

"I don't think I like the idea. We'll find a better way. The last one died, right?" He turned his head back to check the traffic light when it turned green.

"Yeah, but I saw the pickup. I'll recognize him. He won't catch me off guard like he did Grace." Her hand trembled. She tucked it under her leg so Josh wouldn't notice.

"Did you ever work on an operation like this before? Do you know what goes into it? You plan and you go over every option. For days you practice every detail and still something you never dreamed about pops up."

"And how do you know so much about how to plan and practice? Who made you an expert?"

He paused for several seconds.

"I worked as a stuntman. It's how I got my start in the business. Several materials we used could turn deadly."

She recognized he'd considered carefully before he answered her. Though the answer made sense, he held something back he didn't want anyone to know. She didn't push him on it, and decided his mysteries had nothing to do with this case. Let him keep his secrets to himself. They wouldn't affect the outcome for this night or the ones to follow.

They rode in silence toward I-10. Josh took the exit toward Century City and spoke for the first time in more than a dozen minutes. "You know everyone with half a brain hates this idea."

"I know already," she snapped.

"I'm sorry, but people care about you. We're worried for your safety."

"I'm worried for my safety too, but you didn't know her. He took her, broke her, and left her like trash. Grace was *not* disposable. The detective mattered . . . mattered to me." She turned her face away from him and attempted to watch the scenery, but her eyes, brimming with tears, couldn't focus.

"I'm sorry. I know I haven't known you long, but I don't think I could get over it, if anything happened to you."

"You're the one who got me into . . ." She lost her thought when they pulled up in front of a small building off Santa Monica Boulevard. It looked like a regular garage with the house gone. Painted a bright lavender, the sign in hot pink read *Brad's Magic Hands.* She questioned what the name implied. "Magic Hands?"

Josh laughed. "You wanted someone who can transform

you into a whore. He's your man. He worked on Heather Ballentine for several films. He also did work on two *Planet of the Apes* movies." He got out and came around to the Carrera's other side. "Come on. Brad's a nut case, but he's good." He took her hand and helped her get out, but she still hesitated.

"I expected a woman for this job."

"He's gay, if that helps."

"I don't know what to say. How would that help?"

"I'm saying you can think about him like one of the girls. He's not interested in your business." He grinned and tugged her toward the building.

"You know, we talked to her makeup man on the Ballentine case. It might have been him."

"Probably was. He worked her last film." Josh paused and turned to face her. "He talks a mile a minute to everyone, so you need to watch what you say around him. He can't help it. It's part of his DNA. If he hears anything, it could headline the tabloids tomorrow."

"Good to know." She nodded slowly.

Once they opened the door, she entered a world unlike anything she'd ever seen. The walls were lined with shelves, which held wigs, masks, accessories, and everything imaginable. At the far side, several hairdressing stations sat ready for use. She didn't know where to gaze first until the black stilettos grabbed her attention. One lay discarded beside the other, perfectly lined up with the edge of the shelf. She couldn't stop her mind. It went there. *Grace before, Grace after.*

A tall muscular man came around the side from a curtained area. He filled out his T-shirt and jeans in the right places, but when he greeted them, she understood he'd never take any woman for a lover. Her mind went back to *Grace before, Grace after.* The shoes mesmerized her while she stared at them.

"Hey, Josh. How's it hangin'?"

"This hot lady needs to turn into a working girl ASAP. You got time to help us out? It's an emergency."

Brad motioned for her to do a turnabout. She obliged. He motioned for her to keep at it. She continued to twirl. He put his arm down, and she stopped to face him.

"She's a stunner all right. What particular type? Give me the specifics."

"Brunette hair, cover the shoulders, red lips, a little darker complexion, and clothes to show off her stunning figure," Josh said.

"It's a sin to cover her hair. Does our guy favor school girls, nurses, or what?"

Josh frowned. His shrug implied he didn't know.

"You must have a role in mind. What's the character in the script into? It'll help me give you what you need."

"Street walker. Trashy," she finally said.

"Okay. I can work with that." He put his thumb under his chin, his forefinger along the line of his jaw, and stared at her for a full minute. "Okay." He nodded, turned, and walked behind the curtain.

Grace before, Grace after. The shoes still kept her attention.

She heard various items being thrown around and searched through.

"I'll only take a minute," Brad called to them. Several minutes later, he came out and carried a fake head with a long black hairpiece.

"I didn't get a chance to organize everything after I repainted, but this is the one I need for our hooker. Her blue eyes are heavenly, but do we need to make them brown?"

"We can't take time to let her eyes adjust to contacts. I need her in front of a camera tonight. I don't want them to blink or water."

"Yeah, with the heavy makeup, it could make a mess on my

gorgeous work." Brad studied her again. "With the right shadow and liner, he'll never notice the aquamarine color."

She pulled her cell phone out from her pocket and checked the time. "We need to get a move on. We've got a six o'clock deadline back downtown."

Brad looked aghast and stared at Josh. "You want miracles with no time to produce them. I'm not the fairy godmother."

"I told you I had an emergency." Josh shrugged.

Brad grabbed her by the arm and pulled her behind the curtain. "Okay lose the bra. A hooker's tits would never be so bound. The straitjacket needs to go."

She glared at him like he'd lost his mind. "Not with these." She'd never gone anywhere without her bra since her first one at twelve years old.

"You want this guy to pay you for a roll in the sheets, you need to convince him. Give a little preview. Show off the merchandise. You've got to *be* the part."

"Shit," she mumbled and motioned for him to turn around.

He laughed, but did as she requested.

"I need something to put on to cover myself." She put her fingers on the top button of her blouse and turned her back to him.

"Here, put on this duster until we decide what you'll wear. Strip down to your panties, and we may lose those if they show under your final costume."

She frowned but put on the clothing. It did cover the required parts, but she was still uncomfortable without her bra.

Once Brad turned around, he nodded his head. "Nice rack. We'll make you up so the guys can't stay away."

"Just what I always wanted." She shook her head and rolled her eyes as she walked from behind the curtain.

Brad pointed to the chairs he'd set up for hairstyling and makeup. She sat in the one he offered.

"First we need to get your natural hair bound up so it doesn't come loose." He took her hair, twisted it up, and pinned it tightly. He placed an elastic cap on top and pulled it down. He taped the edges with flesh-colored tape and slowly turned the chair around to hunt for any loose strands. He seemed satisfied with his handiwork and stopped with her face toward the mirror.

When he worked on her face, he added light layers that built her color darker so it appeared natural down into her cleavage. She gritted her teeth every time he got close to her breasts, but she'd do whatever it took for this job. He drew her eyebrows darker, forming perfect arches.

He built up dark black lashes, added ebony liner, and painted her lips a sultry crimson. The smoky shadow added mystery to her exquisite eyes. He crowned her with the black wig and fastened it with lots of hairpins. The bottom fell loosely over her shoulders, and he teased every curled tress into place.

"Doesn't she favor a young Catherine Zeta Jones?" Brad put his hands on his hips and surveyed his creation.

"I would never have agreed before, but damned if she doesn't."

She stared at the stranger in the mirror and didn't recognize the alluring woman.

"Now for the right clothes. I keep a bandana blouse for times like this. We could tie that up under her breasts with a short denim skirt. It could give her the farmer's daughter flair." Brad studied her with squinted eyes.

"I think our guy prefers a more Hispanic type, but not too loud on the colors," she said.

"Hispanic, hmm." Brad took off behind the curtain again. He came back with a creamy thin peasant blouse. Tiny red trim edged the neckline. For the bottom, he paired scarlet spandex pants. "Try these. It only hints at ethnic, but with your figure, it will look killer."

"You can see everything. I can't go out like this."

"A woman of the night advertises. You gotta flaunt what you got," Brad said.

She swallowed and grabbed the clothes, but she didn't say a word.

"Tell her. She must commit to the part and become a wanton woman to get her man. She must convert into the seductress who will to do anything. She has children at home to feed." Brad stared at Josh and with hand motions encouraged him to join in.

"He's right. You'll need to act trashy enough to entice any man. Let's see you in it." Josh nodded toward the curtain.

She took the garments and vanished. She didn't think about this part when she planned to do this. You could plainly see her nipples through the blouse. The pants were tighter than a second skin layer. Worse, you could see her panty line.

When she came back out, Josh's mouth dropped open. Brad wolf whistled. She covered her breasts.

"I can see your panties. Take them off. No one wears full grannies anymore." Brad tossed her a pair of ebony lace thongs.

"Now, what about shoes?" Josh walked over to ruby colored platforms.

"No. I want the black ones over there." She walked to the black stilettos. She took several moments before she reached up and grabbed them. *Grace before, Grace after.*

She held them a moment, then slid them on. "I'll need a purse large enough to carry a gun, handcuffs, and other junk."

"Are you okay? Should we wait another day?" Josh started toward her.

She put up her hand to stop him. "I'm fine. The shoes reminded me what my purpose is. That's all."

"What are you talking about? This is for a movie, right? I expected credits on a movie," Brad said.

"Not exactly. It's for a benefit. I can't explain right now, but I want you to put everything on this. Give yourself a nice tip for the quick turnaround." Josh handed him a card from his wallet.

Brad rang up their total, but you could see the questions fly through his mind as he handed Josh the slip to sign his name. "You couldn't give me a clue?"

"I can't possibly. It's top secret. You'll find out soon enough," Josh answered.

"Aren't you cryptic."

"I suppose, but I don't mean to be."

She stopped the chitchat by holding up her cell phone, showing Josh the time. They both rushed from the building toward his vehicle.

Josh backed out and took off.

They'd gone only a block when her phone rang. She glanced at the screen before she answered. "What's up?"

"I heard a rumor you've turned into a streetwalker," Bob Underwood said.

"Who told you?" She arched her brow and stared at Josh.

"Trin sounded concerned about your reaction to their detective's death, but I know he's worried about you. What gives?"

"They've got someone out here who kills prostitutes. I think it's related to our case. I intend to find out. For the record, I can't believe he called you."

"Paige, you need to come home. The city's budget is tight. We're shorthanded without you."

"I can't leave now. You'll make me look like a fool. Besides, I received an expensive makeover by a Hollywood makeup artist. I'm already dressed for the ball."

"You've got two days. Then your ass better get on the plane home." He sounded serious.

"He might not bite in two days. We need to put him away."

"That's LA's problem, not ours. You were sent out to solve the Ben McCall case."

"But they're related. I'm sure of it. We will catch this guy, and it will prove the other case."

"You heard me. I said two days, and that's two days too damned many." He hung up.

She sighed and threw her phone on the dash.

"What's wrong?" Josh asked.

"My boss gave me a deadline. Forty-eight hours to finish this. Then I'm supposed to head home."

"That sucks, but I'll admit I don't want you to go out there because of what happened last night. It's too dangerous."

"We've already discussed this. I'm going." She grabbed the phone from the dash and threw it in the bag that contained her other clothes and the purse. When they arrived at the PAB, she got out of the car and turned back to Josh. "I'll see you later at the house. It'll be late before we're through for the evening."

Josh nodded and drove off.

She entered the building. Curtis Sampson and Sonny Harmon came off the elevator. She immediately felt the need to hide. Curtis stared at her as she walked past but didn't try to stop her. Puzzled for a second, she then remembered the disguise she wore. She glanced down and saw her nipples outlined beneath her blouse. Her cheeks burned with embarrassment. In the elevator, she grabbed her other shirt from the bag she carried to cover up. She didn't need to flaunt anything until later.

She entered the room where the task force waited. Trin turned and stared at her. She silently dared him to say a word. He shook his head and grinned.

"What's so funny? I already feel exposed and silly in this getup." She walked past him and sat close to the door.

Trin moved closer to her and whispered, "Actually, you look perfect for the assignment. I'm surprised they convinced you to wear it. Let's just say, your normal wardrobe tends to be a little less revealing."

"And much more comfortable to wear."

"We'd better get your tracking devices planted. With that outfit, it could be tricky. We'll put one on you and one in the purse for backup."

"Sounds good. So what did you do while I turned into a painted lady? Did anything interesting happen?"

"We made an unexpected trip to San Diego."

26

Earlier in the afternoon

When Trin got back upstairs, the LT held the phone to his ear. The lieutenant talked for a few more minutes, came out from his office, and walked toward them.

"Another interesting development came up. The San Diego PD found a body. Male this time. Someone messed the victim up bad with a bat or pipe. I told them we'd send someone down to check it out. It could be our guy. Are you interested in a road trip, or do you want me to send someone else?"

He deliberated for a second. "Can we make it back in time for tonight?"

"Use lights and sirens if you need to get through traffic. You know more than anyone what to look for to recognize if he's our perp."

"I'd like to see the crime scene and the body to rule it out. This unsub's interval started at one a day. That's unusual to begin with. I'm sure it has nothing to do with his fantasy but someone who challenged him. Especially with the unusual bullet at the crime scene before this morning's event. Maybe he found the owner of the second blood pool. It might have been a necessary kill. Let's go see." He nodded at Buck and Vern. "You game?"

"Sure. We've wasted enough time here. Maybe he screwed up and left us something. It's out of his norm," Buck said.

"Let's go find out. Call and ask them to hold the scene for us to arrive." He walked toward the door.

When they arrived a few hours later, three squad cars still guarded the surrounding area. The trunk was raised on an old Chevy in a grocery parking lot. When he slipped out from the Nitro, he recognized the place as only a dump site. No blood spatter on the ground anywhere around the car.

They introduced themselves. He walked over to the vehicle and examined the inside. They'd removed the body, but the victim remained on site. The ME loaded the deceased onto a gurney that sat next to his van. He still wanted to see if anything useful remained in the back of the automobile.

"Don't let them touch this yet. I'm not through with it, but I want to view the body so the ME can remove it." He moved toward the official.

"Vern, I'm going with him so I can put it in the report," Buck said.

"Estimate on TOD?" he asked.

"Lividity has come and gone. I'd guess late Tuesday night, early Wednesday morning, but it's hard to pinpoint closer than that. He's cooked for several days in the sedan. Thank God it's not summer," the medical examiner said.

He noticed the angle of the head and the amount of muscle that attached it to the torso. The handiwork appeared similar to their unsub. He felt certain this killer was the same one they pursued.

"You think it's our perp?" Buck asked.

"I think it is, but we need to go over this car and the body closely. It's not his normal pattern. Let's see if he made a mistake."

The two detectives from San Diego nodded.

"I'd like a copy for everything you've gathered and anything else you manage to find sent to the FBI in LA. I can pick it up there. I want it ASAP. I'm sure it's connected to our case. Put attention to me on the package." He gave them his card so they'd have his name and email.

"We'll get it to you ASAP." The medical examiner zipped the body bag closed.

"I'd like you to take a swab for DNA testing on the places the weapon made contact. We could find trace from our other victims. It's a long shot, but worth a try. You can send it with the autopsy results, and put a rush on them both if possible."

He walked back over to the trunk while the ME's vehicle left with the victim inside. He studied the blood pool there for several minutes. He moved around to the driver's seat and observed the ashtray, which overflowed with butts.

He followed the trail of the Marlboro stubs lying on the ratty maroon carpet, but each one matched. He took an ink pen from his pocket, and gently moved several cigarette ends around in the ashtray. One of the top butts was a Camel. Paige had found a Camel at an earlier crime scene. He called a tech over.

"I want you to photograph it, bag it, and label it. I'll take it with me, so do whatever paperwork is required on your end and I'll sign it. We're on a time crunch. I'll need you to fill out the forms now, please. We need to get back to LA for our operation this evening." He watched the young man to make sure he picked up the correct butt, and thanked him as the tech handed it over.

He asked the detectives a few more questions and found out the officers who canvassed nearby didn't locate any viable cameras. The CCTVs put up for security purposes got shot out immediately by a local gang. No help there.

They headed back to LA. A few miles up the I-5, Buck mumbled something.

"Son of a bitch. We found another guy in a trunk back in LA. They called us out. He killed the perp with the same MO. We didn't think he was our man, but I bet he was. We found one of our victims in a motel several blocks away. I didn't put the locations together at the time. Damn, I missed it." Buck looked at Vern. "Hell, you missed it, too. It's time for us to retire."

"Nobody catches everything. You're not ready for the scrap heap, yet." He rummaged in the file that contained the information on the cigarette butt Paige found.

Josh drove several blocks away from the police building to a covered parking garage. He pulled up next to Tony's black Escalade. He climbed out from the Porsche and reached into his pocket for two hundred-dollar bills. Greta sat behind the Caddy's wheel. He walked up to her and opened the door.

"Greta, you're a lifesaver." He handed her the cash.

"I like the young lady, too. I'm glad you'll be protecting her."

"This should get you home in a cab, but you can keep it no matter which way you go home. Thanks for bringing Tony's car."

She glanced down at the two bills in her hand. "Anytime."

"You want me to call you a cab?"

"Naw. I saw a bus stop right back there. It'll work fine for me."

He watched her walk toward the elevator and pulled a small cooler from the back, along with a sack that contained snacks. At least these days, he didn't need to pull down surveillance without food or water.

Once he returned to the Cadillac, he pulled a rifle case from the back seat and assembled it with ease. He loaded it with hollow points and racked one into the barrel. The gun felt familiar in his hands, like an old friend. He opened the glove box and reached for the Glock inside. Thanks to the chip planted near her shoulder blade, Paige couldn't go anywhere without him following.

The minutes ticked by as he waited for her location to move on his display screen. Over twelve years had elapsed since the last time he'd pulled duty on a target. His focus and patience remained untried since South America, but his training prevailed. He wouldn't lose her like the cops lost their detective the night before. Paige mattered too much to him. He planned to keep her safe no matter what it took.

Paige walked down a street in the middle of their perp's prime territory. The guys chose this corner after they charted where he'd picked up the other victims and studied the new map it formed. Her feet hurt. She didn't like the exaggerated sway of her hips, but she strolled toward her designated location anyway. With two short nights to lure in her predator, she didn't have time to waste.

An older black Lincoln slowed down beside her and brought the first customer. The john wore his blond hair short with a side part. This guy wasn't her man, but she needed to play along. If their mark watched, he must think she was a real prostitute. She agreed to blow the perp for two fifty and got into his car.

They drove a mile and stopped.

"I need the money up front. My old man will beat the crap out of me if you don't pay." She stared him in the eye like she did this every day.

He shifted in the seat. "I don't know. You might rip me off."

"Hey, you're wastin' my dime. You want a good time, you fork over first."

He gave her a look that conveyed he believed he held all the power, when he'd been the one to stop and ask her for the favor.

She shrugged and started to open her door. "I got other jobs to do. No pay, no play."

He grabbed her wrist and pulled her back. Way too rough for her liking.

She slammed him in the chest with her purse. "Listen, ass wipe, don't touch the merchandise before you pay. Those are the rules."

He lifted his arm to backhand her, but she pulled her gun from the bag she carried. "I wouldn't if I were you." She tossed him handcuffs. "You can wear these until we sort this out."

LAPD cops approached the car. They dragged him from the vehicle and frisked him. After a stern warning, they made him drive her back to her corner where they started the process over again. By three in the morning, they gave it up for a lost cause.

Josh watched her tracking device move back toward the PAB. He parked beside his Porsche and waited for twenty minutes to make sure they didn't leave. He switched cars and raced home. The Carrera needed to arrive before she did. He yanked his shirt over his head while he raced to his room and changed clothes. He wanted to show concern, so he ran his hand through his hair several times.

Half an hour later, he heard her arrive. He walked to the garage area and intercepted her path to her room. "How did it go?"

She was startled for a second before she recovered. "We busted half a dozen perps, but not the one who mattered. I'm not LAPD so we had to let them go. Hopefully, he'll bite tomorrow."

"I still don't agree with your method, but I'm glad you're safe for tonight."

THE NEXT MORNING Paige left for the PAB by ten. Several late nights without much sleep made her groggy and slow. She wished she drank coffee like the rest of the world, but even at her worst, she couldn't get it down. Pepsi didn't get the job done this morning. Neither did the run she'd worked in before she left the house. Finally, to clear her head, she stopped at a convenience store to grab caffeine pills.

As she stood in line to pay, she spotted the news displayed on the television. They'd found another prostitute. She slapped a ten in front of the cashier, waved the pills so he could see, and ran out the front.

She walked into the room assigned to the task force. It appeared empty. She saw LT Bennett in his office through his open door. She didn't know him well, but she needed to check in with somebody. At his threshold, she hesitated and waited for him to finish up.

His piercing brown eyes studied her for a moment. "Last

night ran late. I'm glad you took your time coming in. How do you feel after your first night?"

"I'm okay. My body didn't want to wake up this morning. I overslept. No one's had much sleep for two nights. I'm sorry I missed the crime scene. If you give me the address, I can still go there."

"I didn't get a chance to make your acquaintance. This seems a good time. I understand you and Trin worked together on a case in Tulsa. He speaks highly about your abilities."

"He saved my life. I'm afraid he's the one who deserves the credit." She never felt comfortable when she talked about the strangler case.

"He claims you slowed the perp down a lot."

"A little. How is Grace's father doing?" She attempted again to change the subject.

"It's been tough for him. She's his only child." He looked down.

No one ever liked death to land close to home. It made their own life seem more vulnerable.

"I can't imagine. I only met Grace on this case, but we shared several life experiences. I liked her a lot. If you talk to him again, tell him how sorry I am for his loss. He must feel devastated."

"I will, but I'd like you to answer a question. What's your stake in this? Why did you place your life on the line?"

"Police are my family. You know how it goes. I met Grace. She and I clicked. The perp killed her. He took one of our own. I have to do this for her."

LT eyed her. "And that's it?"

"Trin and I saw the truck. I believe I can recognize it if I see it again. That gives me an advantage over any other female you could put on the case. We both know he won't stop until we take him off the streets."

He nodded. "If you ever want to leave Tulsa, give me a call. I'll find a place for you."

She took the address for the crime scene from his outstretched hand. She didn't expect the offer. She nodded, turned, and left his office.

Before she left the main squad room behind, she walked over to the desk Trin used. She wanted to write a message in case she missed him at the newest location. The papers slid around while she rummaged for something to write on. Under several forms, she saw the edge of a photograph. When she pulled it out, it was the one of Tom McCall she'd seen from his driver's license. She glanced up for a second. Why the hell did Trin have a copy?

She stared back down at the picture with the dark hair and blue eyes, and it jarred her memory. *Oh My God. It can't be.*

TRIN LEFT the green Nitro and walked toward the crime scene. The two detectives followed him. The deceased appeared fresh from the night before. The unsub chose an open ditch to leave his victim, but the head detached from the body got his attention first. The beating left it an unrecognizable mass made up of bone, brains, and tissue. He could hardly tell the lifeless form resembled a human. Something must have set the killer off. Though he escalated to a certain extent with each victim, this displayed nothing but pure rage.

"What the hell pissed him off this time?" Buck approached him.

He nodded at the head. "I didn't think he could get much more violent, but obviously I was wrong."

Vern moved over to the torso and lifted the skirt. "Again, no signs of sexual activity. Everything's intact. Well, not the head, of course."

One leg lay shattered, and the lower left arm hung by an inch of skin and tissue. Blow flies landed on the body and head faster than they could wave them away. He wanted to say the hell with it and walk away, to leave the unspeakable view behind. His stomach roiled. He'd seen plenty of horrific crime scenes in his life, but this surpassed the worst.

They each drifted apart and walked the crime scene. His eyes searched for anything that could possibly give them the break they needed, but the killer left them nothing. The SID unit bagged and tagged, and the photographer documented everything in the general area.

Finally, Gene Shaw, the ME showed up. They could examine the body more closely after he was done. This time the killer positioned the body with the victim's purse under her leg. So they couldn't check for an ID until he finished his examination.

Eventually, Buck walked back to him. "You heard from Stone this morning?"

"No. I've wondered about her too." He gazed away from the grid he worked. Paige never missed out on the action. He was glad she couldn't see this mess. If she knew this could be the end result, it would only make it more difficult for her to go out on the street tonight.

Gene took a thermometer out, stuck it in the body, and measured for liver temperature. He glanced up and hunted for Buck. "I'd say, TOD somewhere between nine and ten last night. COD presents as a broken neck, but it's not official until I'm through with her on the table." He wiped the instrument off and put it back into its case.

"Let's move the torso first so we can get an ID. Gene, you through with it?" Buck asked.

"Let me go over her a little better. Then I'll bag her." The ME lifted her good arm and studied the limb from shoulder to wrist. He gave the rest of her body a closer examination and nodded once he finished.

A moment later, they lifted her right side enough to get the handbag out. Brains and blood covered the purple clutch. When they pulled her credentials out, a crime scene tech held a bag for it.

The driver's license read Barbara Steen, twenty-five. A voter registration card showed St. Francisville, Louisiana for a past residence. He considered it an odd item for a hooker to carry with her, but it could remind her who she'd been before this city drove her to something less desirable. A damn shame she didn't get her chance to get out of the life before this happened.

Someone put a black body bag on the ground close to the torso. Several officers lifted the deceased onto the bag. The ME still scrutinized the head, but finally stood and motioned for them to take it. He stepped away while they retrieved the sticky-looking glob.

As everyone moved away from the area, he saw light reflect off something gold. The unsub had left an object under the head. Instantly, he understood why the guy had been so pissed off. He saw detective Grace Helston's badge.

Buck walked up beside him. "So our perp didn't like our detective getting so close."

"It would seem not."

Now that their target knew the police were closing in, what would that mean for Paige tonight?

27

Paige scrambled out of the green Dodge two blocks up the street from her corner. The stilettos already made her feet ache, the unfamiliar footwear rubbing blisters on her heels. She made several trips up and down the sidewalk. Still no sign of the old pickup.

A man approached her, one hand clutching his side. Something was off about his gait. She assumed he was her first customer until he spoke.

"What the hell do you think you're doing on my corner? Only Terrell's whores work this place. Get your ass on out of here." He shoved her hard, stumbled, and lost his footing. He grabbed his side again.

She stumbled backward, turning her left ankle, but managed to catch herself. She slammed a knee into his groin. He dropped to the ground.

She bent over him and whispered, "This is a police matter. You'd better leave if you don't want to get arrested."

He stared up at her for a minute. Once he struggled to his feet, he shuffled off toward the back of the building, still holding his ribs. She heard him mumble something about *kill the bitch* as he lumbered away from her.

She positioned her back toward the street so no one could see her mouth and spoke to the officers listening. "I'm okay. A dumb pimp attempted to run me off. I threatened him with arrest. We shouldn't have any more problems with him."

When she circled back on her route, she spotted the truck moving her way. She increased her pace because another hooker stood close by.

"He's mine," she called to the other woman who gave her the finger. *She doesn't know I saved her life.* Her eyes focused on her mark who drove closer.

I WATCHED the woman across the street. She seemed different. Her stride wasn't quite like the others. She flipped her hair away from her shoulder, and the familiar longing filled me. I exhaled the smoke from my lungs and stubbed the cigarette out. As I reached for the key to my truck, a black dude approached her. I stopped every movement. I felt certain the man was the pimp I'd left for dead the other night. *Son of a bitch.* While I watched, the whore kneed the man in the nuts. He went down, and she said something to him. Eventually, the pimp got up and staggered away.

The woman stood up to him. The one trait I longed for in a female. I couldn't say why it affected me so much, but it pulled at something deep inside. Flashes from my past strobed through my mind. I wanted to talk to her more than the others. I promised myself I wouldn't kill her, but lately, I'd made the same promise every day. The reason she had more strength than the other hookers intrigued me. She would give me the breakthrough, I was certain. Then I would never kill again. If I could remember, it would fix the brokenness in my memory. I continued to study her. The fierce craving inside grew ravenous.

I started the pickup, swung out into traffic, and pushed the right turn signal down. I went around the block so my passenger door would stay on her side. When I got a better view, her beauty startled me for an instant. The others couldn't compare. It reminded me to turn on my charm. I nodded at her and produced my most enticing smile.

She paused for an instant and moved in my direction. "Care for a ride?" Her voice contained a whiskey gruffness that made me want her, but I wasn't here for sex. I needed to talk to her about the pimp she'd stood up to. I felt closer than ever to the elusive woman locked inside my brain.

"How much for your time?" I forced myself to smile with innocence though I wanted to get her away from here.

"Two fifty."

"Get in."

"Money first please." Her cocky grin mesmerized. This one was different from the others. Up close she didn't look seedy enough. But I felt certain she had the answers I searched for.

I hitched my hip up so I could get to my wallet. I counted the money out and handed it to her.

She tucked the cash into her huge purse. The beauty opened the door and climbed up onto the seat. Before she managed to get settled, I hit the gas. She swung halfway out the vehicle. The hooker scrambled to hold on, and finally slammed the door closed. As I made a left turn, she crash landed on her purse.

"You must be in a hurry." This time her smile seemed fake and a little scared.

I didn't bother to answer.

~

TRIN SAW the old truck immediately. Certain it matched the brown Ford they'd seen before, he radioed everyone to get ready.

Paige sashayed toward the vehicle and made several gestures with her hand. He heard them discuss the price. When she climbed up into the truck, it took off. Her door flew open. She fell onto her side and grabbed for the armrest. After several attempts, she slammed it shut. The sound from her microphone still gave off traffic noise, but he could no longer hear Paige's voice nor her john's.

"Son of a bitch. The first device isn't moving. I think she lost it when she nearly fell out the door. I can still hear traffic though."

The vehicle took a hard left. Her head vanished from view and came back up. He glanced down at his screen.

"What the hell? The GPS tracker in her purse quit working." He stared at Buck while Vern sped up to keep the truck in sight.

"Did you get the tag number? We're blind right now." He held on as the SUV rounded a left corner. The screech from the tires were barely audible over the beating his heart made.

Buck half turned in his seat. "I got a partial. All but the last two digits."

He recited what he'd written down. The computer keys in the backseat sounded like a machine gun firing off repeated rounds. Then silence filled their green Nitro.

28

———

J osh sat inside Tony's black Escalade a block and a half away and watched Paige shove the black man backwards. A little bit later an old pickup pulled up beside her. This looked like the truck Paige described. He sat up straighter and pulled the binoculars from the seat beside him. After he focused them, he saw FORD spelled out across the tailgate.

He reached for the keys and turned the motor on. The killer could strike quickly. He needed to stay close but keep out of the cops' sight. They didn't catch on last night. He wanted the situation to stay that way. He'd spotted at least three unmarked cars they used the night before. Tonight, he'd spotted a fourth.

One, a green Dodge Nitro with three men inside, eased out from the curb ahead. Once the truck made a hard left, their car followed. He noted they trailed much closer than they did last time and wondered why.

The red dot on his computer moved steadily ahead. He kept an eye on both the screen and the street before him. When the pickup turned right onto a freeway ramp, he observed the Nitro didn't make the turn. *What the hell?* A yellow Mustang cut them off, but he continued to follow the target.

TRIN KEPT an eye on the vehicle in front of them while he worked to trace plates that could match their partial. Several seconds later, his computer screen flashed. He gazed down to study the list for every possible match from the tag numbers he typed in. Nothing on the list matched a pickup. "The tag is probably stolen. None correspond to our truck."

"Son of a bitch." Buck turned back to the front. "Stay with them, Vern."

The streetlights flashed by. The traffic moved with a constant flow. A faded billboard featured Katy Perry in a skimpy outfit. He chewed his bottom lip and mentally kicked himself for letting Paige go out there.

A yellow Mustang squeezed in front of their Dodge, and the driver tossed a beer bottle out the window. He swayed in the seat as they swerved to miss a collision with the vehicle. He sat back up. The pickup vanished from sight. He turned his head slightly and saw the truck drive up onto the freeway.

"They took the ramp! Where's the next entrance?" he yelled.

"Two miles ahead," Buck said.

"That's too far. Take the next right and go back to it. We've got to get back on them right now."

JOSH GUESSED the police switched out cars, leaving one to follow the truck at a time. They probably hoped the killer wouldn't notice the tail. So they used four different vehicles, and the Nitro must have taken the first turn, because he didn't see any of the other three cars following the Ford.

Worrying about them would distract him. No time for it. He needed to keep the truck in sight and make sure the red dot continued to blink on his computer.

They'd traveled about two miles when the truck exited the freeway. He'd lived in the LA area for a long time, but he didn't know where the driver was headed.

The red dot weaved its way through a maze of streets and made a U-turn. He saw the vehicle come straight back toward him. He made a quick left, and went around the block to get behind them again. When he circled back, the pickup had vanished.

He looked back down at the red dot. It still blinked, but it didn't move. They'd stopped. Had the driver noticed him? He had to drive on, or they would know he followed them. He turned right and pulled over on a side street. His eyes never left the computer screen.

By the time they got the green Dodge turned around and back up on the freeway, Trin noted the truck had disappeared. Vern floored it, and pushed him back into his seat. The speedometer closed in on a hundred and soon passed it by fifteen. Silence reigned inside their vehicle.

"It's been five miles. Where are they? We should be right behind them. They probably turned off. Son of a bitch." He slammed his hand against the door. "I should never have let her talk me into this."

"Surely she recognized the perp if we did," Buck said.

"Damn it! This can't be happening. First Grace and now this?"

"I'll get a BOLO out on the pickup. Hopefully, our patrols will find it." Buck picked up the radio and gave the alert.

In the backseat he called for an FBI helicopter to join in the search, but he knew they were screwed. Hank would never get over a loss like this. He racked his brain to think of anything that could help. "Turn around. Their taillights were distinctive. If we haven't yet, I don't think we will. Head back to that exit a couple miles behind us. They probably left the freeway there. At least that'll give us something to try."

I STARED at the sexy woman who hugged the door. She'd offered herself to me for money, but she didn't act like any prostitute I've been with before. My father preferred trashy women. Most hooked. A few didn't. I shook my head and attempted to clear the puzzle from my mind. The woman lost in my memories held the answer to something important. I needed to focus on her.

My father also liked to drink and brutally beat his women, but until recently I'd never felt the need to knock any woman around. Now, I'd turned into the same monster he'd been. I didn't want to kill this beautiful woman, but I didn't know how to control the rage that festered and breathed inside me. *When it explodes, I can't stop the animal I become. If only she can help me remember.*

I saw an old dump ahead. The sign blinked, a third of the letters missing. I pulled into the Westgate Village Inn and put the truck in park. "Here. Go get us a room." I handed her a hundred bucks.

She took the money and climbed down from the vehicle.

As she meandered up to the office, I saw a flash of the other dark-haired woman. The same one who'd looked so familiar before. The vision vanished before I could remember. I concentrated on the hooker's movements, but the image of the other woman didn't come back to me.

She came out of the office several minutes later and gestured for me to follow. Her hips swayed gracefully while she walked to room thirteen and unlocked the door.

I pulled the pickup in front and went inside. The dingy room was spacious, offering plenty of room for her to move around. "Do your walk for me. It gets me going," I lied.

"What walk?" She faced me, hesitated, then stuck her hand down in her red purse. "My lips are dry. I need gloss."

Her arm moved around above the top edge of the bag. "I don't care about your damn lipstick. I want you to strut like you did on the street."

She flashed a dazzling smile. "Okay, okay." She shrugged and walked toward the dresser. Her eyes locked with mine in the mirror. She sauntered and stopped once she neared the far wall. She turned. "You ever been to Tulsa?"

The question fired an alarm through me, but I didn't know what it meant. "No, I don't think so." I shook my head, but the word "Tulsa" brought flashes like a strobe light that illuminated memory splotches from the past.

TRIN WANTED to throttle himself and everyone remotely related to this case, but mostly he wanted the damned pickup to appear in front of them. They took the exit he figured they should try, but his hope ebbed low. Too much time had passed.

"Do you know this area at all? Are there any motels or parks close by? Those are his primary crime scenes." He grabbed the edge of the backseat with all his might to release tension, but it didn't help.

"Definitely plenty of crummy motels in this area. I don't remember any parks," Buck answered.

"Radio any patrols in the area to search motels for his pickup."

"Will do." Buck lifted the transmitter and relayed the request.

Vern turned twice and pulled up to their first one they saw. They made a slow sweep around every side and searched for their target. No old brown pickups.

29

J osh figured he was close, but he didn't see the pickup anywhere. The red dot barely moved before it stopped again. Four rundown motels and several cafes sat in his view. Normally, he wouldn't come alone to this part of town, but he hadn't seen any of the police vehicles after he got on the freeway. That meant Paige was in this alone except for him. He grabbed the Glock from the glove compartment and checked to see the gun remained loaded and ready.

He pulled into the first motel and slowly circled the rooms on each side. He pushed the button to lower his window. He wanted to be able to hear in case anyone called for help. Anticipation tensed his shoulders and spine. He continued to slow his breathing and listened for Paige's voice. Nothing.

He drove on to the next motel and repeated his actions. He longed to yell out, do anything to find her, because he knew time was running out.

PAIGE PAUSED in the repetitious sauntering back and forth, back and forth across the room and tried to engage the man. "So what do they call you?"

She paused to face him. He seemed so young, yet so much like his brother.

"What the hell is it to you? I pay you to walk. I need to remember." He nodded at her to start again.

She knew who he was. Something had clicked when she saw Tom McCall's photo in Trin's papers. The first time she'd seen a picture of Ben's father, she sensed something about him was familiar, but wrote it off to resembling his son.

But now she remembered. She knew exactly who this killer was. The thirst for justice that had consumed her since she'd seen Grace's mangled body was now tangled up, her emotions conflicting.

"Sometimes I like to know who I work for. You sure you never been to Tulsa? It's in Oklahoma." She started her trek across the room one more time and kept her eyes on him.

"Let it alone. I don't want to talk about some damned town I've never been to."

"I heard you say you needed to remember. What's that about?"

He moved, reached down to the floor. He held a bat by his leg. She sauntered back to her purse and the gun inside it. The green light still flashed on the recorder she'd started when she went for her lip gloss earlier.

"What the hell are you doing? I told you to walk." This time he pointed with the Louisville Slugger and urged her on.

She picked up the purse, dangled it over her arm, and swung her hips, flipping her hair over her shoulder.

∾

Josh drove slowly toward the back of the second motel. As he came around to the front, two guys walked up to the Escalade.

"Are you scoping out our turf?" The first one stuck his head in the window. The second pulled a gun from behind his back.

"No." He gave them a pointed expression. He didn't have time for their bullshit. "I'm looking for someone. A brunette about five eight or nine. She's gorgeous. I think she went into a motel around here. I need to find her quick. Now get the hell out of my way, I've got business to tend to."

"You dissin' us? That ain't no respect, man. It could get you hurt." The kid boasted a tattoo on his neck, likely gang-related. He lifted his gun, leveling it at Josh.

Trin heard the rotors of a helicopter passing overhead. No one had spotted the truck yet. Vern drove around one motel after another, but time continued to slip away. With it, the chance of saving Paige dwindled. His stomach filled with acid, which no amount of Tums could fix. He ran his hand through his hair several times.

He dialed central command again and checked for any disturbances in the area. Someone had reported a woman screaming several blocks away. He gave Vern the address, and they took off, Vern driving like a maniac with a death wish.

The dilapidated clapboard house didn't feel right. He and Buck departed the vehicle and moved toward the sagging porch that fronted the old house. Dark and silent, it towered before them.

"The unsub's never taken a victim to a house before, but this one appears deserted. Let's get this over with." He pounded on the door. "Police! We have reports of a potential domestic altercation. Open up!"

Buck swallowed and took a deep breath. He came up beside him. Buck kicked the door open. He went through, flashlight in hand, and illuminated the way. The main room in front revealed no inhabitants of the human variety. Cobwebs and layers of dust covered an old sofa with padding sticking out of the arms. A filthy trash can lay on its side, the contents spilled across the floor. He smelled the acrid bite of a fired weapon. The situation didn't bode well for the screaming woman. He told himself it wasn't Paige. The unsub didn't use a gun, but he was aware their guy might possess one. Or he might have taken control of Paige's. *Son of a bitch.*

"Are you ready? Let's slice the pie," Buck said.

He nodded to the left, which meant he would take that side. They went down the hall, Buck on the right.

He ducked and entered the first door. He moved the light around the room and stayed low.

"Clear."

Buck entered the door on the right and flashed his Maglite into every corner.

"Clear."

"I got something here," Buck said as he entered the next door on the right.

Trin's stomach felt like it dropped a foot. He entered the room. The scent of gunfire got stronger. He breathed again once he saw the clothes were the wrong ones. *Thank God.*

"It's not Paige. The victim is a teenager." Buck holstered his Glock.

"Call it in. Can you stay with the body until the police arrive? We've still got to find Paige. I'll take Vern and the car. Get loose ASAP. I can give them my statement later." He glanced at his watch. "Ten twenty-one."

~

Josh stared at the two young punks before him. *Stupid teenagers.* "I don't want to mess you up, but it's what'll happen if you give me any more shit. I need to find this woman. She's in trouble. You see an old Ford truck pull into any of these motels in the last few minutes? It's important. How about a hundred bucks for the information?"

"How about you give us everything in your wallet, and we don't give you shit?" The kid's hand on the window displayed a cross inked on it. He looked barely old enough to be out of high school.

Stupid kids. Josh shrugged, yanked the handle, and slung the door wide in a split second. The teen sprawled in the street, his head landing with a *thud.* He slammed the door back against the truck and stepped into a kick that caught the tattoo-necked boy in the hand. The boy's gun clattered to the ground.

After the young punk swung with his fist, Josh grabbed it and twisted the teen around until the arm wrenched against the kid's back. As the kid lifted his leg to stomp his foot, Josh tripped him and continued to hold the arm in place. Tattoo boy hit the ground face first. Blood spurted from his nose.

"Wise up, before someone kills you both for your stupidity. Know your enemy, or you won't get much older." With his knee still on his back, he zip-tied him and the other one who remained out cold. He left them in the street. Not his problem. He only cared about finding Paige. He got back in the Escalade and continued his search for the truck.

~

Paige watched him lift the Slugger to his shoulder. His massive biceps bulged as he adjusted his grip on the handle.

She needed to get his attention. "Why did you kill your father?"

He stopped. So did she. She studied him, uncertain how to attack next. Her hand moved slowly inside the bag she carried and hunted for the grip to the gun. She backed a step away from him.

"Why did you stop? I only pay if you continue to walk." He slammed the baseball club down on the bed. A dust plume flew up.

She peeked down for a split second to better place her hand on the gun he couldn't see.

"What did you ask me?" He shook his head like he wanted to clear it.

"I asked why you killed your father, Tom McCall." She faced him and showed no fear but clenched her teeth to keep them from chattering.

"Who are you?"

"Someone who wants to keep you alive. It's not too late. Drop the weapon and let me help you."

"Are you joking? I ain't never dropping this. It's my lucky friend. Besides, that asshole deserved to die."

Stillness filled the room for several moments while he stood there and stared at her. "He'd lost money, again. A bunch. He borrowed money from a loan shark. The bastard had to know Mark Bader would kill him if he couldn't get the money to pay him back. He complained for days about his pissy life. One night he drives to Malibu. Pulls into a huge place on the coast. When the door opened, I see an older version of me. The guy slams the door in his face. By this time, I figure the guy's related to me. Has to be. He looks exactly like me, and my old man knew him."

Paige knew better than to push, as much as she wanted to skip to the end of the story, to the murder.

He sat down on the bed. "All my life people said I looked just like some dumb actor, but my father never mentioned he knew the guy. I figured it was just a fluke, but the old man cuts around to the side of the house. About thirty seconds later I followed. I'm real curious about this other person who's my double, and he's rich. After I come around the side, there's the old man drinkin' beer from the guy's bottle. I hear my father threaten him. Swears he'll tell the truth about the man's mother." He paused for a few seconds.

When he didn't continue, she asked, "What happened next?"

"I had no idea what was goin' on. The man who's my spittin' image told my old man to screw himself. Said he wouldn't give him a dime and walks away from my father down the beach. I watched him stand up to my old man, something I'd never been able to do. Here I am stuck with the meanest bastard in the world, and all this time my old man's held out on me." He pulled a pair of gloves from his front pocket. "My old man killed women too, you know."

She saw the gloves and panicked. *Pigskin.*

"I know he killed your mother in Tulsa. My guardian worked on the case. We believed he took a child, but we could never find McCall or you. You both disappeared."

His expression changed drastically. He continued to move his head like he wanted to pop his neck in a bizarre way. She'd triggered something in him, but she didn't know what. Surely, Trin and Buck should have arrived by now. *Where the hell were they?*

He stared up at her and pleaded with his eyes. His voice sounded much younger when he spoke. "Why wouldn't you leave him? I begged you for us to go. He treated you so mean. I felt certain he'd kill you, and I was so afraid I'd get stuck with him. Why? Why couldn't you take me and leave?" He raised his bat to his shoulder and swung.

She heard the swish and ducked. The edge caught her wig and moved it out of place. She stepped back and struggled not to stumble. She knew what he could do, and yet, she was so unprepared for his quickness.

"I don't want to kill you. Please, don't make me kill you." She pulled the gun from her purse and tossed the handbag back into the corner behind her.

He stepped closer. She moved around the side of the bed but still faced him. He pursued, the Slugger clutched in his gloved hands. She stepped onto the bed and jumped over. She couldn't let him corner her.

Desperate to stall him, she grabbed for the bedspread and yanked it in his direction. If she could trip him up, she might manage to get him handcuffed. The crack sounded loud as the club connected with her wrist. The gun flew across the other bed onto the floor by the wall. Pain zipped up her arm, so intense tears formed in her eyes. She didn't have time to think. The piece of wood flew toward her again. She threw herself at his feet and hoped to get him on the ground. While he stood, he would continue to swing.

She landed and rolled under his feet. He fell forward, knocking his head against the bed support. She heard the thud. Their legs tangled. She scrambled and wiggled under the first bed, hoping to get to the other one where the gun lay.

He stayed quiet for a second. She turned her head and saw his dazed expression. "Damn it. I cared about you. I asked Hank about you every day. I prayed for you. I worried your father might kill you."

"It would have been better if he did." He moved again and came closer.

His hand found his weapon. He grabbed it and poked at

her under the bed. His lucky friend slammed into her side. She scooted to the far side of the bed and moved toward the gun.

He got up, ran between the beds, and kept her trapped under the first. She scooted back to the middle, and he continued to prod at her from the edges with his weapon. After several attempts to get at her without success, he moved to the end of the bed and lifted the mattress. He threw the massive object against the wall with the window that faced the street. Quickly, he lifted the box springs, and she managed to slide and squirm under the second bed.

"You bitch!" he yelled. The unwieldy piece followed the first and landed close by.

Fear choked her, and sweat formed on her brow. She had to stop him. The second mattress lifted in his hands. She struggled to find the gun that lay against the wall. At first, she couldn't understand why she couldn't get a hold on it. Then she glanced toward the pistol. Bone poked through the skin, and blood flowed steadily from her wrist. Her fingers wouldn't move no matter how hard she tried. *Shit!*

She repositioned herself and stretched with all her might. Her left hand searched frantically for the gun. She felt the barrel while the huge mattress landed over near the first. The second box springs rose. She turned the gun and managed to get a grip on the handle. It felt wrong in her left hand, so awkward. Finally, she got it turned in the right position to fire.

He lifted the last massive springs. She could see her enemy, but her left hand remained trapped beneath the bed frame. She worked desperately to get the gun to point up between the slats.

When the last obstacle left his hands, he grabbed his bat where it leaned on the wall and took out the wood strips in one swipe.

"I don't want to kill you!" she screamed as the boards flew over her hand and nearly knocked the gun from it.

He pulled the club over his shoulder, muscles bulging. "You're gonna have to, or I'm killin' you." He paused for a split second to give her a choice.

The door flew open with a crash and smashed into the wall. Josh fell over the bedding into the room.

She saw the killer change his focus to Josh, but the piles of bedding tripped him. Josh couldn't get his feet under him to get back up. Everything seemed to unfold in slow motion. The young man turned, and his muscles tightened once more. The Louisville Slugger slashed through the air with deadly force.

She didn't take time to aim. With the wrong hand, she would need a miracle to wound him. She pulled the trigger anyway. The kid's body dropped and landed over the bed frame by the door.

30

Paige's eyes moved to meet Josh's gaze. The gun still shook in her left hand. "Is he dead?"

Josh reached for the carotid artery and felt for a pulse. He nodded, stared down at her hand, and sucked in a breath. Fear settled in his eyes.

She remembered the last time she'd used her gun. She'd put three bullets into the serial killer, Grant Windsor, but it didn't keep him down for long. This time, she felt like she'd killed a little boy. If only they'd stopped Tom McCall years ago in Tulsa.

"I'm sorry, Paige, but you're hurt bad. Let me help you up. I want to see what happened to you."

She dropped the gun. Josh grabbed her by her good arm and lifted her to her feet. He took her into the bathroom, closed the seat, and sat her on the toilet. He flipped the light switch on and examined her wrist.

"This is not good. We need to get you to a hospital."

"Get a towel and wrap it tight. The police. We need to call

them. God, that sounds weird. Normally, I'm the police." She felt woozy.

He pulled her to her feet and took care with her wrist. His hand never left hers as his other took his phone out and punched 911. He asked for an ambulance and reported the dead body.

"Let's go outside and wait. We can't disturb the crime scene." She pointed toward the door. Her hand still shook, and she couldn't seem to stop.

He helped her stand and kept his arm around her shoulder while he guided her through the trashed room. Tony's Escalade was parked nearby so he seated her inside. She began to shiver.

"I don't like this. You need treatment for shock, and your bleeding still hasn't stopped." Josh stood beside the open car door and rubbed her shoulder.

After Vern and Trin arrived several minutes later, Josh walked over to meet them. Her mind in a fog, she watched. They talked and nodded several times.

Trin moved in her direction. "We lost communication with you. Somehow, your bugs got taken out when he drove off so quickly. Damn it, Paige."

She attempted to lift her lips into a smile but couldn't force them. "I'm still in one piece. Better than last . . . time."

"Don't remind me. At least I didn't need to revive you." Trin looked down at the blood pooling in her lap.

"Son of a bitch," he yelled at Josh.

She couldn't distinguish words, only noise. Her vision blurred. Her head drooped. She felt herself fall.

Josh climbed into the front. The FBI agent dragged her into the back seat. The Escalade peeled out from the parking lot.

"I've found where she's bleeding the worst. I'll continue to keep pressure on it, but you'd better hurry. She's already turned white," Trin said.

He stomped the pedal to the floor. Tires screamed under the strain as he took a corner on two wheels, but Paige remained passed out.

"Is she still alive?" he asked.

"I've got a faint pulse." Trin kept his finger close to her carotid.

"If she doesn't live, I'm gonna take your hide for this. How could you not protect her?" He remained mad at himself because he failed her. Those damned teens slowed him down.

"I don't know how she lost both trackers we put on her. Who could figure? How did you find her when we couldn't?"

"Some follow their targets better than others." He absolutely didn't want to go there, so he said nothing more.

He pulled under the portico of an emergency room and crammed the gearshift into park. He grabbed the handle and opened the back door to help Trin with Paige. He carried her through the door, back into the emergency stalls, and straight to a doctor. "You've got to get blood into her now, before she bleeds to death. Her wrist has a compound fracture."

The doctor nodded toward a bed. He laid her down while Trin walked back to the admittance area. He rolled Paige onto her stomach and pulled the top down over her shoulder. He had a quick problem to fix.

Before the doctor returned, he took his knife from his cargo pants pocket and cut a tiny slit near the chip's edge on her back. With the blade's dull side, he pushed the tracking device from under her skin and put both in his leg pocket. He lifted the peasant blouse to cover his handiwork and swiftly turned her body face up.

A second later the doctor returned with nurses who scurried around Paige.

AFTER TRIN SETTLED WITH ADMITTANCE, he and Josh both paced in the small waiting area.

"She better make it. You don't know Hank, but he'll make our lives a living hell if she doesn't. Surely, they can get a transfusion into her in time." He chewed his bottom lip as he moved again. He stared over at Josh. "How the hell *did* you find her when we couldn't?"

Josh shrugged. "Better tracker I guess."

He didn't like the idea that Josh did anything better, but his envy came from his own attraction to Paige. He could see the way Josh hovered over her. The concern on the actor's face struck him as far more than friendly. They both desired the same detective from Tulsa. Who wouldn't be drawn to her? She had everything a man could want.

He was too old for her, but Josh wasn't a good choice either. He chased skirts and lived in Hollywood. He'd be damned if he'd move over and let him have her. Besides, something seemed off about the guy. *Better tracker, my ass.*

PAIGE OPENED HER EYES. A strange man gazed down at her. He wore a white lab coat. His name tag read Dr. Pierce. They'd gotten her to the hospital in time. Goose bumps climbed up her arms, and cold settled into her bones.

"You may experience symptoms of shock. Do you feel chilly? We can add another blanket."

She nodded. Her mouth tasted cottony. She didn't think she could speak.

"We stopped the bleeding. You needed several units of blood, but we fixed the problem. In the morning, we'll go in and rebuild your wrist. I've called an expert. He works on our professional athletes here. He's the best." He spread another white blanket over her.

She nodded again.

"I'll let your friends in. They're pacing out there in the waiting room." He grinned.

She gave a lopsided smile, and the doctor turned to leave.

She saw Josh first because he hurried into the room. Trin arrived behind him.

"Are you okay?" they both said in unison.

Finally, she moved her mouth to speak, but it came out like a croak. "Yes."

"You don't sound good. Should I get the doctor back?" Trin looked hesitant before he moved several steps closer to her.

"My mouth's dry is all." Her teeth began to chatter.

"Do you feel any better?" Josh asked.

"I'm cold, but okay. The shock, I think. A fancy doc will fix my arm in the morning."

"What do you know about him? We want only the best," Josh said.

"He's supposed to work on the best professional athletes here. Doc didn't give his name."

"I'll check him out," Trin said as his phone rang. He gave several clipped responses and glanced back at her. "The police want to talk to you, but I headed them off. Tomorrow's soon enough."

"You'll find the guy's confession on a recorder in the purse I carried. Ben McCall didn't kill anyone."

Trin nodded and got up to walk out the door.

"I'm so sorry. I never dreamed you'd get hurt this bad." Josh took her good hand in his. He leaned in close and searched her eyes.

"Hey, I've been through worse. I'll survive."

"If I'd protected you better—"

"If *you'd* protected me better? What do you mean? Trin and Buck had my back, not you." For the first, time she questioned how he'd found her in the motel.

Ben stepped out of the Men's Central Jail, onto Bauchet Street, and squinted in the blinding sunshine. His eyes adjusted to the dazzling light slowly after two weeks inside the dank hellhole behind him. He'd feared he would never see sunlight again and still couldn't believe Paige had managed to free him. He could never repay her for his freedom, but there was nothing he wouldn't do for her now. All she had to do was ask.

His whole attitude lifted once Caroline honked the horn of a nearby black Escalade. She'd come to get him. He hadn't known if she would, but Paige needed to skin his hide for the way he wanted Caroline. He should step away from the gorgeous redhead, but he didn't think he could.

The warm sun comforted his back after two weeks inside. When he opened the door, he noticed her shy smile. She looked like perfection to his eyes. He didn't get this goofy often —like never.

He needed to pull it together, or she would run for the hills. In that instant, he knew he didn't want her to run. He wanted a future with this woman. To make a family with this beautiful creature seemed as right as his next breath. He'd never thought he'd get a chance with anyone who mattered like she did.

He wanted to make a bargain with God to not take her away. Mostly, he figured his mother still prayed for him, or he'd never have met Caroline. The issue with Paige still loomed. She would be pissed at him, and he owed her so much for what she'd done.

"Where are we headed?" He couldn't keep the smile from his lips.

"I'll let you choose. I expected your release yesterday. What took them so long?"

"In jail, the wheels of justice don't move at all, especially in reverse. I'm just glad to be out. I knew Paige was the only one who could help me. I need to thank her."

"Yes, you do. So do we go there or somewhere else first? It's your choice."

"How about a picnic on the beach? I know a private one we can use." He wiggled his eyebrows.

"Sounds good. I haven't been to the ocean this trip."

"We'll stop and buy sandwiches and sun screen on the way."

"You really know how to treat a lady."

"If we go anywhere public, cameras will follow. I'm surprised they didn't show up here."

"I think Josh called and threatened the authorities if they leaked your release information. He's still miffed they arrested you in the first place."

"Where is he? I thought he'd come with you."

"He hasn't left her side once since she proved your innocence."

"He always did take responsibility seriously." He nodded.

"I'm not sure that's the only reason. I think he might care

for Paige. She's hard to read so who knows if she likes him or not."

"We're talking about Josh. I've never seen him get serious about any chick."

"Wait a minute. Paige is much more than a chick. She risked her life for you."

"I didn't mean it that way. I'm just surprised you'd think Josh would feel serious about her. I means she's beautiful, but it's Buzzkill we're discussing."

"You can see for yourself when we get there. I'm sure he'll still be by her side."

His phone rang.

"Okay. I'll pay close attention. This should get interesting." He answered his mobile.

"I hear you're a free man, and I'm damned glad of it."

"Tony Strete, as I live and breathe. I haven't heard your voice in too long. How's the movie business?"

"This one's fine. How in the hell is the one I'm partners on? Do we still make our release date? No, seriously, I'm glad you're out."

"Me too. My life took a scary turn for a while. How much longer until you come home?"

"If problems don't come up, about a month and a half. We'll finish stateside."

"The release date might get pushed back. No one's touched our project since this murder situation arose, but we'll celebrate my homecoming with steaks and beer once you get here. Josh and I will grab a head start before then, I'm sure. You know what I mean."

"Yeah, I can't trust you two with anything. What are you up to?"

"I left the jail minutes ago. We're on our way to see Josh

and Paige Stone. You remember her from our adventure in Tulsa."

"I never met her, but I know who you're talking about. Why isn't Josh with you?"

"Paige got hurt killing the bad guy. Josh stayed with her. Caroline says he's smitten."

"So who's Caroline?"

"Paige's friend, and now my friend. She came and picked me up. "

"Is that a nice way to say you're screwing her?"

"God, no. She's not like that."

"Now you've got me worried. Don't tell me she's got *you* by the balls?"

"Why would you say that?"

"Your response. She's not like what? I think you're in real trouble. Shit. I leave you two alone for several weeks and look what happens. Don't find any extra girlfriends for me. I'm immune to the female crap. I can see after I get home, I need to talk sense into you both."

"Say whatever you want. There's nothing wrong with me."

"We'll see. I've gotta run. They're ready for my next scene. I'll talk to you in a few."

He disconnected.

"Is your friend okay?" Caroline asked

"Sure." He ran his hand through his hair and grabbed the back of his neck.

"You do that a lot."

"What? Oh, run my hand through my hair? A habit, I guess. You want to stop at a supermarket to pack our own picnic? Or I can call a little shop and have them put together something fancy for us. Champagne. Caviar. Brie. Whatever you want, you name it."

"I'm more of a DIY girl than a diva. Let's go shopping together. I had my fill of fancy growing up."

"You did, did you? I can't wait any longer. How about you fancy this." He reached for her and kissed her cheek. She grabbed his face with both hands and brought her lips to his.

Paige hovered at the edge of sleep. But when Curtis Sampson entered her room, her eyes popped open, fully awake. *What did he want?*

"I know you're surprised to see me. I gave you a hard time. Sorry." He fiddled with his jacket like he didn't know what to do with his hands.

"Okay."

"I hope you can let my brusque manner pass this once. I felt certain we had the right guy. Our witness lived next door to McCall for years. Who could figure she'd give the wrong identification. Then they found his prints at a double murder site. So we believed we'd found our perp."

"I understand. I talked to her. She was completely convinced, but we didn't know then the real killer favored his brother so much. To tell you the truth, I thought Ben did it in the beginning."

"I'm sorry you got hurt. Someone said you almost died from blood loss."

"That's what I'm told, but I'm fine except my wrist."

"Will it heal okay? What do the doctors say?"

"They don't know for sure, but they're encouraged."

"I hope everything works out. I wanted to check and make sure you're on the mend."

"Thank you." She couldn't think of another appropriate response, but at least he attempted to apologize.

The door opened and Josh walked through.

"I went to three different floors to get you this Pepsi." He saw Curtis and gave her a questioning look.

"Samson, this is Josh Stuart. I'm not sure you two ever met." She glanced at Josh. "He's the detective who worked on Ben's case."

Josh's expression didn't appear friendly, but he shook the outstretched hand.

"I need to leave. Take care and have a safe trip home." Curtis hurried from the room.

"You didn't need to scare him off." She grinned at Josh's harsh expression.

"What did he want?"

"He made an effort to apologize, I think."

"Big of him, I guess. How's your arm?"

"It aches, but I won't take those narcotics the doctor prescribed. Two ibuprofen will do, and don't let the nurses catch you."

"Are you sure? It's a nasty break. I've never seen so much bone stick out before." Josh got a small bottle from his pants pocket and shook two tablets into his palm.

"Compared to the dead prostitutes, it's nothing. Believe me. Did they let Ben out yet?"

"He called while I was running down your soda. Caroline picked him up a few minutes ago."

"You left them alone together? He has designs on her. She's good people. What were you thinking?" She swallowed the pills and chased them with water.

"That they're two adults who can do what they want?"

"That's hardly the point. Why didn't you go get him? You're such good friends and all."

"I couldn't leave you here alone. Besides, they planned it and didn't ask me."

Before she could answer, Ben and Caroline walked in.

"Are your ears burning? We were talking about you." She took her first drink from the cold can.

"Good words I hope," Caroline said

"Mine were, I assure you." Josh walked over to grab Ben in a quick hug.

"Sure. Leave me with my foot in my mouth. How long you been out?" Her gaze moved to Ben.

"Long enough to drive here. We plan to picnic by the ocean eventually, but I couldn't wait to thank you for your help. I also wanted to ask about this guy everyone thinks is my half-brother." Ben directed the question to her.

"Remember, I asked you about one? I figured with the witness so sure, the perp must look a lot like you. He did, but younger."

"You met him?"

"Yes. When he struggled with me. But he tried to kill Josh, and I had to shoot him. I'm sorry, but he wouldn't stop. I think your father messed his head up real bad."

"Wouldn't surprise me. If I'd known about him, I would have paid the old man to let me take him. I wish I'd helped him somehow."

"You can't fix what you didn't know existed." Caroline put her hand on his shoulder.

"True, but I still feel frustrated another person took abuse from my ass—I'm sorry, Caroline. My mouth still hasn't been retrained." Ben glanced back at her. "Will you be alright? My guard said you nearly died."

"Not like the last time. I'll heal." She observed Ben and Caroline holding hands. "Now, Mister McCall, what are your intentions concerning my good friend? I see you didn't take my advice."

"Yeah, what are your intentions concerning me?" Caroline's voice teased, but her eyes searched his.

"I planned to take your advice." Ben nodded at her and pointed at the redhead. "But I'm certain I can't live without Caroline. I'm hopeful she feels the same way."

"I'm going to hold you to it, and it better be legal before you're hands on." She studied him for a moment and believed he did care for her friend.

"I hear you," Ben said as the group laughed together.

31

Two weeks later

Paige took the left curve onto old Route 66 and punched her CD player. Bruno Mars filled her speakers with "Talking to the Moon." Her Cavalier traveled steadily toward Claremore and the cabin where she once died.

This Wednesday was her first trip back since she left for LA four weeks earlier. She looked down at the cast on her right arm and wrist. She now thought of it as her battle scar from her trip out west. Dusk showed off its last brilliant colors of the sunset. She hoped to arrive before darkness covered the night sky.

The shadows lengthened when she drove under the oak and pecan tree canopy. The road remained patched and bumpy enough to shake her car while she maneuvered the country lane. She parked her vehicle just the way she had the first time she came to this place—the night her personal monster attacked her.

She noticed the FOR SALE sign had a SOLD panel attached. Flashlight in hand, she walked down the long driveway toward the log house. The window on the south end of the home waited for her inspection. This time no hidden creatures rustled in the tall grass, no smell of a wood-burning stove stung her nostrils, and the light never quivered as she shined it on the walls of the first bedroom.

When she moved to the second glass, the room stayed empty. After she rounded the corner to the back, the sliding door didn't reveal a pink backpack with a computer inside. And most important, she still breathed normally. No sweat broke out on her back or any other place. She touched her right index finger to her lips and felt herself grin.

She'd never made it this far before without the panic attack. She looked in every window just to make sure she was finished with this ordeal. To prove her point, she walked calmly back to the silver car at the end of the driveway while the smile still lingered. This cabin's hold on her now gone, she looked up at the stars in the clear night sky and believed Detective Grace Helston witnessed her victory.

ABOUT THE AUTHOR

Maribeth Garrett is an avid reader and has always wanted to create stories like those she loves to read. *The Past* is the second book in the exciting Paige Stone detective series. A native Oklahoman who grew up around wheat fields, Garrett now resides on acreage in the northeast part of the state, where her children and grandchildren keep her young and active.

MORE BY ADMISSION PRESS

Looking for your next great read?
Visit www.admissionpress.com